beneath these SHADOWS

MEGHAN MARCH

Visit my website at www.meghanmarch.com.
ISBN: 978-1-943796-79-3

About This Book

The only permanent thing in my life is the ink I put on my clients.

I drift from city to city, in and out of beds, from one tattoo shop to the next.

Every time I start to put down roots, I rip them up.

Until New Orleans.

Until her.

She's everything I'm not.

Full of fire and life. An innocent where I'm a sinner.

I want to consume her. Protect her. Keep her.

But first, I have to escape from beneath these shadows.

Author's Note

Thank you so much for purchasing *Beneath These Shadows*! Have no fear, this book can absolutely be read as a stand-alone, but because it is the sixth book in a series of stand-alones, there will be some appearances by characters who have been in other books in the Beneath series. If you have any questions about other characters, here is where you can find their stories:

Beneath This Mask (Simon and Charlie)
Beneath This Ink (Con and Vanessa)
Beneath These Chains (Lord and Elle)
Beneath These Scars (Lucas and Yve)
Beneath These Lies (Rix and Valentina)

This is also a book where worlds collide. If you're wondering whether Dom Casso has appeared elsewhere, you can find him in the Dirty Billionaire Trilogy and the Dirty Girl Duet.

None of these books are required reading before *Beneath These Shadows*, but if you want to dive deeper, that's where you'll find more on these characters and back stories.

Happy reading!

All my best,
Meghan March

1

Eden

My office. Now.

The text appeared on the screen of my phone with a sharp ding, and I dropped my mascara wand on the counter, narrowly avoiding smearing a black streak down the front of my white blouse.

I reread the text three times to make sure I hadn't misunderstood. Three words. Impossible to misunderstand. Impossible to ignore.

I ran down a mental list of anything I could have done that would have drawn his ire, but came up with nothing. I went to work—the job he allowed me to have. I came home. Everywhere I went, I was chauffeured by a man with a gun in a big black SUV with armored doors and bulletproof windows.

But that didn't mean my father texted me. Actually, he rarely remembered I existed.

A knock sounded on my front door, and I shoved the

mascara wand back in the tube. A summons from Dom Casso, head of one of New York's most notorious crime families, didn't allow for any delay.

I hurried toward the door, catching my stockinged foot on the handle of a bag I'd left next to the couch. My toe slammed into the table leg, sending pain rocketing through my foot.

"Shit."

The knock turned into pounding as I winced.

"Eden, hurry up."

The voice belonged to Angelo, my regular babysitter. *Excuse me, I mean security.*

"Just a second."

"Don't got a second. We need to move."

I shook off the stubbed toe and rushed across the room, avoiding any more potential tripping hazards. I peeked through the peephole as I'd been taught, ensuring that Angelo was alone and not being held hostage at the end of someone's gun.

It appeared all clear. And for the record, I thought that rule was ridiculous. I probably ranked in the triple digits on Dom's list of priorities. Illegitimate daughter fell just below resoling shoes and remembering to pick up a new black golf umbrella.

"I'm hurrying. I swear."

I slipped into a pair of pale pink Tori Burch flats I'd left in a haphazard pile of shoes by the door and snatched a black trench coat from the whimsical iron hooks I'd screwed into the wall with my very own drill—and it wasn't a pink drill either. Don't mind the few pieces of patched drywall where I missed the studs.

I unlocked the four dead bolts and pushed back the

security bar. Angelo, who looked just as tall, dark, and Italian as his name suggested, stepped inside.

He surveyed me from the top of my golden-blond head, which definitely didn't look Italian in the least, to the soles of my less-than-practical flats. But it wasn't like I was walking the streets of New York.

God forbid I should do such a thing.

I shoved my arms into my coat and tied the belt around my waist. "That was me swearing when I stubbed my toe. Don't worry. I'm good."

I stepped out of the apartment, and he waited impatiently while I locked and checked the door before leading the way to the elevator.

"What's the hurry? What's going on?"

Angelo pushed the call button and stepped inside first when it came. "You know I can't tell you nothing. It ain't fair for you to ask me shit like that."

This might have been true, but I also knew that Angelo had a soft spot for me, which was why he'd finally brought me dinner from The Halal Guys's cart on 53rd and Sixth last week after months of me begging him to take a detour during our drives to and from work. Even though I hadn't actually gotten to have the whole experience like I was craving—standing in line, avoiding making eye contact with strangers, yelling my order as loud as I could over the noise—I still appreciated the gesture all the same.

Regardless, it also meant I kept pushing for an answer as the doors slid shut and he became a captive audience.

"It has to be something big. Dom never wants me in Hell's Kitchen. Why now?"

Angelo shrugged and leaned against the mirrored wall. "I'm sure he woulda rather come to your place, but he just don't have time."

I needed the reminder like I needed another credit card in my wallet.

"Just tell me so I know what I'm walking into."

"E, I swear, even if I knew what he was going to say—*which I don't*—I couldn't tell you. All I know is that bad shit is happening and we're on the defensive on every front. Dom sure as fuck don't like being on defense, so he's gonna hit back and hard."

Chills traveled up my spine despite my black trench coat, because even living in the little bubble that made up my world, I had an idea of the brutality that Angelo alluded to. Well, at least I imagined I did. I'd seen *The Godfather* movies, after all.

"So, what does that have to do with me?"

Angelo met my gaze as the elevator door opened in the lobby. "Wish I knew, Eden. Really wish I knew."

Twenty minutes later, Angelo and I stood outside the doors to my father's office on the top floor of a brownstone on the edge of Hell's Kitchen. Angelo knocked, and from inside, someone barked the command to enter.

I hadn't exactly spent hours and hours committing Dom's different vocal pitches to memory, but it didn't sound like him.

Angelo pushed the door open and gestured for me to enter first. As I always did before entering this office, I steeled my spine.

Normally, Dom sat behind his big wooden desk, doing whatever it was mob bosses actually did during the day. I wasn't quite sure what that was because there hadn't been a *take your daughter to work* day for organized crime. Today, the desk sat empty.

I scanned the office and my eyes locked on Vincent Francetti as he turned from the window. Dom's second-in-command had dark hair slicked back from his face in a style I swore came right out of Hollywood. It might as well be called *the mobster.*

He'd always made me uneasy for a reason I couldn't articulate. I'd never been in a room with him without Dom present, and trepidation crept into my veins like a tiny team of commandos.

"Where's Dom?" I hoped he couldn't hear the tremor in my voice.

"Dealing with more important things." Vincent snapped out the words, and the slice of his insult hit the mark.

I shoved my shoulders back and lifted my chin, determined not to let him see how much his words stung. Just because I knew my father didn't care, didn't mean I wanted it shoved in my face.

"I can come back at a time that's more convenient for him." I kept my tone crisp and my statement pointed.

"He needs you gone now."

"Gone?" I choked on the word.

Vincent looked at me like I was a child, and a developmentally delayed one at that.

"Yes. Gone." He strode to the desk and grabbed a thick manila envelope off the leather blotter before holding it out to me.

It seemed like a dare, as if he knew I didn't want to get any closer to him than I had to, but he was going to force the issue.

Digging deep into my stores of poise to appear unaffected, I crossed the room and reached out to take it. Vincent jerked it out of my reach, toying with me.

Now that I was close, he lowered his voice so that not even Angelo could hear. "You're going to take this envelope and you're going to disappear. Don't tell anyone where you're going, especially any of your little friends."

If there had been any room for awkward humor in this situation, I would have laughed at that. Friends weren't exactly part of Dom's policy of enforced isolation.

"There's a number in here to a line you call only in an emergency. If you're not bleeding to death or being held at gunpoint, think twice before using it. Only use the ID, credit cards, and cell phone in here. Don't even fucking take yours with you. Leave it all at home. Do you understand me?"

I dipped my chin a fraction of an inch, indicating that I understood what he was saying, even though I didn't. "I'm just supposed to leave?"

"Lay low. Don't attract attention. And for fuck's sake, don't tell a goddamned person who you are."

"How long?" The question came out a whisper.

"Until you get a text from the number in here telling you to come back."

The orders he issued repeated in my head over and over until they began to sink in. *Disappear. Don't tell anyone where you're going.*

He finally held out the envelope again, and I reached to snatch it from him, praying that my hand didn't shake. But Vincent didn't let go as I tugged.

"Don't fuck this up, Eden. You've been a liability to Dom since the day you were born, so for once in your life, do something to make yourself less of a fucking burden. Don't call Dom. Don't bother him. Just get the hell out of here."

With that verbal slap to the face, I yanked the envelope from his grip and turned away from the distaste stamping his features.

The words sliced at my insides as they played on a loop in my head. *Make yourself less of a fucking burden.* I wanted to scream as Angelo followed me out the door and down the stairs.

I never asked to be a burden. Why can't they understand that?

We walked in silence until I slid into the backseat of the SUV.

"I'm supposed to take you home to pack and then to the airport." Angelo glanced at me in the rearview mirror, and his tone carried an apology.

I nodded, but my brain was already moving forward.

Where will I go? What will I do?

As much as I'd chafed against the restrictions I lived under, I never realized that they also acted as a security blanket until the moment they were ripped away.

It was one thing to paper the bulletin board in my office with pictures of places I wanted to see with thoughts of *someday I'll go,* but all of a sudden, someday was now.

The freedom to go anywhere, all by myself, should have been heady and intoxicating, but instead unexpected anxiety invaded my every breath.

Angelo had spent more time with me than any of Dom's other soldiers, and he recognized the change in my mood.

"It's going to be okay, E. Just pick somewhere, check into the nicest hotel in town, order room service, get a massage, do girly spa shit, and pretend you're on vacation. You wanted a break from all this, so now you got it."

I inhaled a deep breath and let it out. *I can do this. I'll be fine. This is what I've wanted for years.* Regardless of how uneasy it made me that it was being shoved upon me, I vowed to embrace the opportunity. The proverbial door to my gilded cage had been flung open, and it was time for me to explore.

But one piece of this whole thing continued to elude me. "Why is he doing this? What happened?"

Angelo's gaze dropped away from the rearview mirror and fixed on the road. "I thought Dom would be there and he'd tell you what's what."

"Apparently he couldn't be bothered."

"I'm sure it's not like that." Angelo's words came out stiff because we both knew it *was* like that, at least for the last decade, with no signs of changing anytime soon.

"Just tell me."

He stopped at a light and turned around to look at me. "You can't tell anyone I told you any of this."

I lifted the manila envelope. "And who am I going to tell while I'm in exile? Hell, who would I tell *here*?"

"Cash houses got hit this morning, and so did some of the businesses."

Unease bloomed in my belly. "Which businesses?"

As much as I wasn't supposed to know that the spa where I kept the books—clean, legit books—was a front, I wasn't dumb enough to ignore the comings and goings of Dom's people, and the briefcases and duffels they carried.

"The spa. It . . . it was bad. That's why you gotta go. They don't know if it got hit because you work there or if it was just part of the overall plan. Either way, I'd get you out of town too."

The dozens of questions I wanted to ask were wiped

away in the wake of the most important one. "Was anyone hurt?"

Angelo glanced up at the rearview mirror, his face apologetic for a beat before taking on a hard cast. "They threw a Molotov cocktail through the front window before they shot up the place from a car out front. Four of the girls went to the doc to be treated, but no one died."

Oh, thank God there were no casualties. But still, the thought of any of the girls being injured twisted my gut in knots.

"Do you know who? What kind of injuries?"

His eyes back on the road, he shook his head. "Didn't get any details."

"Then why am I going to some undisclosed location and not a safe house somewhere?"

Angelo's shoulders tensed. "No fucking clue. Not like Dom and Vin explain themselves to me. But if I had to guess, I'd say they're worried the organization has been compromised. If no one knows where you are, no one can tell."

You've been a liability to Dom since the day you were born.

I stayed silent for the rest of the drive to my apartment.

"You've got twenty minutes to pack, and then we need to be on the road before it gets leaked that you're leaving town."

Angelo's words started my internal clock ticking down as soon as we stepped into my apartment. My mind chaotic, I strode into my room and stared at all the clothes in my closet for a full minute before I realized I couldn't pack anything until I decided where I was going.

Spinning around, I headed for my office and the bulletin board of all my *maybe somedays*. Clippings from magazines, printed articles, postcards, and pictures of skylines covered it. *Must Do* lists for each city hung along the bottom.

Just pick one, I told myself. But decision paralysis set in. What if this was my only chance to see a piece of the world?

"Can I leave the country?" I yelled to Angelo.

"Are you fucking nuts? No, you can't leave the fucking country."

Disappointment slammed into me, but I shoved it down. *Good-bye, Paris, Rome, Dublin, and Barcelona.*

Focus on the positives. It narrowed down my choices. I paced my small office, my gaze flicking to the bulletin board with every pass.

"You got fifteen minutes, and I don't hear any fucking packing," Angelo called.

"Stop rushing me!"

"I'm not fucking around, Eden. We gotta move when your time is up."

"Fine. Now stop yelling at me."

Just pick a place.

Pictures of San Francisco, Nashville, Seattle, and Miami all hung there, but my gaze zeroed in on something else.

New Orleans.

I'd seen ads on top of cabs for the last two weeks, advertising an upcoming Mardi Gras party at a club, and wished that someday I could see a real Mardi Gras parade.

I'm taking it as a sign.

I was going to New Orleans. I reached out to grab the *Must Do* list, but snatched my hand back. If someone came into my apartment and noticed it was the only one missing . . . wouldn't that be giving away my location?

I reached out again, grabbing the lists for both New Orleans and Nashville off the bulletin board.

Spinning on my heel, I ran for my bedroom and stuffed

my carry-on with all the clothes I could possibly make fit before exchanging my ID, phone, and credit card for five thousand dollars in cash from the safe bolted into the back of my closet. I stripped out of my trench coat, skirt, blouse, and pantyhose, and tugged on jeans, a polo shirt, and a lighter jacket.

When I wheeled the bag into the living room, Angelo was staring at his watch.

"You ready?"

Ready to leave the tower and experience life without a bodyguard dogging my every step?

"Yes. I'm ready."

When we pulled up to the curb at JFK, I gave Angelo a quick hug and a kiss on the cheek.

"Take care, big guy."

"Be safe, Eden. If you need anything—"

He cut off his offer because he knew I couldn't call him.

"Thank you for everything."

When I got to the ticket counter, I pulled my new ID and credit card from my wallet. When I laid them on the counter, I got my first look at my new name. *Elisha Madden.*

"I need a ticket on the next flight to New Orleans. One way."

2

Bishop

WIPING BLOOD AND INK FROM THE SMOOTH, pale skin beneath my tattoo machine should have been calming, but today, the fine lines of the butterfly mocked me. I wanted this tat over and done with. I should have made Delilah take the girl, but we were taking turns on the flash work that got so much action during Mardi Gras season.

The girl, whose name I couldn't remember, kept glancing up at me from beneath her fake lashes in a way that was probably supposed to be sexy, but didn't stir my interest in the least. I'd had enough party-girl pussy thrown at me in the last week to put me off the species completely. If it wasn't a challenge, then what the fuck was the point?

"How much longer do you think? I can't wait to get back out and grab a drink."

Even her voice annoyed me. Too breathy and high pitched.

"Ten minutes," I said, trying not to breathe in the cloud of vanilla perfume wafting off her in clouds.

"Is it cool that I'm going to go back to party after it's done? I've never had a tattoo before, so I don't know the rules."

I lifted the needle away from her skin as she shifted for the fiftieth time in half an hour. "You can do whatever you want. Care sheets are on the counter out front if you want to do it right."

Her lips twisted into a pout at my answer, but it didn't deter her for long.

"You wanna come?" Her glitter-slicked lashes batted again as she twisted around to face me. "My friends and I would show you a real good time."

"You quit moving and we'll be done a lot quicker."

She returned to the position I'd asked her to take with a huff.

What in the hell would make this girl think I was remotely interested in joining them? I'd done nothing but shut her down over and over when she tried to start a conversation. Customer service at its finest, right? My boss would probably kick my ass, but then again . . . maybe not. He had as little patience for this shit as I did.

"Just think about it." She didn't move this time, but the plea came through loud and clear.

"Got plans."

My short answer finally did the trick. She let me finish my work in silence, and the minute I taped the clear plastic over the tat and snapped my gloves off, I stood.

"You can settle up with Delilah."

I had to get the fuck out of the room before her heavy perfume suffocated me, so I strode out into the main area of the shop. My sister's laughter followed me as I headed straight for the front door and fresh air.

"Can't get any peace, can you, Bish?" Delilah tapped a pencil against her sketch pad as she grinned at me.

It was her running joke that four out of five female clients would hit on me, and the fifth would hit on her. I wouldn't have been surprised if she actually kept track of it. But she was the only family I had, and I loved the shit out of her.

"Don't go too far, hot stuff. I'm heading out to pick up our food in a few."

I flipped her off and ducked outside to suck in a lungful of fresh air. Well, as close as I was going to get in this town. Pockets of smokers congregated among the crowd, clouds wafting away from them, but the urge to light up didn't hit. *Damn, maybe I've actually outgrown that shit.*

I leaned against the window and cracked my neck on both sides as I watched the crush of people waiting for the parade to turn down Canal Street. I didn't know or care which parade this was; I only cared that I was out of the shop and the next piece of flash that someone wanted inked on their body was Delilah's problem.

It made me wish my boss didn't have a policy about blocking off time that appointments could otherwise have filled during these three weeks of the year. So instead of challenging artistic pieces, I had tourists wanting shamrocks on their asses and names on their arms.

I scanned the crowd, trying to pick out the next one who'd walk through the door. I didn't actually care who it would be. I only wanted the distraction.

But I had no idea how big of a distraction I was about to find.

Elisha Eden

I'D PICKED THE ROOSEVELT BECAUSE I FIGURED I couldn't go wrong with a Waldorf hotel, even though I'd never actually stayed at one. When the cabbie dropped me off, excitement warred with anxiety as I climbed out of the cab. Sucking in a deep breath as the bellman opened the door, I walked into the lobby covered with gold gilt and intricate tile work.

I can do this, I told myself.

But apparently I couldn't. At least, not here.

After I waited ten minutes in line, the front-desk clerk stared at me like I was an idiot when I asked for a room and informed him I didn't have a reservation.

"We don't have any vacancies. I'm sorry, ma'am, you're unlikely to find anything close to the French Quarter with Mardi Gras coming up next week." His words, in that condescending tone, seemed to carry an extra punch to crush the excitement I'd been feeling.

Mardi Gras. How could I have forgotten?

"Do you have any suggestions where else I could try?" I asked, trying to keep a positive attitude.

The front-desk clerk was already looking over my shoulder and waving the next person forward. "I'm sorry, I really have no idea. Maybe someplace out near the airport?"

Dismissed.

I forced a smile and thanked him as I dragged my suitcase across the lobby. When I'd pictured all the traveling I would do while tacking things to my bulletin board, it had never occurred to me that I wouldn't be able to find something so simple as a hotel room.

Making my way through the brass-framed doors, I stepped out onto a sidewalk that swarmed with people. Screams and cheers came from half a block away, and it seemed like that was the direction everyone was heading. CANAL STREET, the sign in the distance read. I heard the music next, and my frustration at the hotel clerk's lack of assistance faded away when I realized I was going to see my first Mardi Gras parade.

A wide smile tugged at the corners of my mouth. For the first time in my life, I'd be able to check something off one of my *Must Do* lists. *This* was living.

With my suitcase trailing me, I tried to see what was happening in the street, but at five foot six, I didn't have a height advantage on many. All I could see was the back of people's heads as I reached the crowd.

"I see a better spot across the street. Wanna go?" a girl dressed in a neon-green bikini top, tiny black shorts, and fishnet tights yelled to her friend who was similarly dressed. The other girl nodded, and I made a snap decision to follow them as they pushed through the mass of people. Nothing was going to stop me from seeing this parade.

Avoiding elbows and shouts, I plowed through, lifted my suitcase, and ran across the street.

My first clear view of the street showed the parade still a good hundred yards away. I dodged the people gathered on neutral ground and crossed the next lanes without incident. The crowd swallowed me up on the other side, and a shaft of claustrophobia speared through me when I realized I couldn't see over them either.

"Show us your tits!" The raucous calls came from every direction, and beads were tossed through the air like confetti.

The *Must Do* list also mentioned catching beads on Bourbon Street (without showing my boobs), but before I could decide whether catching beads on Canal Street was a suitable substitute, a body crashed into me, catching me off guard. I lurched sideways, tripping over a woman wearing a pair of snakeskin boots that stretched up to her thighs.

"Whoa, watch it!"

I started to apologize, but her elbow flew out and caught me in the ribs, and sent me stumbling further.

Holding on to my suitcase with a death grip, I reached out to catch my fall with my other hand, but my palm connected with something fleshy. My gaze zeroed in on my fingers, and I yanked my hand away.

Oh my God, you cannot be serious.

A penis, painted gold. Connected to a man who was completely naked but for the gold, purple, and green glittery stripes covering his soft body.

"I gotcha, darlin.'" Slurred words accompanied the hands that gripped my arms and pulled me upright.

The naked painted man is touching me. Ewww.

Why couldn't he at least be hot? Seriously, would that be so much to ask?

Abort mission. Abort.

Holding on to my suitcase, I barreled through the crowd and didn't slow until I reached a break in the chaos at the mouth of an alley, once again behind the crowd blocking the oncoming parade. *Crap.* Focused on finding another place to stand that would give me a view, I didn't see the man who reached out and grabbed the back of my pink-and-white polo shirt.

"Hey! You don't have any beads." He jerked me around before a huge guy wearing a leather vest with nothing under it yanked me toward his hairy chest.

"I can fix that for her," the man in a similar vest said from beside him.

"I'm not interested in any beads. I'll thank you to take your hands off me now." I twisted, trying to get out of his hold, but the other man grabbed my arm as beer splashed between us, splattering my shirt.

"Hey, you need a place to stay, girl? I got room for you in my bed." Hairy Chest released me to grab his crotch.

I reared back, latching onto my suitcase as the other guy lunged toward me. I opened my mouth to scream, but a deep voice ripped through the crowd behind me.

"You're late for your appointment. I don't like to wait."

Both men's attention broke away from me as they turned in the direction of the voice.

What the hell? Appointment?

The voice came closer. "I haven't killed anyone in a long fucking time, but I'm happy to change that if you don't get your hands off her."

Immediately, both men released me, and apprehension

crawled up my spine.

"Sorry, man. Thought she was someone else."

"Fuck off. If I see you assholes around here again, they'll find you floating facedown in the Mississippi." Heat met my back, and the voice rumbled low in my ear. "Come on, cupcake, let's go."

My gaze landed on the two men who were now raising their hands and backing away, tripping over themselves, actually.

I didn't want to turn around. If they were afraid of the voice behind me, how much scarier did the body it belonged to have to be?

Then again, he'd run off two guys on the pretense of some appointment. *What was that about?* The wall of heat dissipated behind me, and I found the courage to turn around.

The blue-and-red neon lights of the sign attached to the marble building on my right read VOODOO INK.

A tattoo shop?

Immediately, my attention caught on the back of the man striding toward the door.

A tattoo appointment?

People stepped out of my unlikely rescuer's way as though he were a force of nature unto himself.

His brown-and-gold-streaked hair was twisted up in a knot at the back of his head, and broad shoulders stretched the back of a black T-shirt with the same logo on the back. Ink covered every inch of his visible skin.

He was a man-bunned, tattooed giant.

A man-bunned, tattooed giant who had saved me from being assaulted by drunk, grabby men.

The space he'd left on the sidewalk filled with people, threatening to swallow me up again, and I made my decision based on nothing more than a shred of instinct.

I followed him.

Eden

*T*HIS IS A BAD IDEA. NO, NOT A BAD IDEA, A TERRIBLE *idea.*

Misgivings of every shape, size, and volume buzzed to life inside me as my hand landed on the doorknob. I didn't have a tattoo, and more than that, I'd never even thought about getting one. Girls like me, the kind who watched the world from the outside looking in, didn't go to places like this.

Before I could decide whether to twist the knob or walk away, the door flew open and I jerked back. A brunette stormed out, wearing only ripped jean shorts and a push-up bra with enough padding to turn her boobs into cannons.

"What an ass. Who turns this down?" She wasn't talking to me, at least not until she almost collided with me. "Good luck with that prick. Maybe he goes for the good-girl vibe you got going on. His loss."

My gaze lifted over her shoulder to see the back of the

man-bunned giant inside the shop, and no one else.

I didn't bother to reply that I wasn't trying to get him to touch me because she was already melding into the crowd that I was trying to escape.

But she did make my decision easier. The chime jangled as I slipped through the open front door and shut it behind me. The giant didn't turn around for several long seconds.

One look at his face, his arms, his hands, his . . . everything, and I knew I should walk right back out that door.

If there could be a universal picture of *dangerous as hell* embodied in the male form, the man-bunned giant would be it. Muscles rippled beneath the black T-shirt as he lifted a hand to his beard-covered face.

The world had apparently decided to throw me a bone. He was gorgeous, and I hadn't accidentally grabbed his penis. *Go, me.* I could definitely see why she was pissed he wouldn't touch her.

Unfortunately, the world had bestowed all that . . . *man* . . . on me. Also known as someone who needed to start at the beginner level, not the *more man than you could ever handle in three lives* level.

I'd had two crushes in my life, and one of them didn't count. Gianni was replaced as my security when he "accidentally" grabbed my ass as he helped me out of the car, and Angelo had seen him and reported the incident to my father. It was the closest any guy had gotten to third base, and I'd gotten a cheap thrill. Unfortunately, that thrill had been killed when it had come out he'd stolen some of my panties. *Ick.*

Before Gianni, there was my aunt's yard guy, Marcello. For three years, he'd trimmed and mowed and edged while I drooled from the window. Compared to this guy, Marcello was a gangly child, and my lady parts were sending out an SOS from disuse.

My brain snapped back into the present as my rescuer's green eyes, almost emerald, scanned me from the soles of my Sperrys to the top of my blond head.

"Where the hell were you headed? The country club?" His voice seemed even deeper and louder in the confines of the black-walled tattoo shop.

"I wouldn't wear jeans to a country club." My response was instinctive, yet ridiculous. It wasn't like I'd spent much time at the club, but even I knew they wouldn't let you in wearing jeans.

His lips quirked as if he might smile, but they smoothed back into a lush line.

Lush? Wow, Eden. Simmer down.

Why had I thought following him in here was even a fraction of a good idea? Scratch the fact that my body thought he was the most delicious thing it had seen since that piece of triple-chocolate Almond Joy cheesecake Angelo had brought me last week when he picked me up from work. Apparently my body was waiting for the notification from my brain that this guy was beyond out of my league.

"I can just go." I made a lame gesture toward the door. Getting a tattoo in New Orleans wasn't on my *Must Do* list, anyway.

His expressive mouth turned downward. "You go back out there and you're gonna get more of the same. You look exactly like the fucking tourist you are carrying that bag around. Makes you a target, if you haven't figured that out yet. Why the hell didn't you leave it somewhere?"

"Because the hotel didn't have a room for me, and told me no one else would either. I didn't exactly plan this."

"Which hotel?"

"The Roosevelt."

He didn't roll his eyes, but it was a close call. Maybe he was staring up to the ceiling for divine guidance?

"You just showed up there thinking you could get a room a few days before Mardi Gras without a reservation? You fucking serious?"

I bristled at his tone. I was so freaking sick and tired of being scolded like I was a child.

"Hey—" I started, having no clue what I was going to say, but I was going to say *something*, dammit, and it was going to be good. But the giant interrupted me.

"Did you have a plan? Walk all over town looking for a hotel? Probably get fucking mugged, if not raped, in some dark alley too?"

The brunette who had stormed out of the shop had been right. He was a prick, even if he was the most beautiful man I'd ever seen.

I propped a hand on my hip and injected confidence into my voice. "I'll find something. Not every hotel can be booked."

He shook his head. "Any hotel room within ten miles is booked. Even the ones that rent by the hour."

My very first chance to venture outside the insulated world mandated by Dom Casso, and I manage to pick the one city with no vacancies. *How is this fair? Maybe I am just a liability.* The negativity welled up, but I shoved it down. I would not fail at this.

Straightening my spine, I gripped the handle of my suitcase tighter. "Then I guess I better start looking somewhere else."

He pointed to one of the chairs lining the wall beside

me. "Sit. Don't go anywhere. I have an idea."

I dropped into a seat at the authoritative command and froze as he turned his back to me.

How long had I been blindly following orders? And from some random stranger, at that? My judgment was clearly faulty.

I started to stand, but an inconvenient thread of curiosity kept my butt in the chair. If he had an idea, maybe I should stay. What other choice did I have right now? Run back outside and fight my way to a taxi to take me and have it take me to the airport Holiday Inn? That would be giving up my one shot at this adventure, and I wasn't ready to admit defeat.

Besides, even if he was a jerk, his first instinct had been to protect me. That said something, right?

I stayed seated while he pulled out his phone and tapped something on the screen. When he was done, he leaned back on the counter and shook his head.

"You've got no business wandering around this city alone, and I don't have time to be your keeper."

Before I could retort that I didn't need a keeper, the door chimed, and I jerked my head around to see a blue-and-black-haired woman in a retro neon-green leopard print dress, complete with black petticoat fluffing out the skirt, strut inside.

"Working during Mardi Gras season sucks." She held up a brown paper bag in one hand and a drink carrier in the other. "But I got the food. And coffee. So hopefully we can get through tonight and worry about tomorrow, tomorrow."

Her gaze landed on me as she lowered the bags and drink carrier onto the counter. "Well, well. Don't you look like a little lost lamb? You here for some ink, sugar?"

The man-bunned giant let out some kind of half laugh, half scoff. "She look like she's here for ink?"

"Guess that means she doesn't fall into your hands-off rule then, Bish."

What did that mean?

The dark glower that took over *Bish's* face had me poised on the edge of my seat to run. Man-bun plus beard plus all those tattoos plus angry scowl finally tipped the scale from dangerously gorgeous to just flat-out dangerous.

"I think I should get out of your way."

The woman cocked her head to the side, and her inspection sealed my decision to take my chances on the street. I'd be fine. Probably.

I shoved out of the chair but only made it a few steps toward the door with my bag in tow before long fingers wrapped around my wrist. Fight-or-flight instincts burst to life as I turned with my hand balled into a fist.

"If you actually knew how to throw a punch, you wouldn't tuck your thumb under your fingers." He dropped his hold on my wrist to pry my thumb out of my fist. "Otherwise, you're liable to break it."

I tucked the knowledge away in case hand-to-hand combat came up in the near future. His scowl had lessened, but I didn't like the patronizing expression.

"You shouldn't just grab people," I said, tugging to release my hand from his grip, but Bish held fast.

"If you hadn't jumped out of your chair so damn fast, I would've told you I'm trying to get you a place to stay."

I looked from him to the woman who watched us like a zoo exhibit. Her black eyebrows rose so high, they disappeared behind her blunt-cut Bettie Page bangs.

"You're . . . you're trying to find me a room?"

"During Mardi Gras?" the woman interjected. "Damn, Bish. If I didn't know you better, I'd think she already blew you in the back to get that kind of help."

I stiffened at her insinuation. I wasn't the kind of girl to . . . blow a guy in a tattoo parlor. Although now that she'd put the idea in my head, I couldn't keep my gaze from dropping to the level of his belt buckle.

Whoa. There's a bulge.

"Shut it down, Delilah."

I jerked my head up to look at both of them, hoping no one had caught where I was staring.

The woman, Delilah, smirked rather than replying, and heat burned up my cheeks. She'd definitely caught me. The wink she threw me sealed it.

A quiet buzz sounded from Bish's phone, and he tapped out something else. When he looked up, he nodded. "I got a place for you to stay for a couple days, but I need to clean up before I can take you."

"I can go myself if you tell me where. I'm not completely helpless."

He shook his head. "Not fucking happening."

Delilah followed him as he disappeared into one of the small rooms toward the back of the shop where they must do the tattoos. It was actually a really cool place. The interior said gothic voodoo plus a touch of heavy metal and rock 'n roll—at least, that was my interpretation of it. Regardless, I could see why Delilah had given me such an odd look. It was way too cool for me and my polo shirt and Sperrys.

Part of me wanted to take a closer look at the pictures of their work on the walls, and maybe even stick around to watch them give someone a tattoo, but I knew that wasn't in the cards. Instead, I stayed by the door, one hand wrapped around the handle of my suitcase as part of my brain told me to grab the door handle and run.

Delilah had plenty of questions for Bish, and her voice carried well enough for me to overhear.

"What the hell are you doing? You don't get involved and try to help people *ever*. Where the fuck did you find a room, anyway? You taking her home?"

My fingers grasped the knob. There was no way I was going home with him. But before I twisted the knob, he replied.

"Fuck no, I'm not taking her home. A friend saved me a balcony room at the Royal Sonesta for a few days to party. I wasn't in the mood to party tonight, so I was gonna let it go. Now I'm not. Simple as that."

I released my grip on the door handle with a rush of relief. *A hotel.*

"You're gonna give up a balcony room on Bourbon during Mardi Gras to help some girl you've never met? What the fuck happened while I was gone, Bishop?"

Bishop. I rolled the name around on my tongue, surprised at how much I liked it—and how well it suited him.

"Nothing happened. But you know as well as I do from one look at her that she doesn't have a fucking clue what she walked into."

"And since when do you care?"

"Leave it alone."

Delilah backed off, and I dropped my gaze to the black-and-white-tiled floor and pretended like I wasn't exercising mad eavesdropping skills.

Bishop strode toward me, his face impossible to read. "Let's go."

Decision time. Based on Delilah's shock, this wasn't

something that was in character for Bishop. My hesitation must have been obvious, because he stopped in front of me.

"Your choice, cupcake. Hotel room or take your chances on your own. We both know the smart move here."

Delilah followed behind him, her heels clicking on the floor. She propped a hand on her hip and her gaze swung from him to me.

"He's not gonna hurt you, sugar. He might be an ass, but he's the kind of ass you can trust with your life."

What choice did I really have?

I forced my lips into an imitation of a polite smile. "Thank you. I appreciate it."

He grunted in response before peeling back my fingers to release the death grip on my suitcase.

"What—"

My question was cut off when he lifted the carry-on and strode out the door.

"Would you look at that . . ." The words came as a whisper from Delilah. Her eyes cut from the doorway Bishop walked out of to me. "Better catch up with him, because at this rate, who knows what he'll do next."

Bishop

I DIDN'T GET INVOLVED. I NEVER GOT INVOLVED. SO, WHY the fuck was I carrying a suitcase that had to cost more than a month of my rent to the Royal Sonesta with a girl trailing after me who had *prim, proper, and helpless* written all over her?

Because I couldn't let her fend for herself in this mess? Since when did I care about random people off the street?

I glanced back to see if she was keeping up, and slowed when I realized she was lagging more than a few steps behind me.

Pink-and-white polo shirt with no doubt some fancy logo on it. Dark skinny jeans. Fucking Sperry Top-Siders. And then that face and those eyes. Like a sucker punch to the gut.

I wasn't the kind of guy for women like her. The kind that fell into the category marked off with caution tape that read Good Girls – Proceed At Your Own Risk. But for some reason, my brain and my dick couldn't get on the same page.

Not that my dick was going anywhere near her. Fuck, she probably had some kind of force field to keep guys like me away from her pristine self. *Then why does she look at you like that?* I saw the fascination in her eyes when she looked at me, and I was going to fucking ignore it.

She finally caught up, and I shortened my stride so she could keep pace. Questions burned on the tip of my tongue, but I shut them down.

I don't get involved.

But seriously, what the fuck was she doing in New Orleans with no hotel room during Mardi Gras? That didn't scream *sophisticated world traveler* to me. Something wasn't adding up.

Doesn't matter.

I kept my eyes straight ahead, scanning the streets, moving to dodge people and glancing down at her no more than once every thirty seconds to make sure she wasn't falling behind again.

But that excuse was bullshit because I never let her out of my peripheral vision. Still, that was how I saw her drag her gaze up to my face as though she was trying just as hard to figure me out when she should have been keeping track of the pavement beneath her feet.

"Fuck," I bit out as she caught a toe on the uneven cobblestone and pitched forward toward a girl in a silver bikini top and not much else. Cupcake's arms shot out to brace her fall, but before her hands could make contact with the girl or the ground, I wrapped an arm around her waist and yanked her up beside me.

The cry of surprise I'd expected to hear when she was falling didn't come until she was flush against my side and the scent of something beachy and citrus invaded my nose. *Of course she has to smell better than any woman I've ever gotten close to. Fuck me.*

"Thank you." The words were hushed, probably because her face was buried in my shoulder.

I stilled and waited for her to unwrap her fingers from around my wrist and disconnect us.

As soon as she became aware of how she'd clung to me, she jumped away like she'd just learned I was a leper.

"Watch yourself."

"Sorry. I'm not usually this clumsy."

I wasn't sure I could believe that so I started walking again, and she hurried to keep up. When the door on the side of the Royal Sonesta finally came into view, relief and disappointment punched into me.

I just needed to get the key, get the girl in the room, and get the hell back to the shop. My good deed for the day— more like for the year—would be done, and I wouldn't have to worry about what would happen to her on her own. *And I'll never see her again.*

The crowd parted ahead of me, and I tugged on the knob of the side door. It didn't budge.

Fuck.

"I . . . uh, I think you have to have a keycard to get in." She gestured to the gold plaque and the card reader beneath it.

Shit. This was why I only agreed to party in a hotel room if someone I knew was already there or I already had the key. Dealing with front-desk managers wasn't my thing.

"Come on." I wrapped a hand around her arm and pulled her toward the service door that led into the parking garage under the hotel. She stiffened but followed.

I inhaled the combination of exhaust, brake fluid, and gasoline that finally drove her scent from my nose. *Better that way.*

Inside the garage was a door that led to the hotel, and I reluctantly released my hold on her before pushing it open and gesturing for her to enter ahead of me. We made our way through a maze of hallways until we reached the lobby.

The desk clerks looked overworked and underpaid as they dealt with drunken partiers and answered the nonstop ringing phones.

I caught sight of Leon and joined his line. The girl hung back, which was fine by me.

Leon, a client of mine whose ink was completely hidden by his uniform, smiled when he saw me. "Hey, man! Didn't think you would actually take me up on the room and let me pay off a little of what I owe you."

"I appreciate it, brother. How many nights did you block this one off for?"

His eyebrows went up and he checked the computer. "It's blocked until Wednesday morning, but only comped for two nights. I can't comp it the whole time without getting fired."

"That's no problem." Her voice came from beside me as she slid a credit card across the counter. "You can use this for whatever you need to charge."

Leon looked from the girl to me and then down at the card before swiping it. "That works for me. Thank you, Ms. Madden."

Ms. Madden. Now my curiosity was beating at me because I needed to know her first name but I wasn't about to ask in front of Leon.

After he returned the credit card and slid two room

keys across the counter, she stepped away. Leon smiled and winked at me. "Enjoy your night. I know I would if I were you."

"Thanks, man. Consider us even." I didn't address his comment because I was sure he figured I'd be fucking *Ms. Madden* six ways to Sunday in the room tonight, but that wasn't on the menu.

As I followed her to the elevator, I got my first good look at her from behind. Long blond hair tumbled over her shoulders to the middle of her back, and her ass filled out those jeans in the best way possible.

If she were on the menu, I'd fucking devour her.

My dick jumped in agreement, and I had to force myself to think about something else. Like the fact that hooking up with a girl like her would lead to nothing but trouble, even if she had been throwing out the signals that she was interested, which she wasn't.

Even better. I was picturing her ass cupped in my hands while I lifted her up against the wall of the elevator we stepped into, and she was trying to pretend I didn't exist.

Heavy silence hung in the air as she stared at the floor and I pressed the button for the third floor.

The mirrors told the truth, though, and she sneaked more than one glance at me before we stepped out.

Ms. Madden started down the hall ahead of me.

Ms. Madden. Way too frigging proper. Gave me all sorts of ideas about teaching her just how improper she could be.

Not happening.

"What's your name, girl?" The question came out more like a bark, fueled by frustration with my inability to lock my shit down.

She jerked around at my harsh tone and nearly tripped

over her own feet on the carpet.

"Uh . . . E-Eden," she stuttered, and then shut her mouth so quickly her teeth clacked together.

Once again, I reached out to steady her, but was slow to drop my hand from her hip.

"Watch yourself." It was as much a warning to me as it was to her.

"Sorry. It's been a long day." Her gaze met mine for a moment before dropping away.

I reached up, and she froze as if expecting me to touch her again, but I pointed at the wall behind her.

"Looks like we found your room."

Elisha Eden

WOW. *I SUCK.*

The first time I needed to give my name on my new ID, and I totally choked. I was the worst mobster's daughter in the history of mobsters' daughters.

I spun around and faced the door to the room, hoping to hide the panic at my mistake.

Bishop reached around me to slide the keycard into the reader, and the heat from his body radiated against my back. I held my breath, wondering if he'd press against me, and then gave myself a mental slap for even considering it.

He was a perfect stranger. A *dangerous* stranger. *Who found me a place to stay when I would have otherwise been out of luck.* It didn't add up.

But the puzzle of Bishop poofed into a cloud of smoke when he pushed open the door, and I took in the scene before me.

Two women. Naked. One spread-eagle on the bed, and

the other licking and sucking a path down her body as her fingers pumped in and out between her legs.

Oh my God. Live porn. Right in front of my face.

I tried to back away but slammed into Bishop's chest. "Uh, wrong room?" I turned toward him, desperate to get out.

His arm wrapped around my waist, stopping my attempted flight. His chest rumbled as he murmured, "Fucking Leon."

"Hey, baby. We were wondering when you were going to show up. Don't worry; I'm getting us both fired up for you."

My gaze darted up to Bishop's face but all I could see was the hard set of his jaw, which didn't look very excited at what had to be most men's fantasy laid out before him.

"Did Leon tell you I wanted you here?" His tone didn't sound welcoming, rather the opposite.

I turned slightly, as though I couldn't hear her answer just fine without seeing her. *Mistake.*

The girl on top withdrew her fingers from the other girl and sucked them between her lips.

Oh. My. God.

"Of course. Who wouldn't want us here?" Her attention landed on me and the arm Bishop had around me. "You don't need her, baby. We'll take care of you all night long."

The girl on the bottom finally opened her eyes and spoke. "I've been waiting for that big cock of yours, Bish. Kitty's fingers just don't fill me up."

Kitty scooted off the bed and stood. She was built like the girl who'd slammed her way out of the tattoo shop. Tall and slim, with legs that went on forever and boobs that defied gravity. The girl beneath her looked to be of a similar and equally unfair build.

Where did all these girls come from? He'd turned down the one, but what guy would turn down *this*? Another thought followed. *Is this his type?* If it was, there was no way I could ever compete.

Why was I even worried about competing?

"Not tonight. You need to go." Bishop's tone was devoid of hesitation.

Kitty—what the heck kind of name was that, anyway?— looked at me with derision.

"Because of her? She looks like she's got a stick shoved so far up her ass there'd be no room for you in her cunt."

My mouth dropped open at her rude and incredibly coarse words. *Wow. Just . . . wow.*

Bishop's entire body stiffened behind me and his arm around my waist tightened. "Get your clothes on and get the fuck out. I don't know what made you or Leon think this little party of yours was a good plan, but you were both dead wrong."

She huffed, and the girl beneath her sat up. "Don't talk to her like that."

"Both of you. Go. Now."

"You're a dick." That came from Kitty.

"Don't make me tell you again."

Bishop unwrapped himself from behind me and strode forward to scoop tiny scraps of clothing off the floor and toss them on the bed. Looking back at me, he said, "You want to go try to find a housekeeping cart to get a clean set of sheets? I doubt you want to sleep on those."

He was right. It also gave me an excellent excuse to get the hell out of the room as quickly as possible. Five minutes later, I'd raided a linen closet at the other end of the floor that hadn't been shut all the way, and headed back to the room, hoping the girls would already be gone.

I should have taken a little bit longer, because they were just leaving when I returned.

Both girls looked at me with daggers in their eyes. "Fucking bitch. You better believe we won't forget this. You wouldn't even know what to do with a guy like him." Kitty's tone was pissed. "No one else ever gets a second shot with Bishop, and you fucking stole mine."

Second shot? I didn't even want to think about the fact that she'd had a first.

"She does not exist for you," Bishop said, anger threading through his voice. "Not another goddamned word. Get the hell out."

I slipped into the hotel room, desperate to get away from them. Actually, right this moment, I wasn't too keen on being around him either.

Anger and disappointment rolled through me, and I didn't want to think about why that was. I didn't know him. Didn't care who he screwed or how many at the same time.

I stalked across the room and froze before I could drop the fresh linens on the desk. A room key and four lines of white powder lay across the glass.

"Whoa. Is that—"

Bishop was behind me before I could finish my sentence. "Fuck." He grabbed the trash can and swept the powder into the bin.

I'd seen the movie *Blow*; I'd just never seen cocaine in real life.

Bishop dropped the trash can back on the floor, strode to the bed, and tore off the sheets. When he was finished, he balled them up and tossed them in the corner before snatching a clean sheet from the stack I still held in my arms.

I didn't know what to say, so I rounded the foot of the bed and helped remake it in silence.

When the job was done, Bishop backed toward the door. "You should be good. Room is comped tonight and tomorrow, but after Saturday morning, it's on you. Room service and anything like that is on your card too." He tucked his hands into the pockets of his jeans. "Look, I'm sorry about Kitty and her friend. I wouldn't have—"

I held up my hands, palms out, hoping he'd stop right there. "It's okay. You don't need to say anything. I mean, I might have to burn the garbage—wait, would that get me high?"

He choked out a laugh and shook his head. "Hold on." He crossed the room and grabbed the trash can before disappearing into the bathroom. The next thing I heard was a flush. He came out and dropped the can back in place next to the desk.

"You're all set. I'll make sure Leon didn't give out any more keys. If he did, I'll have him rekey the room and call you to come down to get a new one."

More than anything, I wanted to ask him why he'd bothered to help me, but I couldn't find the words to put together. Instead, I went with my sincere thanks.

"Thank you. I really do appreciate everything. I'm not sure what I would've done without your help."

Bishop shifted, looking uncomfortable at my words. "Thank me by staying out of trouble."

He turned, pushed open the door, and disappeared.

Bishop

7

I KEPT THINKING I SAW HER. *EDEN*. FUCKING MIND WAS playing tricks on me.

But it wasn't the blond cupcake coming into the shop when the door chimed today. No, she should still be tucked away at the Royal Sonesta—or long gone.

I told myself it didn't matter which, but I was full of shit.

Last night when we'd walked into the hotel room to find Kitty fucking her friend, I'd expected a full-on meltdown from the girl who had surely never seen anything like that before. But she'd barely missed a beat. She didn't make any shitty comments about the fact that two girls were about to get it on in the bed I'd told her she could have that night. She just brushed it off and did what she had to do. Even when she ran across the lines of coke on the desk, she hadn't freaked completely. She'd been shocked and confused, but didn't blink twice after I swept it away.

I hadn't expected resilience from her, but that's what I

saw. Now I couldn't help but wonder how long she was staying, or where the hell she was headed next.

Footsteps neared my room, and I finally looked up at the new arrival. Another familiar face.

"Hey, Bishop." The smile in JP's voice was impossible to miss, as was the hero worship in her stare.

The girl was relentless. I'd done work on her sleeves and shoulders, and she'd been trying to get me to take her out since the first sitting. Besides the fact that my dick wasn't interested, she was too young, and I would have been breaking my rule about not touching any female who walked into Voodoo wanting a tattoo. But JP couldn't or wouldn't take the hint.

"What do you need, girl?" I couldn't find it in me to be mean to her because she was just a kid with a crush, no matter how irritating it was becoming.

Her entire face lit up when I stood from my chair and set my book on the counter behind me. "What do I always need when I come to see you?"

She was an ink junkie, a feeling I understood well. "What do you have in mind this time?"

"Maybe a picnic on the riverbank followed by dessert at my place?"

I suppressed a frustrated groan. One of these days, she was going to have to learn to take a hint. "I meant for your ink. You know the other ain't happening."

Her cute smile fell into a frown. "I'm not too young. I swear it."

"You don't get to decide that for me. I call the shots. So, what do you want for your ink? Or you just here to shoot the shit?"

"Fine."

Her huff was cute, but that's all she was. Cute. Before I'd thought she was too innocent for me, but even JP came off as more worldly than Eden, and my dick didn't seem to mind that.

Stop fucking thinking about her, you little bitch, I reprimanded myself mentally, and forced her from my mind.

"Will you draw me a piece for my back? I'm ready to start it. I was thinking something with skulls and flowers. Like girly voodoo stuff."

At the mention of designing a tattoo, my mind went to Eden again. The first time I saw someone, especially someone without ink, my brain instantly snapped into *create* mode. With Eden, I pictured the ink I'd put on her shoulder blade as soon as she'd followed me into the shop and it was clear she'd never been inside one before.

Even the thought of tattooing her virgin skin had my dick taking notice. I shifted on my stool to readjust, not wanting JP to notice.

Pushing Eden out of my head and willing my dick to go down, I turned my attention back to JP. "What are you thinking?"

"The magic Bishop touch. Whatever you think. I just want it big, and covering the top half of my back so it ties in just under my epaulets."

Now that, that I could do. I loved it when clients let me have free rein to design. The best work always came when someone wasn't dictating every little detail and let me flex my artistic muscles.

"Let me think about it. I'll start drawing it up today. I might be able to fit you in for a sitting next week. I think I have someone who's going to cancel."

"Awesome!" JP clapped her hands, her enthusiasm

impossible to ignore. "You sure you won't change your mind about the date? Just give me a chance. I'm not a kid."

"It's my rule. No touching the clients. You'll find a guy. It just won't be me."

Her expression fell and hurt flashed across her features. Even if I felt guilty, it was better that way. I didn't get involved. That wasn't my thing.

Then why did you help Eden? Fuck if I knew the answer to that one.

Tearing my gaze from the hope lingering in JP's eyes, I looked out toward the front window—and caught a glimpse of the back of a blonde with curves in all the right places.

I shook my head. No way it was Eden.

And why the hell did I keep looking for her? She wasn't coming back here.

End of story. Time to put her out of my head.

Eden

SUNLIGHT STREAMED THROUGH THE GAPS IN THE drapes, dragging me from a sleep that was more like a coma. I'd lain awake for so long last night, I thought I'd never doze off with the raucous noise from the never-ending party on the street below invading my room.

But apparently I was wrong.

I rolled out of bed and walked to the French doors to pull back the blinds. I needed to make sure this morning was real and not a dream.

The iconic buildings that lined Bourbon Street stared back at me from beyond the balcony, and a rush of feelings invaded.

Anxiety. Excitement. Nerves. Anticipation.

I was a girl forced from my home because of whatever messed-up stuff my father was involved in, and I'd proven yesterday that I wasn't nearly as street-smart as I thought I was. Reading about adventuring to new places wasn't exactly the same as doing it in real life. The confidence I'd had when I stepped on that plane at JFK had faded when I'd nearly gotten assaulted.

But today was a fresh start. The city didn't seem quite so intimidating with the morning light, and I could pretend I was a normal girl on vacation. I could start on my list and do all the things I'd dreamed about doing.

I remembered Angelo's orders—*stay in your room, get room service, get a massage.*

Sorry, Angelo. I couldn't pass up this opportunity.

And then Bishop's words as he left last night popped into my head. *Stay out of trouble, kid.*

I certainly wasn't going to go looking for trouble, but I wasn't going to let yesterday stop me. Today I wasn't going to be carrying around a suitcase like the target he'd told me I was. Today I could blend in.

When would I ever have another chance?

Staring into the mirror, I gave myself a pep talk. "I can do this. I don't have to go far. I can just walk around the French Quarter and be *normal*. I'll be fine."

Rationalizations in place and confidence buoyed, I showered and got ready for the day. Obviously, I hadn't had the luxury of time to deliberate over what I packed, so I pulled some of the mishmash of clothes from my suitcase.

Jeans, a white cami, and a pale pink cardigan wouldn't stick out during the day, right?

I slipped into my Sperrys and headed out of my room, feeling like today was the beginning of something completely new. My first taste of real life and the uncertainty of how my choices would play out. No safety net or security here. Just . . . me.

It was long overdue.

I found the green-and-white-striped awnings of the famous Café du Monde about the time my stomach was grumbling to be filled. Once I was seated at a little table, I devoured the delicious powdered-sugar-covered confection that was their famous beignet and guzzled a cup of coffee while I people-watched. It was a habit of mine honed from years of living on the sidelines and watching life go by.

I refused to acknowledge that I might have been scanning the crowd for a certain man-bunned giant. *Maybe I should walk by the tattoo shop . . . see if he's there.*

I didn't know where that idea came from, but it was a terrible one. I would do no such thing. Even if he had been the most intimidatingly beautiful man I'd ever seen, I had no business seeking him out. It wasn't like he seemed eager to stick around and get to know me either.

Which was good because *no one* could get to know me here. I was still kicking myself for giving him my real name. How could I possibly screw up something so basic and important?

You're not going to see him again, so it doesn't matter.

It wasn't like we would cross paths. New Orleans was a big city. And we especially wouldn't cross paths if I stayed away from a certain tattoo shop. Not that I had a reason to walk by there, anyway. It wasn't like I wanted a tattoo or something.

Right?

It wasn't something I'd ever considered. Getting a tattoo hadn't made any of my lists because it had literally never crossed my mind. Until now . . .

Pushing the ridiculous thought away, I left my seat at Café du Monde and stepped onto the sidewalk. It was terrifyingly exciting to know that there would be no security trailing me through the streets. Tendrils of freedom wrapped around me, and I savored them.

At least until I remembered that if something happened to me, like yesterday when those guys grabbed me, I'd be completely on my own without any way to defend myself. Except now I knew how *not* to throw a punch.

Why hadn't Dom insisted on self-defense? Oh, that's right, he never expected me to be outside the bubble I'd existed within.

Deciding that I'd keep a close eye on my surroundings, I walked toward Jackson Square and watched street artists create their works as jazz from a brass quartet filled the air. I stood for long minutes, letting the music sweep me up, and inch by inch, I began to relax.

This city had its own rhythm, and I was feeling it in my blood.

I tossed the handful of change from Café du Monde in the open trombone case and continued to explore. I made my way around the Square, soaking up every detail of the architecture, the vivid colors, the eclectic street performers and artists, until a decadent sweet scent hit my nose. Letting my senses lead me, I turned in a slow circle to figure out where it was coming from. A woman stood in the window behind a hand-painted sign that read FRESH PRALINES.

Just because I'd stuffed myself on beignets didn't mean I couldn't enjoy more of what New Orleans had to offer. I stepped toward the door, but a familiar voice caught me off guard.

"Hey, sugar. Didn't expect to see you again."

Coming out of the store right in front of me was the black-and-blue-haired woman from the tattoo shop. Delilah. Apparently New Orleans wasn't nearly as big of a city as I'd thought.

"Delilah. Remember me?"

I shook off the momentary surprise at running into someone who wasn't a stranger. "Yes, sorry."

"No big deal. It's good to see you looking a little less lost than last time." She adjusted the bag over her shoulder. "So you decided to stick around, I see."

"How could I not? This city seems to be a pretty special place."

The smile that stretched across Delilah's face was sincere. "It certainly is. I came with friends in 2005 for a weekend and never left. Definitely more my speed than Omaha."

One look at her blue hair, retro Hawaiian print dress, tattoos, and vintage yellow Mary Janes would tell anyone that Omaha wasn't exactly where Delilah was meant to live.

"So, now that you're sucked in by the lure of this awesome place, are you ready to get a little wild and crazy like the rest of the Mardi Gras partiers? Maybe tattoo that virgin skin of yours?"

My earlier thought slammed into me. A tattoo meant seeing Bishop again, and as much as I wanted to deny it, the idea was tempting.

Maybe he could be one of your New Orleans experiences . . . That thought had to be from an inner troublemaker playing devil's advocate, but I pushed it away.

"I should probably start with something a little less drastic." I nodded at the door I'd been about to go in before she came out. "Like pralines."

Delilah lifted her bag. "I got you covered. I had a major

craving today and this is the only place I'll buy them. And . . . if you want to get the inside scoop on all the non-touristy must-dos to check off while you're here, I'm your girl."

My inner list-lover surged to life at her tempting offer. "I'd love that."

"Then come with me and prepare to be wowed. We'll eat pralines until we're sick, and see if you can get Bishop all stirred up again." She winked at me, and I immediately regretted my hasty acceptance.

"Maybe that's not such a good idea."

Delilah's dark eyes shined with mischief. "I think it's the best idea I've had in forever. Come on. I won't take no for an answer."

And that's how I ended up allowing myself to be dragged back to Voodoo Ink within a half hour of deciding I wasn't going to walk past the tattoo shop ever again—no matter how badly I wanted to.

"Dirty Dog is my absolute favorite for clothes. Some of their vintage stuff is a little pricey, but not overpriced, you know what I mean? It's just good stuff. For eats, you have to check out the Cookery and Desire. I could literally give you a list as long as your arm. If you want to get out of the Quarter, it gets even longer."

My anxiety rose with every step we took toward the shop, but Delilah's cheerful monologue about awesome restaurants and shops helped drown it out, even if I didn't think I'd recall the name of a single place. Before too long, we stood in front of the door I remembered all too well. When she yanked it open, I wasn't ready.

My gaze scanned the vicinity for any kind of delay I could grasp.

The sign on the building next door read YOUR FAVORITE

HOLE with a giant donut as the O in *hole*.

Coffee. They liked caffeine.

"Do you want me to grab some coffee from next door to go with those pralines?"

Delilah paused with her hand on the door as the chimes tinkled. "I sure wouldn't turn it down."

Grateful for the momentary reprieve to get my thoughts in order, I stepped away from the door of Voodoo like someone had put some kind of spell across the entrance specifically designed to keep me out.

As soon as I walked into Your Favorite Hole, I realized my mistake in running away from the inevitable.

Because there he was. Standing in line one person ahead of me. He was unmistakable with that mane of brown-and-gold hair wrapped up in a man bun. At five foot six, I considered myself average height, but he had to have at least eight or ten inches on me.

I wonder what else is eight or ten inches. Where the thought came from, I had no idea, but I silenced it . . . although not before dropping my gaze to the worn jeans that cupped his ass below the hem of his black Voodoo Ink T-shirt. The memory of yesterday's bulge stepped onto the center stage of my brain.

Bishop turned around, coffee cup in one hand and a brown paper bag in the other.

First the single-take. Then the double-take. Followed by the fleeting look of surprise.

"Eden."

A stupid thrill ran through me when he said my name. *I shouldn't be impressed that he hasn't forgotten it in twelve hours.* And yet, I kind of was.

"Uh, hi?" I waved awkwardly, my wristlet dangling from

my waving hand.

Wow. Smooth, E.

He backed away from the counter and came toward me. The woman in front of me in line turned and dragged her gaze from the thick black soles of his boots up to the top of his man-bunned head, all but salivating at the sight.

"How was the room?" he asked.

"Good. Fine. Great. Really nice. Thank you. I appreciate it. Really."

He stayed silent after my word vomit.

The woman in front of me paid for her coffee and donuts and moved toward the counter, where the barista would undoubtedly set up the drinks.

"Ma'am, what can I get for ya?" the woman behind the cash register asked, providing the interruption I needed.

Bishop's attention stayed on me and his feet remained planted on the floor. I opened my mouth to order before realizing I had no idea what kind of coffee I should order for Delilah.

Chancing another glance up at Bishop, I found him still watching me. "Do you know what Delilah drinks?"

His brows knitted together. "You're coming to the shop?"

"Oh, hon, that's all you had to say," the cashier said. "We'll whip her order right up. You want anything else?"

I turned from Bishop to the cashier. "Two of whatever Delilah gets is fine."

"No problem."

The heat from Bishop's stare dissipated, and I glanced over my shoulder.

He was gone.

No *good to see you again*. No *stay the hell away from the shop*. Nothing.

The cashier read the confusion on my face when I faced the counter again. "Ah, don't worry about Bishop making a quick exit. He don't talk to many people, no matter how much they might want to talk to him."

Her description echoed what I'd gathered yesterday.

"Do you know him well?" I asked as I handed over a twenty.

"As well as anyone, I guess. He comes in twice a day like clockwork, getting his caffeine fix and ignoring the ladies." She jerked her head toward the woman waiting by the barista, whose eyes were fixed on the door Bishop had just exited. "And don't forget those two." She nodded toward the comfy seating area in the corner where two other women sat, their expressions disappointed and wistful all at the same time.

"They come in here at least three times a week to stare. He's like our own little attraction drawing in customers 'round here, because they sure as hell don't come for the donuts."

I believed it. They didn't exactly look like they ate a lot of donuts, given the way their knit blouses clung to their thin frames. Actually, I kind of wanted to buy a few donuts and drop them in front of the two women and walk away slowly.

Once the image evaporated from my mind, I turned my attention back to the cashier, whose name tag read FABIENNE. "This place is amazing. I can't imagine you need an attraction to get people to come in here." The wall of donuts behind her tempted the crap out of me, even though I'd already had beignets and planned to devour pralines.

If I work up the courage to go into Voodoo.

Fabienne smiled back at me. "It ain't Starbucks, but we do all right. You want a donut to go with that order?"

"I've got some pralines waiting for me, but I'll definitely

take a rain check."

The barista set two cups on the end of the counter. "Delilah's order is ready."

I moved toward the end of the counter and thanked her.

"Make sure to come back and try one."

"I will, definitely."

I refused to acknowledge that my promise meant that I'd be so close to Voodoo.

I collected the coffee and decided that regardless of what or who was next door, I would be back.

Bishop

9

THE DOOR CHIMED, AND I JERKED MY HEAD AROUND to see if she'd actually come back.

Who the hell else would walk into a tattoo shop wearing a pink sweater?

Play it fucking cool, man. Lock this shit down.

I didn't react to women like this. Certainly not ones who were as innocent and naive as Eden. I needed to treat her like any other customer. Except she wasn't even a customer, so I didn't know what to do with her. Dragging her into the back to find out if her lips were as sweet as the cupcake she made me think of when I saw her wasn't an option.

Delilah strolled out of the employee break room and met Eden as she crossed the black-and-white-checkered floor of the shop.

"Caffeine. Lifeblood of the gods. Thank you. I'll repay you with all the pralines you can eat before you puke. But you have to clean up your own puke. Shop rule."

Eden's brows went up. "I'll try not to puke." She held out a cup to Delilah. "I asked for your order, and the woman at the counter said this was it."

"Four-shot skinny latte with a dash of cinnamon. The only thing that keeps me going some days."

"I got the same, so it's good to know you don't drink black-tar coffee or something." Eden sounded hesitant, like she had no idea why she was here.

That made two of us.

Delilah dropped the open box of pralines in her hand on the counter, and I pretended I wasn't watching as Eden studied them and pulled out a candy.

Now I'm a fucking creeper. What am I going to do? Watch her eat it?

"Hey, Bish, you want one?" Delilah called to me. "Might sweeten you up a little."

I sucked back a too-big mouthful of coffee, burning my tongue.

"I'm good." Almost as an afterthought, I tacked on, "Thanks."

Delilah's eye roll was almost audible.

"Don't mind him; he's just cranky. Bish is still recovering from the girl who committed the cardinal sin after he dropped you at the hotel last night—she touched his beard *and* she grabbed his ass."

People who talked about you like you weren't there were fucking fabulous. But Delilah was the only family I had, so she got a pass.

"Oh wow. That's pretty . . . forward." Eden's surprised gaze finally landed on me, and I held it for several long moments before it dropped to the floor.

"It gets way worse, and sad to say, he gets the brunt of it."

Delilah glanced back toward my station. "I don't know what it is about a guy with tats and a beard that makes them think they should just grab on to whatever they want."

"That's enough, D. I can hear every word."

She turned around with a smirk. "Obviously. Why else would I talk about you?"

Eden's gaze darted back and forth between us like she didn't know what to make of this kind of banter.

"Because you're a pain in my ass."

"And you love me anyway. Get out here and say hi to Eden. You know you want to."

Eden's face flamed red, but Delilah didn't seem to notice she was embarrassing the hell out of the girl.

"It's okay. I don't mean to bother either of you. I was just . . ."

I rose from my stool and came out into the main area of the shop as Eden's words trailed off.

"You were just doing what?" I asked.

"Exploring. And trying new things." Her dark eyes met mine after a beat of hesitation, and I could think of a dozen new things I'd like her to try.

Why did corrupting her innocence seem like the best idea I'd had in years? I should feel like a piece of shit for even considering touching her, but something about her called to my most basic instincts.

Protect. Defend. Claim.

I hadn't felt that fucking primal in years—and I needed to *lock that shit down*. My life was simple, and this girl had *complicated* written all over her.

"She's about to try her very first praline," Delilah said. "You sure you don't want one, Bish?"

"I'm good. Have at 'em."

Eden, looking grateful for the interruption, lifted it to her lips. When she bit into the praline, a quiet moan escaped her mouth and echoed in my balls.

Fuck. Fuck. Fuck. She shouldn't be bringing out this kind of response in me, and I needed to get it under control before I did something I wouldn't be able to take back.

I turned my attention away and walked behind the counter to check the appointment book, even though I knew exactly what was on the schedule for the day.

"Oh my God, these are delicious," Eden whispered after she swallowed.

"Best in the city, in my opinion. So, what really brings you to New Orleans if you aren't here for the craziness of Mardi Gras?"

It was a question I wanted to ask too.

"I always wanted to come here?" Eden's reply sounded a hell of a lot more like a question, but before she could say more, the door swung open and chimed again.

I swung my focus to the entrance, ready to glare at whoever came inside, but I couldn't.

"Charlie! It's been way too long, stranger! Where have you been hiding, girl?" Delilah's excitement sent her voice into the next octave.

The women hugged, and Charlie smiled over Delilah's shoulder at me. "Hey, Bishop. How's it going?"

"He's cranky as usual," Delilah said. "Tell me, what's new? This place isn't the same without you around. I know you're up in Simon's fancy-schmancy place doing all that noble charity stuff, but we miss you down here."

Charlie was the shopgirl before I started here. I'd only met her a few times when she'd come in for touch-ups on her tats. Full sleeves graced her arms, and her back was fairly covered. She was notorious in her own right, the daughter of the man who committed the biggest fraud to ever hit the investment world.

I wondered if Eden would recognize her. Most people didn't, given that she'd made a one-hundred-eighty-degree change from the days she spent as a society princess.

"We've been so crazy busy. Between Simon taking over the CEO position from his dad, and me running the non-profit, I swear, we barely get to sleep anymore. But I had to get down here to say hi and see if you could squeeze me in for a quick touch-up."

"Anything for you, girl. Anytime."

Charlie turned to Eden and held out a hand. "Sorry to be rude. I'm Charlie Duchesne. I used to work here."

"Best damn shopgirl we've ever had. And we haven't found a new one who would stick since. Sad state of affairs." Delilah motioned to Eden. "This is our new friend Eden, who up and decided to come to New Orleans on Mardi Gras but didn't know what she was getting into. I'm just waiting for the real story."

Eden stiffened, and my guess was that she didn't appreciate being put on the spot.

"Umm . . . there's really no story."

Charlie sized her up. "You sure? Because that's what people usually say who have the best stories."

"I really just always wanted to come here. That's basically it."

"How long are you staying?" This question came from Delilah.

Eden shrugged. "I don't know. I haven't decided."

"Where are you staying?" Charlie asked.

"A hotel, for the moment."

Eden's answers were vague enough to raise more than one question in my mind, but for some reason, I didn't like seeing how uncomfortable the interrogation made her.

"What do you need touched up?" I asked Charlie, trying to change the subject. "I can take care of it right now, if you want."

All three female heads swung in my direction.

Charlie smiled. "Only if it's not too much trouble." She held up her arm and flipped it over. "When this healed, some of the line work flaked. Considering it's my tattoo for Simon, I want it to be perfect." She glanced at Delilah. "And I wanted a reason to come hang out. I miss this place."

Delilah studied her. "Are you sure everything's okay uptown?"

Charlie nodded. "I'm just feeling nostalgic, and I had some free time on my hands."

"Come on. We can get you fixed up." As I headed back to my station and Charlie followed, I could feel Eden's attention on me.

It only took ten minutes to fix the lines on Charlie's eternity tat, and by the time we finished, she was ready to spill.

She dropped into one of the waiting-room chairs and pulled her knees up in front of her. She looked all of twenty years old. "We're talking about trying to have a baby, and I'm kinda freaking out."

Delilah's eyes widened. "Wow. That's a big one."

Eden, who'd been talking about pralines and places to eat in the Quarter with Delilah while I worked, released a breath. "That is big."

Charlie tucked her hair behind her ears. "I love Simon more than I knew I could ever love another human being, and I want to have a family with him. It's always seemed so far off in the future, you know? But now it's getting real. It shouldn't scare me, but it does."

"Change is hard. Especially that kind of permanent change." Delilah's voice was soft.

"Yeah, and I know it's going to be the kind of change that flips our entire life on its head, and I'm trying to figure out if I'm ready for that. I like our life. It's good. It's amazing. What if this screws everything up?"

"What does Simon say about it?" Delilah asked.

Charlie shook her head. "I haven't told him any of this. I don't know how. I don't want him to think I'm not excited for a family, but I'm . . . I'm just worried."

"You've gotta talk to him about it. He's a man; he can't read your mind."

Again, all three female heads in the room swiveled around to face me. Even I was surprised to hear myself offer up the words.

Delilah offered a small smile to Charlie. "He's right. You have to tell Simon what you're thinking. That's the only way you're going to be able to figure out if right now is the time to do this."

"I know. But he wants it so much, and I feel like there's something wrong with me because I need to really think about it."

"There's nothing wrong with that. It's going to affect you both, so you both have to be ready."

Charlie inhaled and released a deep breath before un-curling herself from the chair and standing. "Okay. I'm going to talk to him today."

"Everything's going to be fine. That man loves you like crazy." Delilah hugged her tight. "Now, don't be a stranger."

Charlie hugged her back. "You know I won't be." Then

she looked at Eden. "If you need a place to stay for longer than a couple days, let Delilah or Bishop know. My old land-lady is crazy as hell, in the best way possible, but she's got a place she keeps empty most of the time. It was exactly what I needed when I was new in town and trying to find my way. Something tells me you might need the same thing."

10

Eden

THE WAY CHARLIE LOOKED AT ME, STUDYING MY features, made my heart hammer.

I recognized her. She'd been on the front page of every newspaper in New York for a couple of months while the FBI was trying to track her down. But she hadn't looked like this then—no tattoos and purple-and-red hair had made the front page. She was the privileged daughter of the biggest investment swindler to hit New York since Bernie Madoff.

Just knowing she was from the same city made me worry about being recognized. But I'd never been in the papers. We'd never crossed paths. It was impossible.

Still, Charlie's offer made it seem like she saw too much.

"Thank you for the offer," I said. "I appreciate it."

She smiled at me again before she left the shop.

I had to be more careful. I couldn't risk being identified. I was supposed to be laying low, and here I was acting like a tourist.

Dumb, Eden. Why do you have to be so dumb? Maybe because my life hadn't exactly prepared me for this.

As soon as the door chimed behind her, Delilah turned her attention back to me.

"So, what are you going to do with yourself while you're here?"

I knew what I wasn't going to do—stay holed up in my hotel room and not get to experience anything. I could go back to New York and do plenty of nothing.

The thought hung in my head like a punishment. *Why would I want to go back to that?*

Then my next thought. *It's not like Dom would give me a choice.*

Realizing I'd let the silence go too long without answering, I met Delilah's gaze. "I think I'd just like to do some living." It was as honest of an answer as I could give.

"Well, sugar, I think you've come to the right place for that. Between me and Bishop, we can show you almost everything this city has to offer."

Bishop didn't offer his support for her suggestion, and I filled the awkward silence that followed.

"That's okay. I'm sure I can figure it out. I've got a list. My plan is to work my way through it."

"A list? How very organized of you. Do tell."

Bishop pulled out his cell phone and frowned down at it. He turned and walked down the back hallway without a word.

Delilah and I both watched him go before she turned back to me.

"Look, I don't know if you've got your sights set on the big guy, but he's tough to read. I've never seen him react to someone the way he did with you, so I have no idea what to make of that. I probably shouldn't interfere, but . . . that's kind of what I do. So, you want the scoop?"

Do I? I almost snorted at my own stupid mental question. *Of course I do.*

Bishop
11

I BREATHED IN STALE SMOKE UNTIL IT CLOGGED MY *lungs as the pain from my broken ribs threatened to take me to my knees again. I'd crawled all the way from the alley, where they'd left me broken, to find everything that mattered to me had been burned away.*

Rage filled my veins as I vowed revenge.

I jerked awake from the nightmare, sweat coating my skin, sheets sticking to my body, and my lungs heaving for breath. It had been months since it had ripped me out of sleep and tossed me into a past I couldn't run far enough from to forget.

I sat up in bed for a few minutes, letting my racing heart calm down enough to assure myself I wasn't having a heart attack, before accepting that there was no way in hell I was getting any more sleep tonight.

After splashing my face with water, I stared into the mirror. The long hair, the beard, the tattoos. Behind them was the punk kid who'd thought he knew how to fix everything and hadn't considered what his actions could cost him.

Everything.

Whiskey. That was the only thing that would drive the smell of the smoke from my nose and chase the memories away. I stumbled into my kitchen for the bottle on top of the fridge, but as soon as my hand wrapped around it, I couldn't stomach the thought of sitting at my table drinking alone.

Too much silence to dwell on the past. I needed noise. People. Not to interact, but to distract.

I headed back to the bedroom to grab a pair of jeans off the floor. I shoved my legs into them before reaching around in the darkness to find the nearest shirt.

After I dragged my boots on, I tied my hair up into a knot at the back of my head and shoved a knife in my pocket. Old habits die hard, even though most people would think twice about fucking with a tatted-up guy my size. But then again, tweakers and drunks didn't always care.

Maybe that's what I needed tonight. When I left my apartment above Voodoo and headed toward Bourbon Street and the perfect distraction of nonstop partying, I was more than ready to take on a fight, if that's what found me.

I didn't admit to myself that I was going to walk past one specific balcony, hoping to catch a glimpse of a girl I knew better than to think about.

Eden

I TRIED TO FIND SLEEP AGAIN, BUT TONIGHT IT WASN'T happening. Too many thoughts and possibilities made it just as impossible as the dull roar coming from outside.

Fear kept me in my hotel room. Fear that I'd attract the wrong kind of trouble and wouldn't be able to defend myself. Fear that I'd be recognized somehow. Fear that I didn't know how to live, even when given the opportunity.

How pathetic is that?

Twenty-four years old, and I was completely clueless about life and scared to take the first step to living it. Maybe it hadn't just been the gilded cage keeping me trapped, maybe it was *me*.

So, get out there. Live.

I peeked out the curtains of my balcony window and watched as the partiers milled about in the streets with drinks in hand, or exited one bar only to enter another.

I could go down there and have a drink. Step a few

inches outside my comfort zone. Finally have a life experience not dictated by someone else.

Did I really want to do it? No. It would be easier to stay here, in my bed, where I could find another book to hopefully hold my attention. But something inside me told me I had to do it. I owed it to myself.

As I pulled back the duvet, a vision of the two naked girls who had been on this bed before me entered my mind—along with the guy who'd tossed them out of the room.

If I hadn't been here, would Bishop have taken advantage of what they'd been offering? The one girl, Kitty, had made it sound like she'd already been with him once and wanted seconds.

Not that it mattered. The fumbling loss of my virginity with a hotel bellboy in a beach cabana when I was eighteen and on a trip to Spain with my aunt didn't exactly put me into the category of women who would attract a guy like Bishop.

Why am I even thinking about this?

Probably because everywhere I looked in this room, I felt or saw his presence.

Well, that was one more reason on the "pro" side of getting out of here for a couple of hours.

Decision made, I crossed to the closet and considered my options. I hadn't packed anything that screamed *night out on Bourbon Street*. Probably because I didn't own anything like the girls wore out there.

I'd brought exactly one dress, and it was simple and black with cap sleeves and a square neckline. Otherwise, my choices were jeans and camis and cardigans. I couldn't wear a cardigan on Bourbon Street, could I? It seemed like one of those offenses that could get you escorted out of the French

Quarter.

But a dress? That seemed like too much.

Out of your comfort zone, E.

Without thinking any further, I stripped off my yoga pants and T-shirt and slipped the dress off the hanger.

As I stepped into it and zipped up the side, I examined my shoe options. Leopard-print flats would have to work because wearing my Sperrys with it would definitely get me laughed out of town.

A makeup touch-up followed, and after I clasped a necklace around my neck, I was done. Ready.

I left my room before I had a chance to change my mind.

When I pushed open the doors of the hotel and stepped onto the sidewalk, I couldn't decide if I'd made the best decision of my life or a horrible mistake. I'd convinced myself that I could handle myself out here, but the noise was three times as loud as it had been in my room, and being on the street level made it seem more foreboding than it had from the balcony window.

Revelers dodged around me as I stood like an idiot in their way. One man knocked into my shoulder as he walked backward. His apology was muffled as he tripped over his feet, and I followed his line of sight to see a dozen women lifting their shirts for men on a balcony across the street.

The best description I could give it—tits and ass everywhere.

And I looked all prim and proper in my just-above-the-knee-length dress, flats, and understated jewelry. *Terrible mistake*, I decided.

I was two seconds from turning back to the hotel and retracing my steps to my room when I saw a group of girls around my age laughing and walking down the street. Greek letters were printed on the front of their T-shirts, and from the smiles on their faces and the drinks in their hands, they weren't worried about their safety. I didn't have numbers on my side, but I could get off the street and into a bar with a corner stool that would allow me to people-watch without being right in the thick of it.

That's stepping out of your comfort zone? my inner voice said, mocking me.

"One step at a time," I whispered to myself. "Small steps."

Now, which bar? I turned and surveyed my options. So many of them looked alike. I let instinct be my guide and picked the one with music coming from open doors and windows only a few dozen feet away.

It seemed as good a choice as any, and I didn't have to walk by any dark alleys.

Making my way inside the dark room lit mostly by neon beer mirrors and signs, I snagged a seat at the end of the scarred bar where it curved around and met the wall as a couple left.

The bartender wasted no time before stopping in front of me.

"What can I get you, hon?" Her blond hair was pulled up into a messy bun on the top of her head, and a deep vee cut in the black shirt showed off her generous cleavage.

I looked around the room to see what everyone else was drinking, and spotted a woman with a plastic cup of what looked like some kind of purple punch.

I nodded at it. "I'll have one of those purple ones."

"Ten dollars."

Pulling some cash from my small wristlet, I handed it over and she turned to make the drink.

See, that wasn't hard.

The drink was before me in less than two minutes, and I lifted it in a silent toast to this new chapter in my life. *Salut.*

It was grape deliciousness in a plastic cup. I had no idea what kind of alcohol or how much the bartender used because I couldn't taste it. Someone could seriously put this drink in a sippy cup, and I would have thought it was for toddlers. Well, not quite. But that explained why it went down so fast.

The heat from the crush of people in the bar flushed my cheeks, and I officially decided that this was a good decision.

When I laid another ten on the bar and lifted my cup toward the bartender, she nodded, grabbing the money before going to work mixing another drink.

The second one I sipped a little more slowly, mostly because of the cute guy who took the stool beside me.

"Hey, I'm John."

"Eden."

"You here by yourself?"

Instinctively, I knew I should lie. Smart Girl Bar Rules 101. "My friends are dancing. I'm taking a break."

"Yeah, it gets pretty wild here, especially during Mardi Gras."

We yelled to each other over the music and the noise for a few minutes while he ordered a drink and told me stories of some of the crazy stuff he'd seen tonight. I ordered my third drink and he insisted on paying. I insisted right back that I could buy my own drinks. It started going down just as quickly.

He pointed out another drunk idiot, and I turned my

head toward the street.

And that's when I saw him. Bishop. Like an avenger just inside the bar, his tattoos lit almost neon by the lights, he shoved through the crowd toward me in the corner of the bar. His eyes locked on the guy next to me as I lifted my cup and sucked down another swig.

Before I could lower my drink to the bar, Bishop grabbed the cup from my hand and dumped it down John's shirt.

"What the fuck, man?" John jumped off his bar stool as the purple liquid stained his blue-and-white-striped polo.

Rage. That was the only emotion I could make out on Bishop's face.

"I saw you drop something in her drink. Don't fucking tell me I didn't."

My eyes darted everywhere. From Bishop to John and then to the bartender, a wooden club clenched in her small fist. She looked between the two men, as if unsure who she should be threatening.

"All of you. Get the hell out of my bar."

Bishop didn't say another word before wrapping a giant hand around my upper arm and pulling me off my stool. As he dragged me toward the door, he turned back to John, who was now patting his shirt down with napkins.

"Get the fuck out of this town before I can track you down and show you what I do to guys like you. Piece of shit."

The bouncer, probably attracted by the commotion, stepped to Bishop and looked down at me.

"You okay, miss?" He had to yell so I could hear him.

I nodded because I couldn't think of anything else to do. Was I okay? I thought so. My head was swimming and my legs were unsteady, but that was just the alcohol, right? I hadn't been drugged. Had I?

"That piece of shit dosed her drink. I don't think she had much, though."

The bouncer immediately spun around and stalked across the bar toward John.

Bishop didn't wait to see what the bouncer did before tugging me onto the street. Thankful for my flats, I stumbled along after him.

"Slow down. Please."

I tripped on a crack in the sidewalk and pitched forward toward Bishop's side.

Shit.

He didn't let me land on my face. Apparently, he was good at that. His strong arms wrapped around me, and he caught a handful of boob.

Holy shit. Bishop is touching my boob, was the only thought in my alcohol-soaked brain. My nipple peaked into his hand, which he yanked away before setting me upright again.

"What the fuck are you doing out here by yourself?"

I blurted the only answer that came to mind. "Living."

That's when my knees gave out, and I pitched forward into Bishop's chest.

Bishop

LIVING. THE WORD ECHOED IN MY HEAD AS EDEN'S body collapsed into mine.

Fuck. I scooped her up into my arms.

"Shit, you're hammered. How much did you drink?"

Her head lolled against my shoulder. "Enough. But only a little of the last one. You spilled it."

"No shit. Because you were getting fucking roofied. I thought you learned your lesson when someone tried to grab you in front of Voodoo. You need to smarten up if you're going to spend any time alone in this city."

"Sorry I'm not doing a good enough job for you."

I stepped in the direction of the hotel. She needed a keeper, and it wasn't like I was in the market for another job.

"Where's your room key?"

She lifted her arm to show me a little purse dangling from her wrist.

When we reached the door to the lobby, I set her on her

feet and she wrapped her arms around my neck. "Don't let go."

"You smell good." Her face buried in my neck as I unzipped the purse and fished out the keycard. "Really good."

I shook my head, trying to tell myself that she was just drunk and had no idea what she was saying.

"Come on. Let's get you inside."

Eden untucked her face from my body and looked up at me. "Are you coming inside?"

"You think you can get up there yourself?"

Her brows drew together as she considered it. "I don't know. What was in those drinks? They didn't taste like anything but grape."

From the way she was stumbling, I had to guess it was the Purple Circus Punch, made with Everclear. And I also had to imagine that Eden didn't have a clue what that was.

I slid the keycard into the reader and pushed open the door to the lobby. Keeping her tucked in tight to my side and helping her walk, we avoided too many strange looks in the lobby before we reached the elevator.

Thankfully, I remembered exactly which room she was in, because Eden was already on the edge of passing out by the time the elevator stopped on the third floor. I lifted her into my arms and carried her down the hallway.

"I've never been like this before . . . not even when I raided my aunt's wine collection when she spent the weekend at the spa."

If I needed any more clues to figure out just how sheltered the girl in my arms was, that would have done it.

Adjusting my grip on her again, I used the key to open the door to the room and pushed inside. She hadn't taken it over like most women would—tossing clothes everywhere and covering every flat surface with something girly. She'd kept her suitcase neatly packed, and the only thing disturbed was the bed. The sheets were tangled and a tablet sat on the nightstand.

I lowered her to the bed and she flopped backward on it.

Rage heated within me again at the kid who'd dosed her drink. I wanted to go back and beat the fuck out of him. But if I knew bouncers in NOLA, the kid wasn't getting off unscathed. We didn't take kindly to that shit here.

What the fuck would have happened if I hadn't ended up on Bourbon? If I'd gone to one of my normal places?

I didn't want to think about the alternative. When I'd stepped into the bar, my instincts demanded I scan the entire interior before ordering a drink. Even at the end of the bar, Eden hadn't been able to hide. In a sea of drunken mindlessness, she stood out. I didn't know what it was, but there was something.

And now, seeing her nearly unconscious, I couldn't stop thinking about how fucking vulnerable she was on her own.

She kicked her shoes off and struggled to sit up and reach behind her. "I can't reach it. Can you?"

She had to be talking about the zipper to the dress. I sat down on the bed beside her as she turned her back toward me. But there was no zipper.

"What are you trying to reach?"

"I just want out of this dress."

"Well, how did you get into it?"

Eden released a noise of frustration before stilling. "Crap. Side. Forgot." She lifted an arm but fumbled with the tiny tab.

"Stop. I got it." I tugged it down and the sides fell free beneath the sleeve.

Shit, her skin was just as smooth and white as I'd imagined when I pictured tattooing it.

I needed to step away, but she continued to struggle with the dress. This had to be punishment for something I'd done in the past. My hands itched to touch her, but I knew I had no right.

Then again, I couldn't keep watching her struggle, so I lifted her to her feet and slipped the dress up and over her head. I told myself I'd keep my eyes on her face, but even I knew I was a shitty liar.

Her tits were fucking perfect. Her bra was pale pink with white lace around the edges and completely sheer. Her nipples were a shade darker, and she looked as sweet as I'd imagined.

I had to stop.

I dragged my gaze to hers and she stared up at me. Her expression wasn't horrified but heated.

She liked that I looked. Her tongue flicked out to wet her lower lip, and the combination of lust and innocence made my dick harder than anything I could ever remember in the past. That's when her gaze dropped, and I knew she couldn't miss my reaction.

She swallowed, and after long moments, brought her attention north, but she couldn't quite meet my eyes. I lifted a hand to her chin and tilted it up the last few degrees.

I shouldn't have touched her. Her skin was even softer than it looked. She leaned into my touch, and that's what fucked me over.

Just a taste, I told myself. *That's all.*

I lowered my lips to hers and her hands landed on my chest, her fingers gripping my shirt and pulling me closer.

So goddamned sweet. She moaned and my cock pulsed,

reminding me that it was ready to go.

I tore my mouth away and stepped back.

What the hell am I doing? She was drunk. Could have GHB running through her system. I wasn't going to take any more fucking advantage because that would make me just as shitty as the guy who'd dumped it in her drink.

Before she could say anything, I turned and crossed to her suitcase. Yoga pants and a T-shirt sat on top. "Here, put these on." I tossed them to her.

I waited a full sixty seconds, hoping like hell she would have covered herself by now, and then I turned.

Mistake.

She must have been struggling with her bra like she had with the dress, because now she was naked from the waist up.

"Christ, woman. Put on some clothes."

Hurt tinged her features, but I forced myself to push down the urge to tell her that she was fucking perfect and the edges of my control were fraying.

Eden tugged the T-shirt over her head and dropped onto the bed again before curling onto her side.

"Just go. I know you don't want to be here."

The hurt was in her voice too, and it pissed me off that my shitty judgment had put it there.

"Someone's gotta babysit you tonight, and I'm sure as hell not letting anyone else do it."

Part of me expected her to tell me to get the hell out, but the only response I got was a soft snore. *Out.*

I lowered myself into the desk chair, her taste still on my tongue. It was going to be a long fucking night.

14

Eden

"*F*UCK ME, CUPCAKE. I GOTTA EAT YOU UP."

    Palms landed on my thighs and spread my legs.

"*This is going to be the sweetest thing I've ever tasted.*"

I moaned and my eyes snapped open. I expected to see my fingers buried in brown-and-gold hair, but instead all I saw was . . . tangled white sheets and an empty hotel room.

No sign of the man who invaded my dreams.

I yanked the covers up over my head to hide the embarrassment burning my cheeks, and rolled over to smother myself in a pillow. A piece of paper crumpling against my face halted my movements. I peeled it off my cheek and forced my eyes to focus as the pounding in my head ramped up.

Had to go to work. Take the Advil on the nightstand and drink the water. If you think you're dying, call.

A phone number was written beneath.

There was no doubt who had left the note. His hand-writing was bold but crisp. No fifth-grader man-scrawl for Bishop.

He'd been here. It hadn't all been a dream.

But which parts were real?

Laying the note aside after reading it another dozen times, I rewound the timeline in my brain and stumbled onto the most important fact—I'd been drunk and he'd rescued me, *again*.

Because I'd needed to be rescued. *Again*.

With a groan, I hugged the pillow and began the process of beating myself up.

I failed at following Vincent's orders to stay out of sight. I failed at stepping outside my comfort zone. I was failing at everything.

All I'd wanted was to experience a slice of life outside my little bubble, and I'd ended up with drugs in my drink. A shiver of apprehension rolled down my spine, followed by the prickle of cold sweat. What would have happened if Bishop hadn't been there?

I could only imagine how ridiculous he thought I must be. How naive. How *stupid*.

The women he was used to probably would have seen that guy drop something in their drink and would have slapped him across the face. Or maybe punched him with brass knuckles. What they wouldn't have done was keep drinking like an ignorant idiot.

Why did I care about the women he was used to? I shouldn't. But for some reason I couldn't stop thinking about him. Maybe because he was so completely different from anyone I'd ever encountered.

That's why I need to put him out of my mind. If there was ever a guy I could point to and say "he's totally out of my league," Bishop was him.

I lay in bed for another thirty minutes, torturing myself by cataloging all the reasons I would never wake up to Bishop saying dirty things to me like Dream Bishop had this morning.

Not that I was carrying some kind of torch for Bishop. I didn't even know him. At most, I had some weird fascination with him. That was all. It was never going anywhere. It was the same as having a crush on some unattainable celebrity.

Oh God, I said crush. *I do not have a crush.*

I rolled again, this time to the edge of my bed so I could sit up and make my next stop the shower, where I could drown any misplaced feelings I might or might not have about Bishop.

I spent the next hour alternatively trying not to throw up and trying to talk myself into leaving the hotel again rather than staying in this room until I was old and wrinkly and someone had to carry my body out for my funeral parade.

God, that's morbid.

Although, seeing one of those jazz parades would be cool. I wondered if they had them for reasons other than death? I needed to look that up.

I swiped on mascara and lip gloss before adding some blush to make me look a little more human, and stepped out of the bathroom.

I would not stay in this room all day. I would see more of the city. I would not go drinking. I would not do anything else that would require being rescued. Today I was truly starting over.

A glance at the clock revealed it was already one in the

afternoon, and I blanched. *Jeez.* Had I ever slept until noon before? Even in college? Not that I could remember.

When I gathered my purse up off the desk, the room-service menu stared back at me, reminding me I didn't ever need to leave. I could stay hidden up here until they booted me out.

And how would that be any different from the life I lived in New York, watching the world pass by from the window of my apartment or the window of an SUV?

I wasn't going to waste this opportunity. I was going to *live.*

I looked down at my jeans, Sperrys, and rose-colored cardigan. First things first. I needed to go shopping so I could fit in here a little more. Then, it was time to check some things off my list.

Eden

I FOCUSED ON THE EXCITEMENT HUMMING THROUGH MY veins as I pushed open the lobby door and stepped onto Bourbon Street. The concierge had written down a list of shops that I should try if I wanted to get a true New Orleans shopping experience, along with a map. Thankfully, the list jogged my memory. The place Delilah had mentioned was included—Dirty Dog. I had to resist the urge to pump my fist in the air at the familiar name. Small victories.

In the light of day, Bourbon Street was a completely different experience. It wasn't empty, by any means, and given that Mardi Gras was right around the corner, that didn't surprise me at all. Obviously, there were still the obligatory partiers who either hadn't quit from the night before or were getting an early start, but it seemed that the crush of people from last night had moved on to sleep it off.

The concierge had also been so kind as to let me know that there were several other parades today, each put on by a different *krewe*, groups that organized parades and parties for Mardi Gras. I tucked the information away for later.

The first stop on the concierge's list was only a block and a half away, and I breathed a small sigh of relief when I saw the black sign with red letters on a brick building. HELL'S ANGEL. I reached for the door handle and turned.

Locked.

I checked the hours on the window and groaned. It didn't open until two. Well, that was disappointing. I peeked through the windows to see what exactly I would be missing if I skipped to the next place.

Everything looked either black or red or covered with skulls or spikes—or all of the above. Like the black-and-red corset with skulls on each boob that were covered in spikes.

"Oh wow," I mumbled. "Maybe I should come back to this one later." I caught my reflection in the mirror. Eyes wide, looking like I'd discovered an alien planet.

Maybe I could find something a little more . . . practical. That wasn't unreasonable, right? I mean, how often would I really wear a spiked corset?

Dirty Dog had to be more promising, especially given Delilah's personal seal of approval. Decision made, I twisted the map around to match the configuration of the streets ahead of me. It wasn't far, only a couple of turns and a couple of blocks. Even I couldn't get lost in this perfect grid of streets. I hoped.

The map also noted where I could find Anthropologie and H&M, but I wasn't looking for the same kind of clothes I could buy in New York. I wanted something local. Something that wasn't mass produced and sold in a thousand locations.

I set off down the street, only to be distracted by the delicious scent of coffee and fresh yeasty bread. My feet practically directed themselves as I stepped inside the tiny little café and selected a fresh croissant and the largest coffee they sold.

Nectar of the gods, I thought as I devoured the croissant in three bites and nearly burned my tongue on my sweet praline latte. *Totally worth it.*

Coffee cup in hand, I returned to the street and kept walking.

Distracted by the fabulous architecture, I made it a solid four blocks before I realized I had to be lost.

The pedestrians that wandered the streets of the Quarter had disappeared, and in front of me was a boulevard and a park. Thankful for the easy-to-find street signs, I pulled out my map again and twisted it around to try to figure out where I'd gone wrong.

The freaking café. It had been on a corner, and I'd gone in a door on one street and come out the door on the other street and kept walking. *Honest mistake, right?*

Not willing to let my minor detour get me down, I turned back around and walked in the direction of the café so I could find my way again.

Thirty minutes later, I found myself in front of a big teal-and-white sign with DIRTY DOG wrapped around the outside and a white bulldog in the middle. The front of the building was painted a cheery yellow, and the old dress forms in the window sported the cutest retro dresses I'd ever seen. One was pink with white paisley print and a white belt around the waist, and the other was the same dress, but in deep purple with black paisley.

Immediately, I wondered if I could get away with wearing either of them. Or both.

Please be open. Please be open.

My thoughts were answered when the door chimed and a girl poked her head out. "Hey! I'm JP. Are you coming in?"

"If you're open, I'd love to find a dress or two." I gestured down at my jeans and cardigan and Sperrys. "Actually, I need more than just a dress."

The girl smiled at me. "Well, honey, you've come to the right place. Me and Yve will get you all set up. She's got the cutest stuff in the whole city."

I followed JP into the store. "Thanks, I appreciate it."

She nodded and clapped her hands. "Yve! We've got a live one!"

Her high-pitched voice screeched without warning, and another woman peered out from what looked like a back room, her arms full of dresses.

"Knock off the yelling about customers, girl."

"It's only one customer, and she doesn't mind."

Shifting the dresses to one arm, a gorgeous woman with golden tanned skin and dark hair stepped across the floor toward me.

"Ignore her. She still doesn't have any manners. We're working on it." She unearthed a hand from beneath the dresses and offered it to me. "Welcome to Dirty Dog. I'm Yve, and this is my shop."

"Eden. I'm . . . new in town. Delilah from Voodoo Ink sent me your way."

Yve's tawny gaze lit with recognition before sizing me up. "Ah, you're the one she mentioned might be coming by. She said she hasn't seen Bishop act like that . . . ever. He's turned silence into just as much of an art form as the ink he puts down on skin."

JP gasped. "Oh God, don't tell me you're the one who's going to be responsible for breaking my heart and killing all my bearded and man-bunned dreams."

"Excuse me?"

"Don't mind JP. Her crush is a thing of legend."

"And Bishop keeps shooting me down. He won't touch any clients. Who knew the best artist I'd ever meet would be the man of my dreams with such a stupid rule?" JP's tone was distraught, but clearly overdramatic.

I hoarded the little pieces of information about Bishop like a junkie. *Because that's normal.*

"We've only met a couple times." I didn't want to bring up the fact that he'd rescued me from being possibly raped last night. Today was too nice and new to be focusing on that. Instead, I changed the subject. "So, I was hoping you could help me find some dresses. Actually, for whatever won't make me look like a tourist. I just . . . I need a change."

Yve appraised my outfit and nodded. "I can see what you mean. Let's get started." She spun away, her sunny yellow dress, the color of the outside of the building, swishing as she turned to a rack.

JP was already ahead of her. "As much as it sucks knowing that you can pull this off in a way I never could, and Bishop will probably fall all over himself when he sees it, you have to try it on." She holds up a white dress with pink polka dots. "We have the perfect shoes to go with it too, if you're not on too tight of a budget."

I thought of the credit card in my purse. I had no idea what the limit was, but knowing my father, it couldn't be less than five figures.

"Can I try it on?"

"Absolutely. I'll start putting stuff in the fitting room. You're going to want to try on way more than just one."

"Let's try the teal and the red too. Both of these are fun."

Yve held up a hanger in each hand. The teal dress had a boat neckline that managed to look both sexy and classy, and the red dress had a wide vee that would show a little more without making me feel overexposed.

She carried the dresses toward the fitting room, and I followed. Or I tried. I only made it three steps before a lavender leopard-print dress caught my eye. It reminded me of the one Delilah had worn the other day, but this color was softer and quieter but still fun.

"Oh, I love that one. Delilah has the neon version. She said this was too tame for her inner kitty cat." JP followed the statement with a *rawr* and a clawing motion with her hand, and I could picture Delilah doing exactly the same thing.

It wasn't like I'd be wearing it at the same time and place as Delilah, so . . . "I'll try that one too, if you don't mind."

"Of course not. Try on anything you want. We've got cute lingerie, and some awesome skirts, and vintage tops and tees too."

Yve slipped out of the dressing room to take the lavender dress from JP. "Don't overwhelm the girl, just funnel some of it into the fitting room and she can try whatever she likes." She checked her watch. "I've got a lunch date at noon, so I'll let y'all get started while I fix my makeup."

"Ooh, is that sexy hubby of yours coming to take you somewhere he can have you for lunch instead? And by *have you for lunch*, I mean bang you over a table for your nooner."

A hint of a blush stained Yve's cheekbones, and I couldn't help but grin at JP's unfiltered comments.

"I should fire you." Yve narrowed her eyes. "Tell me again why I haven't fired you?"

"Because I'm irreplaceable."

"You're lucky I love you, kid."

JP puckered up and blew Yve an air kiss. "Love you too, Yve."

Yve straightened and looked to me. "Right this way. And get ready to put a dent in your credit-card limit, because I know you're going to fall in love with these."

Fifteen minutes later, I knew she was right. All four dresses were on the fitting-room hook I'd designated as the *yes* pile. The lingerie that mysteriously made it into the dressing room, by JP sliding it between T-shirts and skirts, also fit and hung on the *yes* hook.

The only things I didn't plan to leave the store with were the three packs of pasties she'd included and the T-shirts that had the names of bands on them I'd never heard of. They were cute, but if someone started a conversation with me about them, I'd feel like a total poser because googling them to learn their history and songs didn't seem quite right.

I stepped out of the dressing room with my arms full and ran smack into the side of a tall man coming into the shop through the back hallway.

"Oh my God, I'm so sorry!"

"Looks like you could use some help." He lifted the dresses from my arms and carried them to the counter, and hung them on the decorative hook beside it.

"JP, you want to ring these up so I can steal that woman of mine away?"

The man wore a perfectly tailored suit. Everything about him—from his casually styled hair, tanned skin, and French-blue shirt to his heavy watch and designer shoes—screamed *money.*

"Lucas, you're early." Yve looked down at her watch. "I've got seven minutes."

"And what makes you think I've suddenly developed a streak of patience?"

Goose bumps peppered my skin at the hungry look in his eyes as he stared at Yve. JP was probably right—Yve was on the menu for lunch. If he picked her up, tossed her over his shoulder, and carried her out of here, I would have trouble acting surprised. It seemed at complete odds that a man in such a civilized suit could give off such a primitive vibe.

"Give me five minutes to get Eden rung up."

"Do you want me to carry you out of here?"

My eyebrows shot up as my thoughts came out of his mouth.

"See, that's all I want. A man who wants to carry me out of places because he can't wait to get me alone. But noooo. Bishop has the hots for Eden instead."

Lucas's attention shifted from Yve to me. "I'd apologize for being rude, but I'm not sorry I'm stealing my wife away. Good luck with the lumberjack."

"He's not a lumberjack!" JP jumped instantly to Bishop's defense as my body shook with unexpected laughter.

"Close enough. Yve, I'm giving you five seconds to back away from the cash register before the entire block hears you scream as I carry you out."

He started his countdown, and Yve turned to me with a smile that told me she wasn't all that upset about the idea of being carried out.

"I'm so glad I got to meet you, Eden. You'll have to come back and let me know how those dresses work out. And if you're going to a parade tonight, make sure you let JP set you up with a fascinator. You absolutely need a fascinator."

Lucas finished his countdown, wrapped an arm around her waist, and pulled her toward the back door. "And it's time to go."

JP and I were both staring down the back hallway when the door shut behind them.

"Well, that was interesting."

JP sighed. "That was alpha." She spun around to look at me. "Now, let's get you a fascinator."

"What exactly is a fascinator anyway?"

"Think Princess Kate's cute little hats that aren't really hats. You've gotta have one."

I pictured myself in the retro dress with a cute little non-hat. *Totally New Orleans.*

"Let's see 'em."

I returned to the Royal Sonesta with two giant bags with the Dirty Dog logo on the side, and a smile on my face. I'd been determined to find my way back without carrying the map in my hand the entire way, and I'd only taken three wrong turns. I considered it sightseeing and was pretty pleased with myself.

The streets were already beginning to crowd with people who were intent on getting started early on their hangovers, but no one bothered me.

See, I can do this. No big deal.

The Royal Sonesta lobby was bustling, and the concierge was handing out maps with the route of the next parade and a coupon for a ghost tour of the Lafayette Cemeteries by horse-drawn carriage afterward.

Score.

I officially had plans for the day and night. I was going to check two things off my list—watching a Mardi Gras parade without getting manhandled or lost, and then a tour of the famous cemeteries. *And* I was going to wear a fabulous new dress and a fascinator while I did it.

Perfect.

Bishop

"**T**HIS PARADE IS GOING RIGHT PAST VALENTINA'S place, so they're throwing a party. You gotta come out and have some fun."

I finished cleaning my station and turned to look at Constantine Leahy. "You're my boss. You're supposed to tell me to get my ass back to work, not try to drag it out of here."

"We're closing the shop for the rest of the day. I've had you and D working every night since the season kicked off so we could scoop up those tourist dollars, but you both need a fuckin' break. Consider this your newest assignment. We aren't taking no for an answer, and Delilah already agreed."

We, I assumed, had to mean Vanessa. "Your wife isn't trying to set me up with anyone, is she? Because I'm out if that's the case."

Con glared at me. "I'm not into any kind of matchmaking shit. Who the hell has time for that? Whatever Van is doing is on her, and I've got no clue what that might be. I just know there's food and booze."

I put the last piece of my machine away and stood. "Fine. I'm in. Where am I meeting you?"

He eyed me. "You're coming with me. If I leave here without you, we both know you'll never come."

Fucker was right, and I wasn't getting out of this. "All right. Let's go."

"Not that I give a fuck, but don't you want to change your shirt?"

I looked down at the black Voodoo Ink logo T-shirt and back up at Con. "Are you really fucking asking me that?"

Con laughed. "Never mind. I'll lock up and we're out of here."

I followed him out the back door of the shop into the alley behind the building. "I can't wait until Mardi Gras is over. Is it just me, or do these tourists get more obnoxious every year?"

I watched a group of kids who didn't even look old enough to drink tromp across the alley wearing their STUPID 1, STUPID 2, STUPID 3 shirts and giant neon sunglasses. Beer cups hung around their necks with their beads.

"Every fucking year. Because they get younger, dumber, and drunker." Con started off down the sidewalk, and I followed.

Con pulled open the door of his sweet-as-hell Chevelle. My bike was tucked into a small half garage built into the back of the building.

I made myself comfortable in the passenger seat and we headed toward the Garden District via the back roads to avoid the bulk of the traffic.

"Anything I need to know about the shop?"

After Con had stopped working there, I'd taken up the

reins as the unofficial manager. Delilah hadn't wanted anything to do with "being management," even though she'd worked there longer than me. Even with her aversion to anything non-artistic, she picked up more slack than she let on. It was the title that gave her hives.

"No, we're good. Money keeps coming in, so hopefully you're good too."

Con nodded. "No worries on that part." He waited for pedestrians to get out of the road before turning another corner. "You think you might want to buy the place someday?"

Buy the place. The words echoed through my head, and visions of sitting in my uncle's tattoo shop in Hell's Kitchen followed. It was where I'd learned and honed my trade. Where everything that had mattered had been centered until he'd gotten strapped for cash and made a bad decision—borrowing money from a loan shark.

When a payment came up he couldn't make, the loan sharks started coming around to collect with threats and heavy hands, so I'd put my knack for blackjack to work earning extra money to cover the interest. Who the fuck was I kidding? I'd counted cards, and I'd been good at it.

Until I got too cocky and destroyed everything . . .

"If you're not interested, just tell me."

I blinked, forgetting I was supposed to be answering Con's question. "Sorry, I was just trying to wrap my head around your question. I've never thought about it."

Con probably didn't realize that even though my sister was here, I never considered New Orleans a permanent stop for me. I had to be ready to move at any time. It might have been ten years since that shit went down, but that didn't mean my demons weren't still hunting for me.

"Think about it and let me know if you've got any serious

interest. If not, we'll keep doing what we're doing."

Con's words hung with me as we pulled up to a wrought-iron fence that swung open, and he parked next to his brother's Hemi Cuda. Lord ran Chains, the most badass pawn shop in town, with his feisty redheaded girl, Elle.

"Damn, you got the whole crew to come out for this?"

"You think Elle would let Lord miss it to work instead?"

"Good point."

The door to the house opened and Vanessa stepped out, clearly waiting for us to show. "You coming in? Elle's already pouring shots, so we're all screwed."

"We're coming, princess," Con called.

I pushed open the car door. "Guess we're all going to be walking home."

Eden

TAKE A TOUR, THEY SAID. YOU'LL LEARN AMAZING history, they said. It'll be fun, they said.

Well, spoiler. *They lied.*

I was standing in the middle of Lafayette Cemetery No. 1 in the dark without a single flashlight beam from my other tour companions visible.

They couldn't have left me here. Seriously?

We were supposed to stay together and follow the tour guide. And I did. Until he bypassed one of the coolest-looking crypts in favor of telling a ghost story about a child who'd died on the other side of the cemetery. I'd stopped and checked out the crypt myself and lost track of time. I'd been operating with a false sense of security because of the tour, but the creepy silence surrounding me ripped it away.

The battery in my cheap flashlight dimmed as I worked my way along the path to the entrance where the carriages should still be waiting.

Seriously, world?

Every tiny noise amplified in my head as I tripped down the path, whipping my head from side to side to make sure the boogeyman wasn't going to jump out and get me.

My *I'm going to lose my shit* meter was edging into the red zone, but I sucked in one deep breath after another. *It's going to be fine. I'm going to be fine. I'm not going to end up cemented inside a crypt by some psychopath.*

Shivers ghosted down my arms, and I broke into an awkward jog in my pink peep-toe pumps.

All I have to do is get out of the cemetery and find a cab. No big deal. I can do this.

"Who dat?" a deep voice called from somewhere behind me.

Oh God. I'm going to die here. Reports of people being mugged or killed while in the cemetery *during the day* ran through my mind.

I flicked my dying flashlight off, not wanting anyone to be able to follow my light, and ran faster.

"You ain't supposed to be in here after dark, girl." The deep voice was right behind me now, and adrenaline shot through my veins.

Run! my instincts screamed, and I sprinted for everything I was worth. The cemetery gate was up ahead, and all I needed to do was get out. The horses had to still be there. The guide had to do a count. They wouldn't leave without me.

Tripping over an uneven chunk of pavement, I stumbled forward, hands flailing. I caught the edge of a crypt and cement abraded my palms, but I didn't fall. Three more steps and then freedom.

Footsteps pounded behind me, but I reached the gate

and shoved it open. Heart pounding and lungs heaving, I paused to scan both directions for the carriages, but saw nothing.

Did I come out the wrong side?

I darted around the corner and that's when I heard it—the *clip-clop* of hooves and jangling of the harnesses. The reflective triangle on the back of the last carriage flashed under the street lights.

No. No. No. That's not possible.

The orange-tinged streetlights lent an eerie glow to the empty street devoid of cabs as I jammed a hand in my hair.

I'm such an idiot.

A few people gathered at the next corner, but I wasn't going to approach them and ask for help. If I were going to do that, I might as well pin a sign that read HOPELESSLY LOST TOURIST to my chest.

No. I was going to find my way back by myself.

My cemetery pursuer hadn't followed, but still I hurried, walking in the same direction the carriages had taken, hoping against hope that the street lights and my no-nonsense pace would deter any unwanted attention.

A sweet wave of relief washed over me when I saw the sign for Saint Charles Avenue up ahead.

Thank you, universe.

The revelers who had watched the parade earlier hadn't all cleared out. The porches and small front yards of the houses on the street were still full of people drinking and talking and enjoying the night. Instead of fearing the crowds as I had before, I welcomed them. They meant it was less likely I'd end up cemented alive in a crypt in an empty cemetery.

"Hey! You!" The call came as I walked by a large yard surrounded by a wrought-iron fence.

Not talking to me, I thought as I kept my head down and continued walking.

"Eden! Where are you going? Come party!"

At the sound of my name, I looked up and tripped over a crack in the sidewalk.

"Whoa, watch yourself!" Delilah hurried down the path from a beautiful house toward the fence. When she reached the gate, she unlatched it and pushed it open. "Come on. Gang's all here. Where the hell did you come from?"

I didn't have a chance to answer her questions before she pulled me inside the fence and around to the side yard where there were more people gathered.

"Bishop, did you see who I found? She was just walking down the sidewalk. That's like serendipity or some shit."

Even with his back to me, I knew it was him before she said his name. Bishop's wide shoulders tensed as he turned to face me.

"What do you mean, *just walking down the sidewalk*? By yourself?" The questions were split between me and Delilah, and his tone demanded answers.

Embarrassment stained my cheeks again. "Uh . . . I was with a group taking a tour of the cemetery at night . . . and I got separated."

It was impossible to miss the glower on his face with the light coming from the back of the house and the paper lanterns hanging in the trees.

"You got separated from a tour. In a cemetery. At night." He ground out each piece of the statement in its own separate little sentence as if I didn't know exactly how stupid I sounded already.

"Whoa, girl. That's not cool. You could've been—"

Bishop held up a hand. "I think we all know, D."

Another woman joined the circle. "Hi, I'm Valentina and this is my place. Welcome. Can I get you a drink?" She looked from me to Bishop to Delilah and then back to me.

"No, thank you. I was just stopping to say hi because Delilah saw me walking home."

"Walking home? In this town? By yourself?" She shook her head. "That's not a good idea. Let me see if I can't scare up a ride for you."

"Oh, that's not—"

"She doesn't need a ride," Bishop said. "I'm taking her back."

"You don't have a car, and you've been drinking for six hours." This came from the woman who'd introduced herself as Valentina.

"I'll just call a cab. It's fine."

Bishop practically growled at me. "And have them drop you off at the barriers the police have set up a couple blocks away from your hotel where you have to walk through the shit show that's the French Quarter tonight? Do I need to remind you what happened last night?"

Crap. I hadn't thought about the fact that a cab couldn't bring me right to the door. Even so, I didn't appreciate Bishop's tone.

"You don't need to throw that in my face. A cab will be plenty close. It's fine. Just freaking fine. You don't need to worry about me being a bother, Bishop. I don't need you to leave your party for me. I can take care of myself." I smiled at Valentina and Delilah. "If you could give me a number for a cab, I'll be on my way shortly. I'm sorry to barge in."

Valentina returned my smile, but one eyebrow lifted. "I'll get that cab for you. Hold on a moment."

When she stepped away, Delilah started talking. "Sweet

dress! I love it. It reminds me of something you'd get at—"

"Dirty Dog," another voice finished as Yve stepped out of the shadows and into the light. "And it looks great on you." She reached up. "Mind if I fix your fascinator? It's a touch crooked."

Automatically, I reached up to touch the small non-hat made of silver netting, and sure enough, it was askew. *Great. Check the box next to* HOT MESS.

Yve adjusted and repinned it before standing back. "Perfect."

"Does everyone in this town know each other?" I asked, trying to get the attention off me.

"A few of us," Yve said.

"And all of us agree that you've got no business walking around after dark by yourself." Bishop's statement left no room for contradiction, but Yve tsk-tsked him anyway.

"She's a grown woman. She can do whatever the hell she wants."

Bishop mumbled something else under his breath that sounded like *she needs a keeper*, but Valentina returned before anyone could pounce on it.

"Cab is on its way. It should be here in ten. Have a drink while you're waiting. We've got plenty of food too. The guys haven't managed to clear it out yet."

Bishop

I WANTED TO PICK HER UP AND SHAKE SOME SENSE INTO her. Maybe then Eden would realize that this city wasn't safe for her to venture out in alone. How the fuck does someone lose their tour anyway? And in a fucking cemetery? At night? Someone was going to lose their job when I tracked down the tour company and reported that they'd left her behind. They should lose their goddamned license too. She could have ended up dead.

At Eden's request, Valentina got her a water, and the girls talked and introduced her to the crew. I fucked with my phone and googled *night cemetery tour companies*. Finally, a car honked from the curb.

"That'll be the cab. You sure you're good to go alone?" Valentina asked.

"I'm taking her." When Valentina opened her mouth, I didn't wait to find out if she was thanking me or protesting. "I'm not leaving it to chance that she gets there in one piece."

Eden crossed her arms over her chest and pushed her tits up close to the neckline of the pink-and-white dress. *Does she own any clothes that don't make me want to strip her naked and eat her for dessert?*

"I'm perfectly capable."

"No shit, you're perfectly capable. But that doesn't change the fact that I've watched more than one person put their hands on you, and I'm not letting it happen again. You think someone's gonna fuck with you if I'm walking you to your hotel? No chance."

The horn honked again and she dropped her arms.

"Fine." Eden turned and the skirt on her dress flared.

Lord stepped up next to me. "Man, you're so fucked."

I swiveled my head around to stare at him as he swigged his beer. "What do you mean?"

"I mean you're gonna go down like the rest of us." He nodded at Eden. "And that girl is going to be the one to do it. I got a feeling about her. She's already under your skin."

"Fuck," I muttered before striding after her. No way was I going to let her have the cabbie leave without me.

Lord's words dogged my every step. *What is it about this girl?*

The cabbie already had the cab door open and was about to help her inside when I shut the gate behind me.

"I got this, brother. Thanks."

The cabbie, a guy on the younger side of thirty, held both hands in the air as he saw me stride toward him. "Sorry, man."

Eden's eyebrows were almost to her hairline when I finally slid into the seat next to her. "Was that necessary? He was being nice."

"You can't assume everyone is being nice. You have to

be on the defensive. Life isn't all cute kittens falling from the sky landing in big piles of cotton candy."

I didn't know where those words came from, but Eden's laughter drowned out the hip-hop playing on the radio.

"Is that what you really think about me? I'm completely and totally naive and live in some kind of bubble?"

It took me less than two seconds to answer. "Yes."

Eden crossed her arms under her tits, again making that little bit of cleavage turn into a hell of a lot more cleavage.

"Seriously? You've got to give me more credit than that."

"Then don't put yourself in situations where you're alone in a cemetery at night in New Orleans."

The cab driver piped up and added his own opinion. "Oh shit, you were in Lafayette at night? No fucking way, girl. That shit ain't cool. You won't last long 'round here if you keep that shit up."

Eden frowned into the rearview mirror. "It was an accident, and I won't be doing it again."

"You're right, because if you decide you're going to go exploring this city at night, you're calling me first."

I didn't know where the offer came from, but it was out before I could take it back. Did I want to take it back? If the alternative was Eden out wandering alone, hell no.

She laughed again, but this time it was harsher and a little fake. "Like you're really going to make time in your schedule to help me explore anytime I want." Eden flashed a forced smile at me. "I'll just limit my exploration to the daytime, thanks."

The cab driver turned into the Quarter and within a few minutes, slowed to a stop at a police barricade. "This is as far as I go." He craned his neck around to face us through the Plexiglas window as he told her the total for the ride.

Eden slipped cash through the divider and thanked him before opening her door and stepping onto the sidewalk.

"Thanks, man," I said.

"Keep that girl on a leash. It'd be a safer choice."

"Only if I had a death wish."

The cabbie's booming chuckle faded when I slammed the door and strode after Eden, who was already fifteen feet ahead of me.

"Wait up, cupcake. I didn't ride all the way over here for you to just walk off on your own."

She spun around on the sidewalk and faced me. "You think I'm ridiculous. That I can't fend for myself. I hate knowing that."

With a grimace, I chose my words carefully. "I don't think you're ridiculous. I think you've gotten into some situations that you should've avoided."

"You wish I would've avoided them because then you wouldn't have to deal with me."

She started off again but I was quicker. I wrapped an arm around her waist and pulled her back against me. "Don't start putting words in my mouth. I never said I didn't want to deal with you. Just the fucking opposite."

Eden's entire body stilled, and I wasn't even sure she was breathing until she responded. "But all I do is cause you trouble."

I thought of the sweet taste I'd gotten of her and how fucking badly I wanted more.

"Who said I didn't like trouble?"

Eden

OH. MY. GOD. MY HEART HAMMERED AS BISHOP'S soft breath coasted along my ear and sent chill bumps all over my skin and heat blooming in parts due south.

Who said I didn't like trouble?

If this were some kind of date-night movie, I'd turn around and lean up on my tiptoes and kiss him, but I didn't have the lady balls to do it.

"Are you gonna walk a little slower and let me actually see you home?"

I nodded, but then realized I should verbalize my response. "Thank you. I appreciate it."

Bishop released his hold around my waist, but reached down to grab my hand.

He's holding my hand. He's holding my hand! Why is he holding my hand?

My brain struggled to understand exactly what was

happening. Basically, I was having a meltdown like a middle-school girl when the cute guy I had a major crush on held my hand.

I wasn't sure whether I should laugh at myself for being pathetic or fist-pump the air because I was *awesome*.

I opted to not go for the fist pump. Playing it cool would work better, I assured myself.

As we walked the two and a half blocks to the Royal Sonesta, Bishop guided me around people and dogs and puddles of things I didn't want identified. When we got to the corner of Bourbon Street, he pulled me in front of him and we walked as one.

The crowd parted before us as we made our way to the lobby door, but all I could think about was the heat against my back and the swirling questions in my brain.

Would he come up to my room? Did I want him to?

All my questions were answered when we reached the entrance and I pulled out my keycard to open the lobby door.

"Are you going back out tonight?" Bishop asked.

I shook my head. "No, I think I've had enough adventure for today."

"Good. Take it easy. You decide you need more adventure, call me."

I remembered the number he'd written on the note when he left this morning.

"I wouldn't want to bother—" I started, but he cut me off.

"Call me. I wouldn't say it just to say it. I'm not that guy."

My heart thumped harder. "Okay. I'll call."

"Goodnight, Eden." He turned and walked away, not melding into the crowd but drawing every eye as he made his way through it.

Goodnight, Eden.

That's it? That's all?

I got all the way up to my room, cursing the man-bunned giant, and pushed open the doors to my balcony. I dropped into the white chair and watched the people in the street.

That's when I saw him. Across the street, leaning against a building. As soon as Bishop saw me, he nodded and pushed away from his perch to walk home.

He waited to see if I made it up to my room. The frustration that built as I'd made my way up the elevator and down the hall faded, and something warm filled my chest.

Unexpectedly sweet.

With happy thoughts filling my brain, I wasn't prepared for a slap in the face from reality. The phone in my purse buzzed across the table.

A text.

I pulled it out and stared down at the screen.

UNKNOWN NUMBER: *Lay low. Shit's heatin up.*

Eden

I F I WERE GOING TO LET THE TEXT CONTROL MY EVERY waking thought, I would have stayed in my room and had room service for breakfast. Maybe if I were smarter, I would have. But I couldn't let the off chance that something was going to happen keep me inside this hotel room.

So after an amazing breakfast at Stanley near Jackson Square, I slipped into the lobby. My heart rate sped up when I saw two men in suits speaking to a front-desk clerk. One of the men sported a bulge that reminded me of Angelo when his shoulder holster hadn't been adjusted to fit well under his jacket.

The men with guns have nothing to do with me, I told myself as I hurried to the elevator before they could turn and see me. *I'm just paranoid because of that text.*

But that didn't stop me from rushing to my room and locking the door behind me. I pulled my phone from my purse. There'd been no more texts and no calls. Wouldn't there be a more specific warning if they thought I was in danger?

I forced myself to act normally and pulled out my list to decide what I was going to tackle today, but the loud ringing of the hotel telephone startled me back into *paranoid as a crazy person* mode. Against my better judgment, I answered it.

"Ms. Madden?"

It took my brain a second to click into gear at the mention of the alias used on the credit card I'd given them for the room.

"Yes?"

"This is James at the front desk. We've had an issue with the authorization on your credit card."

"What kind of issue?"

"A fraud notice. I'm afraid we're going to need another form of payment."

Fraud notice? Trepidation pooled in my belly, but I kept my tone confident. "I'm sure there's some mistake. I'll check into it and be right down."

I hung up, dug the credit card out of my purse, and flipped it over to the number on the back.

Five minutes later, it was my stomach flipping. *This card has been canceled due to fraud concerns*, the helpful representative on the other end had informed me. *However, we are unable to issue another card until certain issues have been fully investigated.*

The second part sent my mind racing toward possibilities of what could be happening. The card was obviously tied to Dom's business. Someone reported it as being suspected of fraud. Who? The FBI?

I pulled up a web browser and tried to log in to my bank

account. *We apologize for the inconvenience, but you are currently unable to access this account. Please call for further details.*

What the hell?

I had to call the number Vincent had given me. I might not be bleeding or being held at gunpoint, but something felt totally off.

No one answered. I tried four more times and got the same generic voice-mail message.

A dark feeling of foreboding crept over me. Pulling up another window in the browser, I searched for New York City news.

I'd only had a bank account frozen once, and that had been courtesy of the FBI. My identity as Dom's illegitimate daughter apparently wasn't a secret with the Feds.

I didn't have to scroll far to see the headline.

Dominic Casso Under Grand Jury Investigation

Holy. Shit.

Racketeering, conspiracy, money laundering . . . the list went on and on. I read the article word for word until I got to the line that explained everything. *Inside sources tell us that all assets associated with Casso and his businesses have been frozen pending the completion of the investigation.*

Jesus. H. Christ.

I dropped back onto the bed. What the hell was I going to do? If they'd canceled the credit card under my alias, undoubtedly the credit cards under my real name were also canceled, not that they'd do me much good in my safe in New York. Dammit, why did the FBI take such pleasure in making life as difficult as possible? *Probably because my dad's a criminal.*

Shit. The guys in suits at the front desk.

Are they FBI? Are they looking for me?

The room phone rang again, and I froze.

Do I answer? Ignore it?

The obnoxious ringing continued, and I made a snap decision.

"Hello?"

"Ms. Madden, I'm sorry to bother you, but we really need you to come down and handle this credit card issue as soon as possible." The front-desk clerk's voice was sympathetic but firm.

"Uh, of course. I'll be right down."

"Great. We'll be waiting."

We'll be waiting.

The hotel clerk . . . and the FBI?

Shit. Shit. Shit.

What do I do? Or an even better question—what would Dom tell me to do?

Get the hell out of the hotel and away from law enforcement.

I dashed to the bathroom and gathered up my makeup before shoving it in my suitcase along with all my clothes.

I have to get out of here. I wheeled the suitcase out into the hallway and headed for the stairwell that would exit nearest the side door. I wasn't taking a chance with the front lobby and the desk clerk.

Yes, I was going to run out on the bill they couldn't charge to my credit card. I would have felt guilty if I wasn't more worried about being taken in for questioning by the FBI.

What if they were expecting me to bolt? What if someone was covering each exit? Yes, my imagination was running wild, but what if I was right?

As I stepped out of the stairwell into the hallway, I looked to my left and froze.

Fire Alarm – Pull Down Here.

Oh Jesus. I was going to hell.

I grabbed the white handle and pulled.

21

Eden

WITH MY SUITCASE THUMPING AGAINST MY thigh, I ran down the streets of the French Quarter away from the Royal Sonesta. I didn't know where I was headed, but I turned the corner and kept running.

My arm and shoulder burned at the weight of my bag, and my lungs began to protest soon enough for me to realize that I was way out of shape. A glance over my shoulder told me I was probably attracting more attention with my running than if I'd just walked like a normal, sane person.

Well, excuse me for feeling the need to flee as quickly as possible.

I slowed to a walk, more out of necessity than anything, and turned another corner.

Canal Street. A red-and-blue neon sign hung from the marble building.

Really, world? Why? What was it that kept drawing me

back here?

Well, I wasn't going to waltz in there and announce I'd run out of the Royal Sonesta without paying what I owed.

Shit. Would Bishop's friend come after him for the money from the night I stayed that the room wasn't comped? With that horrific thought on my mind, I turned my back on the tattoo shop and slipped into Your Favorite Hole next door.

What a freaking mess.

The same woman was at the front counter as the day before, and her smile widened as soon as I crossed the threshold. *Fabienne*, I was reminded by her nametag.

"Hey there, darlin'. You back for more of Delilah's special?"

The coffee had been delicious, but my lungs were still burning. What I really needed was water and a private place to figure out how much cash I had left, so I could work out some kind of a plan. I was officially homeless and on the run.

"Coffee and water?" I asked, trying to sound less out of breath.

"Comin' right up."

I wheeled my suitcase over to a cozy chair in the corner before lowering into the seat and dropping my face into my hands.

What am I going to do now?

I only allowed myself a few moments of beating myself up before I stood and returned to the counter with money in my hand.

Fabienne nodded at my suitcase in the corner when I reached the cash register. "You leavin' town?"

"No. I . . . I'm just changing locations."

Her eyes narrowed on me, and her scrutiny gave me the

sense that she was seeing right through me.

"You in trouble?"

I shook my head, even though it was a lie. I ran out of a hotel without paying my bill, and there were people with poorly fitting shoulder holsters who might have been waiting for me.

Who were they? FBI? Dom's people? Dom's enemies? The possibilities multiplied in my brain while Fabienne waited for an answer.

"I just had some things not work out like I planned," I mumbled as I held out a ten-dollar bill.

She looked down at the cash. "Keep your money. This is on the house. You look like you could use a break."

I looked down at the money and then back to her. "But—"

"Sometimes you gotta pay it forward, hon. So you do the same when you can."

The unexpected kindness clutched at my heart. "Thank you. Really, thank you."

"You're welcome, hon."

While I was waiting for my coffee, I glanced around the interior. I loved the cozy seating areas, tables, and mismatched chairs.

It felt so happy and homey. Like you could make someone smile by simply handing them coffee and a donut. My gaze landed on the Help Wanted sign that hung in the window. If I were wearing an apron and a hat, would anyone really notice my face? Would Fabienne even hire me?

I decided the best way to find out was to dive in headfirst. "Are you . . . I mean, what position are you hiring for?"

There was no judgment on her face when she smiled. "Do you know anything about working an espresso machine?"

I had one in my apartment that would rival most coffee shops, so I could answer that question with confidence. "I do."

"How about a cash register?"

"I can learn quickly. I'm really good with numbers anyway."

She nodded. "I need someone to fill in shifts for now. It's not ideal because the hours aren't regular, but I need someone to plug into my schedule where we've got holes. You want to give it a try for a week or so and see if it's a fit?"

"Yes, that would be great." Excitement zipped through me, and then nosedived. I had to find a place to stay too. Preferably a safe place that took cash and didn't ask questions.

"When would you want me to start?"

"How about Monday? I'll get you the hours and you can see."

"My day is wide open, so I promise I can make it work. Thank you for the chance; I appreciate it."

The door chimed and Fabienne's gaze lifted over my shoulder. "Bishop's usual, if you would please," she called down to the barista.

Really, universe? How is that fair? I had no idea how I was going to explain about the hotel and that I wasn't staying there . . . so for now, I wasn't going to mention it.

But I couldn't avoid Bishop completely. I glanced over my shoulder to look at him. The line between his brows deepened as he stared down at me.

"What are you doing here?"

22

Bishop

EDEN GRABBED HER COFFEE AND A BOTTLE OF WATER as I reached into my pocket for my wallet and slid a twenty across the counter.

Fabienne took it and tucked it away in the cash register before making change. But she didn't drop the change in my hand like I expected. She tightened her fist around the bills before whispering, "You take it easy on that girl. I think she's run into some trouble and probably doesn't have the first clue what to do about it."

We locked eyes, and her deep brown ones were as serious as I'd ever seen them.

"Thanks. I got it from here."

I waited for my coffee before crossing the room to sit in the seat across from Eden. Her suitcase was tucked behind her chair.

What the hell? "You leaving town again?"

I didn't know why the thought pissed me off so much,

but it did. Nothing about this girl made sense to me, including the pull I felt toward her.

"No."

"Then why the hell is your suitcase with you instead of at the hotel?"

Her gaze dropped to the floor, but I waited her out. Pink tinged her cheeks when she finally looked back up at me. "I couldn't keep racking up the cost of the room. I need something less expensive."

I had to believe her pride took a beating with that answer, but she sure as hell hadn't seemed to be worried about money when she'd tossed down her credit card the night I checked her in. Something had changed, and I took a guess.

"Daddy cut off your credit card?"

All color drained from her face. "Something like that."

Fuck. Now she was broke and alone in a city that didn't have a hell of a lot of spare mercy.

"Bishop, your coffee's ready," the barista called.

Before I turned back to collect it, I stared down at Eden. "Bring your shit over to Voodoo when you're done here. Remember what happened the last time you dragged a suitcase all over town?"

She bit her lip but didn't reply.

I stalked to the counter and grabbed my coffee.

Eden

I DRANK MY ENTIRE BOTTLE OF WATER AND ALL OF MY coffee as I considered Bishop's order to bring myself and my stuff to Voodoo. I didn't want to keep relying on him for help because it highlighted how unable to help myself I was.

What would happen when his friend called about the hotel? I didn't have answers that would satisfy him. But maybe I could give him cash and ask him to pay the hotel?

And how would I do that without explaining why I ran? Yeah. *No.*

Why am I such a failure at this? One day I think I've got it all handled, and the next it falls apart. Maybe that meant tomorrow would be better. I had to keep pushing forward. There was no other option.

Ten minutes later, I'd gathered my courage. With my suitcase in tow, I stepped through the door of Voodoo Ink for the third time in less than a week. For a girl with no tattoos, that had to be unusual.

I hoped to see Delilah inside, but there was no sign of her. Instead, I saw Bishop standing behind the counter with a redhead leaning over it.

"Come on, you know you wanna."

I assumed her tone was supposed to sound sultry, but instead it came out whiny and obnoxious. From Bishop's crossed arms, rigid posture, and definite scowl, it appeared that he really didn't *wanna* whatever it was she was offering.

His gaze, rife with annoyance, flicked up to mine as I rolled my carry-on inside. I didn't know what possessed me to do it, but I dropped my bag and ran across the shop before slipping around the counter and throwing myself at him. It was pure instinct, but it was my turn to rescue him.

Bishop dropped his arms quickly enough to catch me as I wrapped my legs around his waist.

"Baby, I missed you so much!" I buried both hands in his hair and crushed my lips to his.

His muscles tensed beneath my hold, and then he did something completely unexpected—he lowered one hand to my ass and slid the other up to the back of my head to tilt it a little to the side. I opened my mouth, intending to pull away, but his tongue slid inside and he kissed me like . . . like I was exactly who I was pretending to be. A girlfriend away for too long and desperate to get her hands on her man.

"Should've figured." The redhead's voice was a distant murmur, barely audible over the buzzing in my ears.

Bishop was kissing me. Holding me. Pulling me closer until I could feel a ridge beneath his jeans pressing against my center.

Holy. Hell.

I lost track of everything but the kiss.

The door chimed, but it was another long moment before Bishop pulled his lips away and lowered me to my feet.

I blinked twice, my hand going to my mouth as it registered what the hell I'd just done.

Mauled him.

In front of a customer.

What in the world possessed me?

Bishop ran a hand through his now disheveled hair and stared at me like he'd never seen me before in his life.

I scrambled for something to say. Anything to dispel this awkwardness. "You looked like you could use rescuing . . ."

His brows rose at my mumbled excuse.

More words tumbled out.

"So . . . I guess that makes us closer to even in the rescue department."

I waited for a response. Any response at all. But I got nothing. Bishop turned and walked away, down a back hallway until he shoved open a door and slammed it behind him.

Well, crap.

Nice going, E. Really. Nice.

24

Bishop

WHAT IN THE EVER-LOVING FUCK?

I dropped onto the couch in the break room and stared at my hands.

Hands that had been wrapped around Eden's curvy ass.

Fuck. Just like that kiss the night I carried her out of the bar, it shouldn't have happened. I should have held her off and set her right back on her feet as soon as she launched herself at me, but I didn't think. I just . . . fucking reacted. The sweet taste of her hadn't changed, and my cock was just as rock hard as it had been that night.

I wanted more.

Shit.

I knew better than to get mixed up with her, but fuck if it wasn't sounding like the best idea I'd had in a long damn time.

You looked like you could use rescuing . . .

When was the last time anyone had ever given enough

of a fuck to want to rescue me? I hadn't let anyone get that close. That's what moving around every couple of years did for you. Kept you light. No roots. No cares. No one to pry into your past and try to dig out your darkest secrets. Nothing to lose. And that was the way I'd always liked it.

So why was I letting myself get sucked in?

I had absolutely no fucking clue.

The door to the employee break room opened and smacked against the wall. I jerked my head around to see if it was Eden, shocked that she might follow me in here.

But it wasn't. It was Con.

"I know I was drunk, but that's the girl from the Mardi Gras party, right? She here for some ink?"

"Yeah, that's her, but negative on the ink. She look like the type to you?"

He tilted his head at me. "That don't mean shit. You've seen Van. Wouldn't think she'd be the type either, but you'd be wrong."

"True."

"So, what's she doing here if she's not here for ink? Waiting for you?"

I jammed a hand into my hair. There was no way in hell I was going to explain what had just happened. Fuck, I didn't even know myself.

"I don't know yet. I'm working it out."

"And?"

"And nothing."

Con's eyebrow rose. "You really expect me to believe that you're not sitting back here avoiding her because you're fucking terrified of getting sucked into the classy-broad trap? Been there. Done that. Never want out."

From outside the break room, I could hear a female

voice.

"Van out there talking to her?" I asked.

Con nodded. "Yeah, and they're probably best friends by now. If you were trying to get rid of her, you're probably screwed."

I dropped my head back until it smacked against the wall. "She's running from something, and I don't have a fucking clue what to do with her. I can't leave her to fend for herself because the next place I'd see her would probably be on the six o'clock news."

"Well, shit. Can't let that happen. She need a place to stay?"

"Yeah." I remembered Charlie's offer from the other day. "But I think I have an idea."

"Charlie?" How Con knew that's what I was thinking, I had no clue.

I nodded. "She was in here the other day and offered up her old place, but Eden was staying at the Sonesta until today."

"Why'd she bail on that?"

"Money, I guess."

Con's eyebrows drew together in confusion. "She sure doesn't look like she's hurtin' for cash."

"I guess looks are deceiving in this situation. I don't know what the real deal is, and she won't tell me shit."

"Then maybe you need to do your own digging."

Heels clicked down the hallway, and Vanessa stuck her head through the doorway before I could decide how to respond to that.

"You guys want me to go pick up something for lunch while you sit back here and brood?"

Con reached out and snagged her hand to pull her

closer. "I thought we were grabbing something."

"That was before I realized Eden hasn't had jambalaya, étouffée, or oysters yet. Someone needs to help that girl get a true taste of New Orleans before she leaves."

"She ain't leavin." The words were out of my mouth before I even thought about speaking them.

Vanessa's appraising gaze landed on me. "I'm pretty sure that's not up to you." She shifted to look at Con. "He sounds like just as much of a barbarian as you do."

Con laughed and lifted her hand to his mouth to press a kiss to it. "You like it when I'm a barbarian."

"True, but I also like showing off my city to people who will appreciate it."

"Fine, but watch yourselves. The city's still lousy with tourists."

Van pressed a kiss to his cheek. "You're starting to sound like a grumpy old man. We'll be back in an hour or so. Is that enough time to go over the books?"

Con nodded. "Yeah. Have fun, princess."

She kissed him again and waved at me. "See ya, Bish."

Van closed the door behind her, leaving Con and me in the office.

"When's your next appointment?" he asked.

"Two thirty." I glanced at the clock. "Should be here any minute."

"Then I guess you better get to it."

I pushed off the couch and stood. "Yes, sir." I gave him a mock salute and he punched me in the arm when I neared the door.

"Don't fucking salute me, you asshole."

I laughed, but my brain was firmly fixed on Eden. Maybe Vanessa would get her story out of her, and then I'd have some kind of clue what I was dealing with.

Eden

EVEN THOUGH I'D MET THEM LAST NIGHT, SEEING the blond couple come into the tattoo shop still flipped all my accepted stereotypes on their head. Vanessa was wearing a skirt and blouse and heels, and Con was wearing ripped jeans and a T-shirt with a chain hanging from his front pocket to his back. Both of his arms were covered in even more tattoos than Bishop had. Objectively, Con and Vanessa looked like the oddest couple I could imagine putting together, but the way his arm wrapped around her waist and how his eyes softened when he looked down at her told me there was nothing odd about them.

What did people think when they saw Bishop and me together? *Except we're not actually together.*

Con hadn't spared me much more than a chin jerk before striding in the direction of the room Bishop had retreated to, but Vanessa stopped in front of me.

"Hey! Eden, right? What are you doing here?"

"I'm . . . waiting for Bishop, I guess."

Curiosity lit her blue eyes. "There are a lot of girls who wait for Bishop on any given day, but from what I saw last night, you seem to be different."

I thought of the girl who'd been flirting with him before I'd literally thrown myself at him. "I'd like to think I'm different. But . . . it's not like that."

She smiled. "Oh, I know how that goes. Trust me."

With Vanessa's easy response, I felt this strange and instant kinship with her. I could only imagine what it had been like when she and the tattooed blond giant had gotten together. The entire time I'd been in New Orleans, I'd had this feeling that by some strange design, the universe was dropping people into my life at the exact moment I needed them. Bishop, Delilah, Fabienne, Yve. Maybe today was Vanessa's day.

She dived right into a series of questions, asking me what I'd seen and eaten. When she discovered that I hadn't gotten a full New Orleans experience, she vowed that she would change it for me before striding off down the hall to follow Con.

When Vanessa returned, she adjusted her purse—Prada, if I wasn't mistaken—and smiled again. "I know we just met last night, and I promise I'm not psycho, but I really would love to take you out for lunch."

I had to go with my gut. "I'd like that." I looked at my suitcase beside my chair. "What do I do with this?"

She reached for the handle and pulled it behind the counter. "No worries. It'll be here when you get back."

As we walked to the front door of the shop, I heard the creaky door open behind us. I whipped my head around to see Bishop standing in the back hallway, his arms crossed over his chest. He said nothing, just watched me leave.

Was he thinking of the way he'd kissed the hell out of me? Because I was. The unreadable expression on his face gave me absolutely no clue. As I pulled the door shut behind me, his gaze stayed locked on mine through the glass until I turned away.

Vanessa must have noticed because once outside on the sidewalk, she said, "Bishop is intense. If it's not *like that* between you two, you'll have to learn to ignore it."

I choked out a laugh. "He's pretty impossible to ignore."

She tilted her head and looked back through the window. "From the way he's still looking at you, I would say definitely impossible."

It took everything I had to keep walking rather than turn around again to see what she was talking about.

"So," she continued, "you've intrigued the stoic Bishop. It's a feat many have tried to accomplish and failed."

This time my laugh was genuine. "I wouldn't go that far. I think I'm more of an annoyance at this point than anything else."

"Oh, hon, I think you're completely wrong about that. If he considered you an annoyance, he'd grunt and tell you to back off. I've seen it firsthand. You, he watches like he's dying to know what you look like naked."

My mind skipped back to the night I woke up to a note on my pillow. Had he seen me naked? I'd woken up wearing a T-shirt and the same panties I'd worn the day before, and if he was in my room . . . yeah, he had to have seen me mostly naked.

Why had I not realized that? *Oh my God.*

Vanessa noted my quiet and her eyebrows rose. "I know we're still closer to the stranger side of the spectrum than the friend side, but sometimes you need another woman to spill to when it comes to stuff like this."

I'd never had that kind of confidante before. And even more than that, I'd never had anything like this to share.

I decided to speak in vague terms. "I'm totally out of my league with him. He's all tough and tattooed and way too sexy for his own good, and I'm over here practically wearing a nun's habit for all the experience I've had in my life."

Vanessa stopped mid-stride and grabbed my arm. "Are you a virgin?"

"No. God, no." *But close enough,* I added silently.

She pulled me toward a little restaurant with a giant oyster for a sign. "This is it. We're going to need wine for this."

Even now, two days later, the thought of alcohol still made my stomach flip. "Can I pass on the wine? I sort of had . . . an incident that wasn't so great."

"I'm sensing a story there. I'll have wine, you eat the bread they bring to the table, and we'll call it even."

For the first time in my entire adult life, I felt the kind of solidarity with another woman that I'd seen in movies. *Should I tell her what happened with Bishop?* What did I really have to lose?

A host seated us at the only empty table in the restaurant, and I let the entire story of the last few days loose, minus the part about why I left the hotel in such a hurry.

By the time I finished with how I quite literally jumped him at Voodoo this afternoon, Vanessa had drained her wineglass and was fighting back a laugh.

"This is the best thing I've heard in way too long. God, I can only imagine how shocked he was when you threw yourself at him." She held a hand over her mouth. "I don't know why I love the idea of Bishop off-balance, but it makes me so happy. He's turned aloof into an art form since the day he showed up and Delilah made Con hire him."

"Aloof is one way to describe it."

"You've definitely shifted his world out of order, and sometimes that's exactly what we need in order to remind us that we're alive. I think Bishop has just been existing for a long time, so this could be the best thing that has ever happened to him."

I eyed the empty wineglass in front of her. "I'm not sure I'd go that far."

"You'd be surprised. Sometimes what we need is the opposite of what we expect. I'm living proof. I never expected to find everything missing from my life in that big tattooed Viking of a man, but I did. It scares the hell out of me to think how different my life might be if I hadn't accepted his dares."

"It sounds like there's a story there too," I said.

Vanessa's smile widened. "Absolutely, but that's for another day and another glass of wine. Let's order some lunch for the guys. Con should be done with the books in a half hour, I hope, and you need to get in touch with Charlie about that apartment so you have somewhere to live."

"Con's working on the books?"

"Yes, his least favorite task of all."

"I can help with that," I offered. "I mean, if he needs or wants a bookkeeper."

"I thought you said you were taking a job at Your Favorite Hole?"

"I can always be busier. It's not like I've got a wild social life taking up a lot of my time."

"You never know how quickly that could change." Vanessa tapped her lips with two fingers. "But I'll mention it. Con's always grumpy as hell when he's dreading, doing, or forgetting to do books. I wouldn't be sad for that to disappear."

"Let me know what he says. My offer stands."

On the way back to Voodoo with the food, Vanessa pointed out more landmarks and things that weren't to be missed, and I shocked myself by actually recognizing a few of them from my earlier wanderings. Without too much effort, New Orleans could feel more like home than New York.

But with that thought came the reminder of the burner phone sitting like a lead weight in my purse. All it would take was one text or call, and I'd be sucked back into the colorless life I'd led before. It solidified my resolve to soak up every moment of my time here.

Before we turned the last corner back to Voodoo, I saw a neon sign in an old window that looked like the panes were due for a wash and the frame had been painted dozens of times. It read Fortunes Told Here with a pair of hands beneath it. Goose bumps rose on my skin, and I slowed. Vanessa followed my gaze.

"Have you ever had your fortune told?"

I shook my head. "I'm not sure I even believe in that kind of stuff."

"What's the harm in hearing what she has to say then? Madame Laveau is practically a legend in the Quarter." She lifted the bag of takeout she'd ordered. "I need to take this to the guys, but maybe you should step inside and see what happens."

"Laveau? Like Marie Laveau? The voodoo queen?"

Vanessa smiled. "She claims to be a distant relation but there's nothing to substantiate that. Personally, I think it's just smart marketing."

"Is it . . . safe?"

At my question, Vanessa's laugh echoed. "Absolutely. You can meet me back at Voodoo when you're done and tell me all about your future."

With another genuine smile, she patted my hand and strode off down the sidewalk, leaving me to stare at the glossy black-painted doorway.

What could it really hurt?

I crossed the uneven pavement and climbed up the single uneven step. A shiver skipped down my spine, but I shook it off.

None of it was real anyway. Right?

I pushed open the door and tiny brass bells tinkled above my head as the wood floor creaked beneath my feet.

"Come on in, child. I could feel your curiosity from out-side." The woman, tall and thin with skin the color of café au lait, greeted me from behind the counter.

"Hi?" My greeting sounded more like a question than anything else.

"What can I do for you today?"

She folded her arms on the glass in front of her and studied me. I wondered if she could see everything.

No way. That would be impossible. I chided myself for letting my imagination get the better of me.

I cleared my throat and pulled myself together. "My for-tune. I'd like to know what you see."

"Ah. We all want to know our future, don't we? Luckily, you came to the right place. Come on back."

She pushed away from the counter and gestured to the gap between it and the wall. I followed her as I soaked up the ambience of the shop. The lower shelves were lined with books and boxes of tarot cards, and the upper shelves were filled with glass jars of different teas and herbs.

Rather than spooky, it felt only slightly unnerving. She led me to a table and indicated that I should sit. Hands folded tightly in my lap, I waited for her to speak.

"Do you have a preference? Tea or tarot?" She nodded to a cup and teapot. "I read the leaves at the bottom. My grandmother taught me when I was a child."

I'd seen the fortune-tellers with their card tables and tarot decks near Jackson Square, but it hadn't occurred to me to stop. But tea . . . that sounded intriguing. What could someone actually tell you from reading tea leaves?

Somehow, it seemed safer too.

"Tea."

She nodded. "Very well."

She set about brewing a fresh pot and placed the teacup on the table. I waited, wondering if this whole process was drawn out to give more authenticity to the supposed fortune-telling.

But my doubts drained away when she started to speak.

"You've felt trapped. Kept away from the things you truly want." Her gaze flicked up to mine. "And now you're finding freedom because that's what your future holds. Freedom . . . but at a price. You face a very tangled web where nothing is as it truly appears, and when it untangles, you will have to make a choice."

Although her words were generic and perhaps could have applied to anyone, they struck a chord inside me.

Trapped. Freedom. Tangled.

"What . . . what's going to happen?"

"I can't see specifics. I only know that you will be tested and when you think you have failed, you must look deeper."

This last part was cryptic, and apprehension curled

through me at the word *failed*.

Failed at what?

I wanted to continue to ask questions, but she rose from the table. "If you have more questions, come back and see me again, child. I'd be happy to tell you what the next cup says."

I stood, with more questions than answers swirling through my brain.

When I followed her out to the front of the shop, I dug into my wallet and pulled out enough cash to pay for the reading and a tip. I knew I should be watching my finances more closely considering I only had cash to rely on now, but one indulgence wasn't going to break me. I handed over the bills, and she tucked them in the register.

"Thank you," I said before turning toward the door. I was already telling myself that the generic fortune she'd read me didn't necessarily have anything to do with my future.

"Consider this my free advice. That inked man is more than what he appears. Guard your heart."

My hand froze on the doorknob and I whipped around. "Excuse me?"

Her smile took on a decidedly feline quality. "Ah. You were wondering if I could truly see anything. Now you know for certain. Take care now."

My hand shook on the doorknob, but I managed to twist it hard and burst out of the shop onto the street.

How could she possibly know that? *Inked* man. There was no way. Fortune-tellers weren't real. Were they?

A cold gust of wind sent more shivers racing across my skin.

This town was a way more eerie than I gave it credit for, and Madame Laveau was either a first-class guesser or she saw something when she looked at me.

I hugged my arms around myself and made my way back to Voodoo.

Eden

W HEN I PUSHED THROUGH THE DOOR OF THE
tattoo shop, everyone turned to stare at me.
Immediately, I dropped my gaze to my shirt
to see if I'd spilled food on it during lunch and Vanessa had
failed to mention it.

Not seeing any stains, and after surreptitiously checking
to make sure the zipper of my jeans was in place, I glanced
back up at Con, Vanessa, Delilah, and a girl I remembered
from Dirty Dog—JP.

Most notably absent was Bishop.

The inked man.

I tried to inject humor into my voice when I asked, "Did
Bishop eat and run?"

Con's elbows rested on the counter with his fork hanging midair over his takeout container. He held off on shovel-
ing the bite into his mouth before answering me.

"He had to take care of something. He'll be back. He

139

took your shit."

Took my shit?

I bolted toward the counter and looked behind it. "He took my suitcase?"

It was quite literally the sum total of everything I had to my name at this moment, excluding my purse.

"Where did he go?" My tone crept up two octaves and Delilah held out a hand.

"Whoa, simma down, girl. He's taking care of shit for you."

"He's got it bad for you. I see it now." JP was back to her melodramatic self, looking heartbroken.

Delilah laughed. "JP, I told you that you needed to lose that schoolgirl crush. Bishop wasn't ever gonna touch a girl ten years younger than him anyway."

"Not even a full ten. I'm going to be twenty-three in a month." Her pixie-like features narrowed. "Just let it be known that if you and Bishop get married, I'm not coming to the wedding and I'm sure as hell not going to be a bridesmaid. You'd pick some godawful dress in revenge for me having a crush on the groom and it would just be petty revenge, so let's just get all that out in the open, m'kay?"

What. The. Hell?

"Wow, she skipped right to the wedding," Vanessa whispered. "Did the fortune-teller mention a wedding? You might as well put JP out of her misery right now. She's going to give up on ever finding herself an alpha of her own, and retreat to her apartment with seventeen cats and eight subscriptions to different wine-of-the-month clubs."

My gaze darted from Vanessa to JP to Delilah to Con. None of them seemed fazed by JP and her crazy little monologue.

"There's no wedding. There's not going to be a wedding."

"I wouldn't speak so soon, sugar. I know Bishop doesn't seem like the marrying type now, but then again . . . you never know." Delilah winked at me. She needed to not do the winking thing anymore. It was starting to freak me out.

"You're all crazy." My voice was rising higher, but the clang of the door chime drowned out part of it.

Con nodded toward the door. "Thank fuck, man. Get in here before your bride decides to leave you at the altar before you've even proposed."

I spun around to face Bishop in the doorway, and pressed the pads of my fingers to my temples. "They're crazy. Certifiably crazy."

He walked toward me slowly, his green gaze glued to mine rather than sliding to the nutty peanut gallery behind me. I expected him to demand an explanation or to tell everyone to stop acting so insane, but instead he shocked the crap out of me.

"You gonna leave me at the altar, cupcake?" He didn't even crack a smile, and his tone was completely deadpan.

I shoved my fingers into my hair and barely resisted the urge to pull it out. "We're not getting married. We've only kissed a couple times. I'm not sure if you actually saw me naked or if I imagined that, so yeah, definitely no wedding in our future."

His lips twitched at that.

"Wait, you don't know if he saw you naked?" JP asked. "How did that work?"

"Uh, yeah, you skipped over that minor detail with me too," Vanessa said meaningfully.

"She wasn't totally naked." Bishop took another step toward me. "And I couldn't give a fair opinion on the subject because I haven't gotten the whole picture yet."

Oh my God. The way his eyes burned over my body, all of a sudden I felt naked again. I had to change the subject before I completely lost my mind and did something insane, like throw myself at him. Again.

"How much is not totally naked?" JP asked.

Bishop didn't release my gaze to answer her. "Not your business, JP."

"Just asking."

This time Bishop did look away, and I turned my head to watch the interaction. "Enough."

From behind me, Vanessa's heels clicked on the tile. "It's okay. We'll find you a big, bad tattooed guy too. There are plenty of them floating around in this town. Practically a dime a dozen."

"Thanks, princess. That makes us feel so special."

Vanessa crossed back to Con. "You're one in a billion, babe, and you know it."

The heat from Bishop's side melted into my skin, and the fortune-teller's words came back to me. *Guard your heart.*

"You ate?" his deep voice rumbled in my ear.

I nodded. "Vanessa brought yours back."

Speaking of bringing stuff back, I needed to find out what the heck he did with my suitcase because he was empty-handed.

"Where's my bag? I need my bag." I reached out, closing my fingers around his forearm. "I can't lose it. It has everything."

Bishop stared down at me. "It's in your new place that's being aired out."

New place?

"What are you talking about?"

He shrugged. "Called in that favor from Charlie. Got you set up a few blocks away. You'll have to go talk to the landlord to get the final approval and pay the deposit, but the apartment is as good as yours, and she's cutting you a sweet-as-hell deal and giving you time to come up with the money if you need it."

"That place is fucking tiny. Barely qualifies as an apartment," Con said.

"But it's safe, and Harriet doesn't want much more in rent than what the maintenance on it costs."

They had to slow down because I wasn't keeping up. Harriet? What apartment? I was so confused that I didn't even know which questions to ask first. I started with the most basic of the lot.

"You got me an apartment?"

Bishop's gaze dropped to mine. "You have somewhere else to stay for tonight?"

"You could've had her stay at your place." There was a smile in Delilah's voice.

"Low blow. Stop, I don't want to hear any more." JP held a hand over each ear like she was a toddler. "I have to go back to work anyway before y'all crush my hopes and dreams permanently." She hurried to the door, not dropping her hands until she turned and said, "Remember, I'm not going to be a bridesmaid."

The entire town had gone insane. I truly didn't know what else to say.

"Your food's got to be cold by now, but you can pop the po'boy into the microwave and warm it up if you want." Vanessa nodded to the other takeout container on the counter beside the one that Con just emptied.

"Or I'll fuckin' eat it right now," Con said. "I don't care.

143

That shit was awesome. Even the friggin' cole slaw, and we all know I don't eat that shit. You shoulda brought me two, princess."

"I want to hear more about the fortune," Delilah drawled. "Especially if there's wedding bells involved."

"She didn't say anything about a wedding," I blurted. "It's not important. I need to get my stuff." I had to get out of the craziness that seemed to pervade this entire shop.

But Delilah wasn't done. "Did she say anything about tattoos? Because I don't think I need a fortune-teller to see that in your future."

The inked man.

This entire world was going crazy. I wrapped a hand around Bishop's arm. "But my stuff is there? It's safe?"

He looked down at my hand on his forearm for a long moment before replying. "Of course. Harriet's place is solid. I wouldn't let you go somewhere that wasn't. Now, I've got an appointment coming. Can you hang tight for a while?"

"Yes. Thank you. I . . . I really appreciate it. But I would've figured out something for tonight."

He pulled his arm from my grip. "You needed a place, and I knew of a place. It's no big deal."

But it was a big deal. And as much as I knew I should have solved this problem on my own because I was done letting people call the shots in my life, the help Bishop offered didn't seem to come with strings. He just did it, and did it in a way that didn't make me feel caged.

Guard your heart. I'd definitely have to take the fortune-teller's advice.

27
Bishop

"Oh my God. This is amazing." Eden's eyes went wide as she turned in a circle in the courtyard.

"Charlie called it her garden oasis, and she and Huck were very happy here." Harriet sounded wistful about missing her one-time tenant. Her normally steel-gray hair was teal, pink, and purple, like that mermaid look girls who came into Voodoo rocked. It wasn't exactly what you expected on a woman heading toward seventy. But then again, Harriet was one of a kind.

"Huck?" Eden asked.

"Charlie's dog. He's a big bastard. You'll have to meet him one of these days," Harriet explained. "Well, I guess you'll do, girl. If you have any questions, just let me know. I'm downstairs most of the time, and I'll leave a note on the back door if I leave the country unexpectedly."

She leaned in closer and added in a whisper, "Sometimes

I have to dodge the Feds. They're always watching."

Eden's face paled, and Harriet laughed. "Just kidding. Mostly. You can slide the rent under the door whenever you feel like it. I'm not too fussy on what day you get it to me."

"Thank you so much. I can't tell you how much I appreciate this." Eden's voice was quiet, but Harriet waved off the thanks.

"Ha. You need to thank this guy here. Probably owe him a few sexual favors too."

She sent me a wicked grin, and I choked out a cough when the sheet-white color of Eden's face was replaced with burning red. This was Harriet being true-to-filterless form.

"I don't just open up this place for everyone," she said, "especially on short notice. I've been having the cleaning girl keep it up just in case Charlie needed to run away from Simon for a night. But that hasn't happened, so someone might as well enjoy it."

"Well, thank you all the same."

"No problem, dear. Now, I'm off to the opera tonight. I'll be going home with a certain gentleman who knows his way around the clitoris, so don't wait up." Harriet turned away and readjusted the champagne bottle cradled in her arm before disappearing inside.

Eden looked at me, her face even redder than before. "Well . . . she's a character."

"That's one way to describe it." I shook my head to get rid of the mental picture of Harriet getting down with some old dude. "You need anything else before I take off? I gotta get back to work."

"No." She looked up at me with something in her eyes I hadn't ever seen before. "But I really appreciate this. So much. I don't know how I can ever really thank you. First the hotel, and then this. Most people wouldn't put themselves out for someone they don't know."

It wasn't just gratitude staring back at me, it was . . . awe. Almost . . . hero worship.

But I wasn't a fucking hero even on my best day, and having her look at me like that made me realize all the things I wasn't and never would be.

My reply came out gruffer than I intended. "Don't worry about it. You don't owe me shit. Just stay out of trouble."

A little of the awe fell away, and I had to tell myself I didn't care, even as disappointment slid into its place.

"I'm sorry to cause so much trouble." Eden wrapped her arms around herself in what I was coming to realize was one of her protective gestures. "I'll be fine. Thank you again."

A mask of absolutely fucking nothing slipped over her features. The words sounded final, like I wouldn't be seeing her again, and it would probably be a hell of a lot better if I didn't.

But if that were the case, why did it feel like a rock had been dropped in my gut?

Street after street, I kicked myself for not handling every encounter I had with Eden better. She threw me completely off-balance and made me want to be more than what I'd become—which didn't make any fucking sense because I didn't even know her.

But you want to know her.

That voice spoke the truth, even if I didn't want to admit it.

She was keeping secrets, and if she were anyone else, I

wouldn't care. Wouldn't bother to dig. But for some reason, I wanted to know what was hiding behind those layers of innocence that kept drawing me in.

And it pissed me off. Because this wasn't me. Besides, how could I demand answers from her when there was no way in hell I'd be sharing the shit from my past with anyone? Outside of Delilah, I'd kept it locked down for years and wouldn't be changing that anytime soon.

I was a block from Canal when my cell rang, ripping me out of my impending trip down memory lane. Leon's name popped up on the screen.

"What's going on, man?"

"Damn, Bish. Were you trying to cost me my job? What the hell?"

"What are you talking about?"

"Your girl that threw the card down for that room I kept for you? Her card got flagged for fraud and she skipped out without paying for the extra night she stayed that wasn't comped. Just straight-up fucking bailed, according to my manager. Didn't even check out."

"What the fuck? Are you serious?"

"Dead serious."

"I'll make sure you get paid. I'll cover it if I have to, and I'm sure as hell going to find out what happened." The anger burning through me came out in my voice.

"You can pay me back since it's coming out of my paycheck. My manager was talking about turning it over to the police, and I told him it was my mistake. I'm lucky he didn't fucking fire me."

"Man, I'm sorry I brought that shit to your door. I'll make it right. I'll get you the cash, and your next sitting is on me."

"You don't have to do that. Just promise me you'll teach that bitch a lesson." Leon's voice dropped low. "Let me know if you want me to handle it."

A shaft of protectiveness shot through me regardless of how fucking pissed I was at what Eden had done—and not bothered to mention.

"Not a fucking chance will you ever lay a hand on her. You'll get your money, and if you want the sitting, it's yours for the inconvenience. Leave her out of it."

"All right, all right. Sorry, Bish. Didn't know it was like that. Figured you'd be done with the bitch by now. By the way, Kitty was pissed that you tossed her ass out. Ain't gonna get another shot at that."

"I'll talk to you later, man." I didn't bother to wait for his reply before I hung up.

I couldn't give a fuck less about Kitty right now. I wanted to turn around and go back to Eden's new place and shake the truth out of her. Shit wasn't adding up. Was that innocence she wore like her pink fucking sweaters just a front? Was she running some kind of con?

I hadn't been played in years, and I couldn't believe some naive girl had done it.

Why would she bail on the hotel bill but shell out money for rent? None of it added up, but you'd better believe I was going to get to the truth somehow.

I checked the time. If I didn't have an appointment in ten minutes, I'd be back beating down her door for some answers.

She couldn't be that good of an actress. I could smell a con a mile away, thanks to my younger years, and Eden didn't give off a hint of that vibe.

I turned it over and over in my mind all the way back to

the shop, and through my whole appointment. Fuck it . . . I'd be going back tonight.

Eden

I WANDERED AROUND MY TINY NEW APARTMENT, WHICH took all of approximately ninety seconds. There was a small bedroom, a minuscule bathroom, and an open area that served as a living room and eat-in kitchen. But the small size didn't bother me. My apartment in New York, one that I'd fought for the right to live in for years before Dom had allowed it, was at least quadruple the size, but I'd never used every room. I hoped this place would feel more like home than that one did.

Harriet had left a bottle of wine on the counter, and I debated opening it, still wary of alcohol.

Leaving it where it sat, I unpacked my suitcase and hung up my limited wardrobe before pulling out the envelope of cash I'd stashed in the lining of my bag. I might not have learned a lot of the *how to be a gangster* rules from the mobsters around me, but at the end of the day, it seemed like there was only one that truly mattered—cash is king.

For the last several months, every week when my paycheck was deposited into my account, I'd go to the bank and withdraw cash. If someone had asked me at the time, I would have said it was rainy-day money, or some kind of response like that. In all reality, it was because my bank account had been frozen once before when Dom was investigated by the FBI. I couldn't even buy myself lunch because I'd always relied on plastic and never carried cash.

As soon as the accounts had been unfrozen, I'd started my stash in case it ever happened again.

I pulled out the burner phone and checked the Internet browser for news. There'd been nothing new the last five times I'd checked today, and I wasn't holding my breath now. The only article I could find was the same one that had been there this morning.

I'd love to think no news was good news.

Once I'd put the money in the safe in the bedroom closet and organized the rest of my few belongings, I sat down on the small sofa. The TV didn't work, and none of the five books I started could hold my attention. Restlessness wasn't a familiar feeling for me, but tonight I had it in spades.

I looked out the window to the fairy lights hanging in the trees and the blue water of the pool that looked almost tropical with the lights coming from beneath the surface.

Is it heated? I hadn't thought to ask Harriet because it wasn't like I'd packed a bathing suit when I was rushing out of my apartment to leave the city.

Deciding to find out for myself, I opened the door and padded down the wrought-iron spiral staircase to the path that led to the pool. It was a magical little courtyard, and I could see why Charlie had called it her garden oasis. I kicked off one shoe and dipped a toe in the water.

Perfect.

Harriet said she was leaving. The pool couldn't be seen from the gate . . . did I dare take a dip sans suit?

I'd never skinny-dipped in my life, but I was turning over a whole new leaf in New Orleans. Daring filled me. *Why not?* I stripped out of my jeans, cardigan, and cami before pausing to decide if I really wanted to go all the way. I could just jump in with my bra and underwear on . . .

Screw it. For once in my life, I was exercising the *go big or go home* mentality. I shoved my panties down my legs and unhooked my bra before stepping into the pool and slipping my entire body into the water. Definitely heated. From water level, I could see the small tendrils of steam rising into the cooler night air. It was so peaceful. Everything about this night seemed perfect.

A new beginning. Maybe a new place to belong. I was filled with hope, and every day that burner phone didn't make another sound, I convinced myself a little more that maybe they'd forgotten me.

My quiet reverie didn't last long, however. The iron gate clanged with someone's entry, and I slapped a hand over my lips to hold in the shriek that threatened to escape.

Harriet? Charlie? Who?

I sank lower into the water, wanting to be completely covered, but sucked in a breath when a tall, broad form entered the courtyard.

No way.

Bishop started up the stairs but paused when the spiral caused him to face the pool. He couldn't miss me.

"What the hell are you doing?" His deep voice carried across the courtyard as he came back down the stairs and toward me.

I slipped to the front edge of the pool, pressing my body against the cement wall. I reached out, intent on grabbing my cami or my sweater, but both were just out of reach.

Bishop stopped a few feet away from the pile of my clothes, and I stared at the thick black soles of his boots. If he came another step closer, there was no way he could miss how well-lit my naked body was by the pool lights.

"You've gotta be fucking kidding me." The words were uttered low and hoarse, as if he weren't talking to me at all.

"Please toss me my shirt," I whispered.

The last thing I expected Bishop to do was shake his head. "Nah. I don't think I will. Because this way, I've got a captive audience and you're going to answer my questions."

Goose bumps rose along my shoulders, and I slipped further beneath the surface so that my chin touched the edge.

"What are you talking about?" I tried to sound nonchalant, but my heart hammered harder with every beat.

"You bailed on the hotel. Stiffed them on the bill for what you said you'd cover. Why?"

Oh shit. I knew that was going to come out sooner or later, but I'd naively hoped for later. Of course his friend would tell him as soon as possible. And of course I didn't have a story to give Bishop . . . yet.

He stared down at me, clearly waiting on an answer.

"I . . . forgot?"

His eyes narrowed. "You didn't forget shit. You ran. What I want to know is why? I have to assume you have enough to pay rent to Harriet, or are you going to skip out before you pay her too?"

"No! Of course not. No way would I do that to Harriet."

"But you thought it was okay to fuck over the hotel?"

My fingers curled around the concrete edge of the pool. "I'm so sorry. Really, I am. I got spooked and bolted. It wasn't planned."

Bishop's stare intensified, as if he were trying to take me apart layer by layer. "You're not going to tell me the real reason why, are you?"

I broke away from his gaze and stared out into the darkness that had settled over the courtyard. "I can't. I . . . if I could, I would." My voice was quiet, but at least my words weren't a lie.

"I heard all the stories about when Charlie was working at the shop and she was on the run, and I gotta say, I see a whole lot of similarities with you. No one can help you if you won't tell someone what the fuck is going on."

A bitter laugh escaped my lips. *Help me? The bastard daughter of a mobster being investigated by the FBI and a grand jury? Yeah, right.*

"No one can help me. But I'll pay for the hotel. Just let me get out and I'll get the money."

He scowled down at me, clearly unhappy with my answer. "We're way beyond you just handing me some cash and calling it good, cupcake. I want answers. You need me to fuck them out of you? Is that what you're waiting for?"

The words came out in a growl, and I jerked away from the edge of the pool, not thinking about how plainly it would put me on display.

He reached for the hem of his T-shirt and pulled it over his head.

"What? No. What are you doing?"

My voice was so high-pitched that I didn't recognize it. I also didn't recognize this even-rougher-than-normal Bishop before me. It was like someone had flipped a switch. I could practically feel the anger radiating off him.

"I'm coming in. Don't want to get my clothes wet."

I wrapped my arms around my body. No man had seen me fully naked . . . ever. I'd lost my virginity in a beach cabana with my cover-up still on, and he'd barely done more than unzip his khaki shorts.

Bishop crouched and unlaced his boots before kicking them off and removing his socks.

I should have been filled with fear, but when he reached for the button of his jeans, my mouth dried and any trace of apprehension disappeared. Heat flowed through me like the temperature of the pool water had been increased another twenty degrees when he lowered the zipper.

Was this the moment I was supposed to look away? Because there was no way I could do it. I wanted to see everything.

I thought of Kitty and how she'd practically licked her lips when she'd seen Bishop enter the room. I'd known what she wanted then, and apparently my body was on board for that same thing right now, even if my rational mind was screaming at me to cover my eyes.

He shoved off his jeans, and I expected boxers or briefs or even boxer briefs beneath them. Instead, there was just . . . Bishop.

A whole lot of Bishop.

Oh. My. God.

I'd seen porn; I wasn't completely unacquainted with dicks. But I was also under the impression that dicks in porn were way larger than the average man. Apparently, I'd been misinformed, because Bishop was . . . big.

He was also totally shameless as he came toward the steps and walked down into the water.

"You're really fucking quiet all of a sudden, cupcake."

The word *fucking*, regardless of the context he used it in, sent my imagination tumbling into the gutter.

"Why . . . why are you doing this?"

"Because I can't seem to get answers out of you any other way, and if we're both naked, I'm a hell of a lot less likely to pick you up and shake them out of you—unless it's going to make you come."

My insides clenched.

"I would tell you if I could, but I swear it's better if you don't know."

He stepped closer to me as I shrank back against the opposite wall of the pool from where I'd stood before.

"That's just too fucking bad, because I'm not leaving without answers."

29 Bishop

I T WASN'T LIKE I HAD A PLAN WHEN I CAME BACK TO Harriet's. All I had was the extra set of keys I'd purposely kept, and the knowledge that I wasn't leaving until I knew whether the Eden I'd thought I was getting a feel for was a fraud.

When I saw her in the pool and realized she was naked, I decided to take the prime opportunity presented to me.

If she was running some kind of con, I figured she'd use her body to distract me from getting the answers I wanted. If she wasn't . . . I guessed we'd see how she'd react.

I stalked her as she paddled backward to the wall and waited until she had nowhere else to retreat.

"What do you want from me?" she whispered.

"I want the truth."

But that wasn't all I wanted. My cock was rock hard and not afraid to remind me that I wanted her body too.

"Just let me get the money. I made a huge mistake. I

freaked out over something stupid. I'm so sorry." She looked away as she spoke.

I released the concrete edge of the pool and lifted my hand to her chin to force her dark gaze to mine. "Not enough. That's bullshit, and we both know it."

Indecision warred behind her gaze, and I wished she'd just fucking spill so I could quit wondering if I was drawn to someone who was a con or just on the run.

She swallowed, her eyes on mine when she finally said, "They told me my credit card was canceled because of fraud, and I thought I saw cops at the front desk and I got scared that maybe they'd arrest me or something. So I ran."

Her explanation sounded sincere enough to be the truth, but my radar didn't seem to operate flawlessly around her, so I needed more.

"Did you steal the credit card you used?"

Eden's eyes widened. "No. Of course not."

"Then why would you think the cops would arrest you if there was an issue with it?"

Her gaze dropped away from mine. "I panicked."

Something wasn't adding up, but I didn't have a fucking clue what it was. "So you're just afraid of cops?"

For a girl like Eden, I couldn't imagine that she'd have any reason not to think cops were the most helpful people on the planet. For a guy like me, I avoided them as much as I fucking could, even though it seemed half the NOPD had decided that I was the guy who needed to do their ink.

"I don't particularly like them," she said quietly.

"You ever broken the law before this, Eden?"

I expected a quick and unequivocal no, but it didn't come as fast as I thought it would.

"I don't think so. I mean, I'm sure I have by accident

sometime. I've jaywalked. But I'm not some kind of criminal."

Well, that makes one of us, I thought.

My anger from earlier started to fade and be replaced by the heat of the knowledge that Eden's naked tits were only inches from my chest, separated by water I could see right through. Last time I'd seen them under her pink bra, she'd been too fucked up for me to take advantage . . . but tonight she was completely sober.

I raised my gaze from her chest, expecting her cheeks to be red when she realized I was staring at her nipples, but she wasn't watching my face. She was staring down at my body.

"Like what you see?"

That got her attention.

Eden jerked her head up to meet my eyes, and the blush colored her skin like I'd timed it.

"You're . . . big."

A booming laugh broke free from my throat at her unexpected response, and her cheeks flamed even brighter.

"No, that's not what I meant. I mean . . . everywhere. Not just, in the . . ." She looked down, then jerked her gaze back to mine. "I'm going to shut up now."

That kind of awkward and fumbling response couldn't be faked, and protectiveness rose in me again. Eden was no con artist. She was a girl who couldn't even say the word *cock* without turning red.

"Ain't no shame in my game."

She reached out a hand and covered my lips with her fingers. "Stop. You're just making it worse. I wasn't checking out your . . . package. I mean, I did before you got in the pool, but that's only because I thought you'd have underwear on because who doesn't wear underwear?" The babbling continued, and so did my laughter.

Hell, I hadn't laughed this much since Delilah had given in to a customer's request and tattooed a flexing veined eggplant cartoon on a client so he could send pictures of it instead of dick pics.

Eden pulled her hand back and covered her face. "I'm going to stop talking now. I seriously can't be trusted to say anything that's not completely humiliating when you're standing this close to me naked."

"I disagree, and since I'm not ready to get out and put my clothes on, you're going to have to deal with it."

She mumbled something under her breath.

"Come again?"

Eden pressed her lips together for a beat before saying, "I don't know how to deal with it. This isn't something I've ever dealt with before."

A crazy thought popped into my brain. "Are you a virgin?"

If there was a red brighter than fire engine, that was the color of Eden's cheeks. "No! Of course not. Really. I've touched a dick before. I mean, just the one, but it still counts. Well, I didn't really touch it. Except, you know, inside me. Oh my God, I'm just going to shut up now."

Realization dawned on me as her babbled protest silenced. "You've had sex with one guy? Once? How old are you?"

Eden turned to bolt, but instead smashed her tits into my arm. I stepped close enough so that only an inch of water separated us.

Her gaze went skyward. "This is so humiliating."

That's where she and I had differing opinions. "Why? Because you haven't fucked every guy you've ever met? What's wrong with that?"

Eden's gaze snapped down to mine and her brows drew into slashes. "Hey, whoa now. You can toss that double-standard crap right in the trash. What if I had screwed every guy I ever met? Would that make me less of a person? I mean, it's not like you probably haven't been with dozens and dozens of women. I'm not judging you. Except for maybe that Kitty girl. I mean, really? You've got to have some standards."

My laughter boomed out again across the courtyard. "Cupcake, just because I can get most any pussy I want, doesn't mean I do it."

"Still, double standards are—"

When she started on another tirade, I decided to silence her the best way I knew how.

I leaned down and covered her lips with mine.

Eden

H E WAS KISSING ME. HE WAS NAKED. I WAS NAKED.
And my hands, mouth, and the rest of my body
decided this was the best idea anyone had ever
had. That was the only excuse I had for why there was no
water separating us anymore, and the hot, hard length of
Bishop's cock pressed into my stomach.

My fingers gripped his shoulders as his hands found my
ass and lifted me higher in the water, sliding his cock directly against my clit, a spot that normally only zinged with
pleasure because of the toys I owned.

I moaned into his mouth and held on tighter. A small
voice told me that this was going to escalate way too quickly
for my own self-preservation, but I told it to shut the hell up
because I wanted a non-self-induced orgasm.

Bishop's hands, no doubt incredibly clever due to using
them all freaking day, squeezed my ass as he groaned.

One move. That's all it would take for him to be inside

me. What stunned me more than the fact that I found myself writhing against him in a pool was the fact that I wanted him inside me so very badly.

Heat licked over my body, and I knew if I didn't stop soon, I wasn't going to have the willpower to stop at all. But before I could call a halt, Bishop jerked back and his hands dropped away from my ass. By the time my feet touched the bottom of the pool, he had backed away until he hit the other side.

"Fuck, cupcake. Two more seconds and I would've been inside you."

He said this like it was somehow going to be news to me.

What was the appropriate response for this? Probably not, *I know, right?*

Instead I blurted, "I don't have a towel. Why didn't I bring a towel?"

His lips turned up into a sensual smile. "Didn't plan the skinny-dipping? Just went with your instincts?"

"Basically."

Thankfully, Harriet had kept the apartment stocked with sheets and towels, but that meant I had to get out of this pool, naked, with Bishop watching me.

Umm. Nope. That wasn't going to work. Looked like I was going to stay in this pool forever—or at least until he left and I could climb out without him seeing the cellulite on my thighs and butt, and the lack of toned muscles due to not going to the gym in the last millennium.

Bishop seemed to read the dilemma on my face. "You going to go get something to dry off with?"

"Eventually."

"Now would be better."

I looked down at the water and pretended to study my

nails. "I'm good with waiting."

"I guess you're going to get a great look at my ass then, because that means I'm going to go get them." With a splash of water, he pushed himself up and out of the pool, and my attention went right to his ass.

Where did men get asses like that? His was *perfect.* The rounded muscles flexed as he put one foot on the ground and then the other.

He jogged up to the spiral staircase and I couldn't help but watch. I think I might have even drooled.

Ink. Muscle. Pure *man.*

My earlier thought about him being completely out of my league came back in spades. And now he knew just how inexperienced I was.

Bishop let himself into my apartment and disappeared for a few minutes before coming out with a towel wrapped around his waist and one in his hand.

He stopped at the edge of the pool and shook it out. "Come on, cupcake. You're going to prune."

Seriously? He's worried about me pruning and I'm staring at the outline of his cock beneath his towel, wishing he was still pressed against me. Apparently I was the only sexually frustrated one in this situation.

But even my sexual frustration wasn't enough to get me to step out of this pool naked in front of him.

"You can leave it on the edge and turn around."

Once again, his deep, rich laugh filled the courtyard. "Cupcake, I'm not sure where you got the idea that I was some kind of gentleman, but by now, you should know that's not the case. The only reason I didn't find out how tight that pussy of yours was is because I don't have a rubber on me."

How stupid was I that I hadn't even thought about a

condom? Embarrassment filled me, and came out as contrariness. "And because I didn't want you to find out."

"Bullshit." He shrugged. "Whatever you have to tell yourself to make you feel better."

Bishop didn't drop the towel, and I was faced with the choice of staying in the pool or giving in.

"Just turn around."

"I've already felt nearly every inch of you, and there's not a damn thing I didn't like, so what does it matter?"

"It matters," I yelled. "Okay? It matters to me."

Instead of laughing at me or refusing again, he turned his back and held the towel out to the side.

I swam toward the stairs, climbed out, and pulled it from his hand. As soon as I had it wrapped around my body, Bishop turned around and his intense green gaze collided with mine.

"I want you. I'm not making any secret of that, but now I'm going to wait until you admit that you want me just as much."

It was on the tip of my tongue to tell him I wasn't denying it, but something held me back. Probably the same embarrassment that had paralyzed me in the pool. I didn't know how to navigate this situation, and I certainly had no idea how to respond.

When I stayed silent, Bishop didn't speak again. Instead, he reached for the knot of his towel and tugged it off before tossing it aside and reaching for his jeans.

His eyes stayed on my face as though daring me to look down like I had before. I was determined to prove that I had retained some self-control where he was concerned.

The hiss of the zipper sounded between us and he bent to grab his shirt. "You're a fucking contradiction. Stubborn, innocent, curious, and a whole hell of a lot of other things I haven't figured out yet." He pulled the shirt over his head. "But I will."

I wasn't sure if that was a threat or a promise, but either way, I didn't know if I'd be able to withstand his scrutiny. I was supposed to be laying low, not attracting attention or raising questions while I waited for my summons. And instead I'd aroused the curiosity of a man who seemed to have the tenacity of a bulldog. I didn't need him to be curious, but the thought of him being anything else didn't sit well with me either.

I watched in silence as he shoved his feet into socks and pulled on his boots. When he was done, he stood.

"I'll be seeing you around, Eden. That's a promise."

Eden

FABIENNE PUT BOTH HANDS ON HER HIPS AND watched as I looped my apron over my neck and tied it around my back. The bright purple coordinated with my white polo and jeans and Sperrys. It wasn't like I could wear one of my new dresses, so this would have to work. Your Favorite Hole was embroidered on the purple hat I fit over my ponytail and secured on my head.

"That uniform makes you look even cuter than normal. I didn't know that was possible," Fabienne said before turning to the espresso machine.

Her words instantly made me wonder what Bishop would think when he came in for his coffee. Would he look at me differently? *What if he didn't look at me differently? God, that would be even worse.*

After he left last night, I'd kicked myself for not stuffing a vibrator in my suitcase. Note to self: next time, make sure to pack *all* the essentials.

I'd pulled up my favorite bookmarked dirty scenes and handled things the old-fashioned way. But even two orgasms hadn't been able to put me to sleep. I'd tossed and turned for hours, and then when I finally drifted off, I'd dreamed about Bishop sitting on the chair in my bedroom, jacking off while he watched me.

For the first time in my life, I considered begging for sex.

Pathetic. I would not beg. But it wasn't like I had the skills to make *him* beg. This needed to be remedied . . . but not right now.

"First things first. You're going to make me the best latte you can, and then I'll give you any pointers to up your game."

Pushing all dirty thoughts of Bishop out of my head, I turned to the espresso machine and unhooked the portafilter from the head and checked to make sure it was empty before holding it under the grinder and filling it with espresso grounds. After tamping it down, I returned it to the head and paused with my finger over the buttons.

"One-shot or two-shot latte?"

"Small is one, medium is two, and large is three. Let's do a medium. We don't do that tall, grande, venti shit here, for the record."

I slid the shot glasses under the spouts and pressed the button for two shots before bending down to open the fridge beneath and asking, "What kind of milk?"

"We do skim, two percent, soy, and coconut. Do skim, and I'll talk you through steaming coconut and soy later."

Nodding, I grabbed the container and poured what I hoped was enough into the metal pitcher and checked the thermometer on the side. From my own personal experience, I remembered that I needed to hit at least 155 degrees. I frothed the milk while the espresso finished dripping before grabbing a paper cup.

"Any flavoring?"

In my peripheral vision, I caught her head tilting to the side. "Amaretto."

Keeping one eye on the milk, I grabbed the amaretto flavoring and poured one shot into the bottom of the cup before adding the espresso. When the milk came up to temperature, I added it in as well, stirring as I went.

"I can't make any fancy designs on the top, though. I hope that's not a job requirement."

I set the milk pitcher and the long metal-handled spoon aside and offered the latte to Fabienne.

"We'll have you drawing dicks in no time," she said with a smile as she accepted the cup.

There's no way I can fit a dick as big as Bishop's on top of a latte. Seriously, how big was that monster?

The thought disappeared as Fabienne brought the cup to her lips. *Moment of truth.*

She sipped and I held my breath. Her expression gave nothing away until she lowered the latte back to the counter and nodded.

"You'll do just fine."

Releasing my breath, my cheeks tugged with the smile that stretched across my face. "Really?"

"Damn right, you will."

The validation I felt from her approval soared far and beyond what I'd felt in years. I thought about holding it in, but cast that aside to pump my fist into the air.

Fabienne's laugh seemed to fill the room, all the way to the tin-stamped ceiling. "Yeah, you'll do just fine here. Now, let's talk donut holes and packaging them up." She swung her gaze to mine. "You've gotta handle them real carefully.

Just pretend they're a guy's balls and you don't want to crush them."

I slapped a hand over my mouth. "Oh my God, you did not just say that." Once again, a mental picture of Bishop's equipment flashed through my brain.

"Sure did, and I bet it helps."

And just like that, I was officially employed in New Orleans.

Bishop

THE LINES OF A GIRL'S FACE STARED BACK AT ME AS I worked on the portrait of a man's daughter on the outside of his bicep. It took all my concentration to make each one perfect because this wasn't the kind of tattoo I could fuck up and live with myself.

"She's going to be seven this year, and I decided this would be the way I'd always remember her. Even when she's got a license and driving and boys are chasing after her, I always want to remember my little girl when I was the only important man in her life."

My client's words penetrated, and I wondered what it would be like to feel that way. With the course I'd set for my life, it wasn't in the cards.

"You mind if we take a break? I could use a smoke."

I was holding the tattoo machine in midair as I let my mind wander, but snapped out of it. "Of course. Take your time." I looked down at my watch. "I'm going to run next door and get some coffee. You want anything?"

The client shook his head. "Nah, just some nicotine."

I put everything on the counter behind me and snapped my gloves off my hands before standing and stretching. Staying in one position for too long told me exactly how much of an old man I was becoming. Thirty-three years felt older than it should most days.

But when I walked into Your Favorite Hole, the feeling fell away as laughter reached me.

Eden was standing sideways, reaching into the donut bins and pulling out selections for a man that had to be eighty if he was a day.

"I mean, come on, it is called Your Favorite Hole for a reason. You have to pick your favorite." Her tone was light and teasing, and the man's smile grew.

"Oh, darlin', if I wasn't fifty years past my prime, I'd have a whole lot more to say to that."

The rush of possessiveness that had been dogging me since I'd met Eden didn't come this time. The old man was harmless.

He turned and saw me. "But this young man, he looks to be about the right one for you. I bet if you teased him, he'd just pick you up and carry you home."

Eden glanced toward me. Her cheeks bloomed with color but her smile stayed intact. "He does seem like the type, doesn't he? I think that's a safe bet."

The old man glanced between us, looking intrigued. "I sense some history here. You have intentions toward this girl? As her unofficial new grandfatherly figure, I feel the need to look out for her."

I didn't know what it was about Eden that made people automatically want to protect and defend her, but I couldn't fault the old man for feeling like that when it was my natural instinct.

Eden leaned an arm on the counter and rested her chin in her hand. "What say you, Bishop? Do you have intentions toward this girl?" Her tone carried laughter, but there was something else underlying it. *Challenge.*

I studied her and considered my response. Might as well lay it all out there. "I've got intentions. Plenty of them."

Eden's eyebrows shot up to her hairline at my answer.

The old man caught on quickly. "I bet you do, boy. I bet you do." He laid money on the counter and reached for the box of donuts. "You better watch this one, Eden. If he's anything like me with my Sally, he might take his time with the decision, but once he's decided, there's nothing that'll stand in his way."

His words echoed in my head. Was that what I was doing? Taking my time with the decision to make Eden mine? I hadn't even considered the possibility of something permanent because my life hadn't left room for it. And then here was Con asking me if I'd want to buy Voodoo, and an old man insinuating that I could have permanent intentions toward Eden.

I'd never let myself give enough thought to my future for permanence to be part of it. Maybe it was time for that to change . . . but that meant the threat that kept me moving every few years would have to be removed from the equation. I had no idea if they were still looking for me, but I knew better than to settle.

"I'm sure he doesn't have any intentions of that sort, Mr. Flowers."

Mr. Flowers studied us both. "I think you'll be surprised by what he intends, young lady. Thank you for the donuts, and keep the change."

He lifted the box and shuffled out of the shop, but not before pausing beside me to say, "I might be old, but I still know how to get rid of a body. You treat Miss Eden right."

I nodded, holding back the smile his words produced. "Understood, sir."

The door chimed as he stepped outside, and I turned back to Eden. Her cheeks were still stained pink as I stepped up to the counter.

"He just threatened to kill me if I treated you badly," I told her, wondering if those cheeks would get darker. They did, all the way to a bright red.

"You can't be serious."

"Dead serious."

She shook her head. "He came in an hour ago and just wanted to chat. It took us forty-five minutes to finally get around to picking out his donuts."

"Guess that's your special magic then. Making people want to spend more time around you."

This time her eyes widened comically. "Yeah . . . I'm sure that's it. Just look at you. You want to spend as much time around me as you would around someone with the plague."

Her statement threw me. "You think I don't want to be around you?"

"Every time I see you, you're gone so fast, it's like you can't wait to get away from me."

"Maybe I don't think you'll be able to handle what I'd want if I stayed."

The red continued to color her cheekbones, but Eden straightened her shoulders and stood taller. "Maybe that's exactly what I want."

I stepped forward and pressed both hands to the purple

laminate counter. "You sure about that, cupcake? Because I'm not exactly sweet and easy."

"I gathered that from the girls waiting in the room at the hotel."

A shaft of regret that she saw them stabbed through me. "Two-on-one isn't my thing, so don't worry about that."

No, if I got tangled up in Eden, had her in my bed the way I wanted her, I wasn't sure I'd be able to let her go. But given my newfound possibilities of permanence . . . maybe I could keep her.

"Well, I'm definitely not into two-on-one, so that wouldn't even be in the realm of possibilities."

The fact that I was standing in Your Favorite Hole talking to Eden about how neither of us wanted a threesome struck me as surreal. I had to dial it back before we got way ahead of ourselves.

"What time do you get off work?" When her eyes popped open wide again, I smiled. "To hang out. Get some food. See what happens."

"I'm here until midnight, and then I have to shower and change so I don't smell like donuts."

"You can shower at my place. I'll find you something to wear."

"I don't think—"

"I don't think you're walking home from work by yourself, and I'll be working until at least twelve thirty on this portrait. Come over when you're done, and you can let yourself upstairs."

The indecision warring inside her played out on her features, but I knew I'd won when she replied. "Are you sure?"

"Yeah. I'll even make you a late dinner."

"You cook?" Her tone was pure surprise.

"I got a few tricks up my sleeve, cupcake. Guess you'll find out what they are tonight. Now, how about a large black coffee and a bag of donut holes so I can push through and finish the rest of this tat?"

Eden

I COULDN'T BELIEVE I WAS GOING TO SPEND TONIGHT with Bishop. Well, not *spend the night*, but it was way past evening, so I wasn't sure what else to call it. I locked up the shop, still marveling that Fabienne had given me a key on my first day, and readjusted my bag over my shoulder.

Bishop had a valid point. I hadn't thought about how I'd be getting home after work on the nights I worked the late shift. As I knew all too well, me walking through the French Quarter by myself wasn't always the smartest move. But as I walked into the front door of Voodoo, and both Bishop and his client looked at me, I wondered if this was an even dumber move.

As Bishop already knew, my experience level wasn't exactly advanced, and I had no idea what he expected tonight.

"Hi." My voice wavered only marginally as I called the greeting. "Do you want me to just—"

My words were cut off as the door chimed behind me

and clicking heels hit the floor.

"Hey, baby. You got time for me tonight? I want ink and cock, but I'd take just cock if you ain't got time for the other."

I spun around at the slurred, smoky voice to find a girl with bright red hair and almost no clothes on. Her body was ridiculous.

Is she a stripper? From the minuscule ripped tank and tiny little hot shorts to the towering six-inch clear stilettos, I didn't feel my mental question was unfair.

Bishop's tone was no-nonsense when he responded. "Out of luck on all counts, Star. Head on home."

Her rough laugh followed. "You know you're interested. Like you got better plans for later?"

Bishop's face stayed expressionless. "You might want to get a cup of coffee on your way home too."

The expression on her face morphed from smug and happy to harsh and downright ugly in a flash, and her attention turned to me.

"What? With this girl? Queen prim and proper? She do that schoolgirl-uniform shit and act like a naughty little slut for you? I know you like that kind of thing."

The muscle in Bishop's jaw ticked, but nothing else gave away what he was thinking. "The next time you need ink, you're gonna have to find someone else because this shop no longer exists for you anymore."

"You never did know a good thing when you had it. Fuck off, Bishop." She turned on her giant heel and clipped her way out, slamming into my shoulder and pausing. "Slut, you won't be able to keep him. No one can."

When the door shut behind her, I turned to Bishop and mouthed a silent *wow.*

"Sorry about that, man," he said to the customer first.

"No worries, dude. You don't have to explain crazy to me. I've got an ex-wife who could give her a run for her money."

"I'll be back in a second."

Bishop lowered the tattoo machine to the counter, snapped off a glove, and came toward me.

"What'd she say to you?"

I shook my head. "Not important."

"What'd she say?"

"Do you mind if I go up and shower?"

Bishop's hand landed under my chin, and he lifted my gaze to his. "What'd she say, Eden?"

"She called me a slut and told me I wouldn't be able to keep you because no one could. That's all. Moving on now."

He didn't move his hand, and the muscle in his jaw ticked again. "If Delilah were here, she'd track her down and kick her ass. Star's drunk, probably hopped up on pills, and what she said was dead fucking wrong."

I nodded. "I know. I'm not a slut."

His expression softened. "That's not all she was wrong about."

My heart beat harder at the words and the possible implications.

"Go on upstairs and take a shower. I'll be up in a little while." Bishop lowered his hand from my chin and laced his fingers through mine. "Come on. The door is this way."

He pulled me toward the back hallway of the shop and stopped before the door next to the employee break room. I'd assumed it opened to a closet or something, but when Bishop pulled it open, I realized I was wrong. Inside was a stairway leading up to a door.

"It's unlocked. There should be a clean towel in the

closet in the bathroom. You can grab a shirt out of my dress-er if you don't want to put your work clothes back on. Hell, you can even wash them if you want. Washer and dryer are up there too, in the big closet by the door."

"Uh . . . okay. I'll be good. Sorry to interrupt your work."

"You're not an interruption, cupcake. You're a breath of fucking fresh air. Go on up. I'll be done soon."

With his words propelling me, I climbed the stairs as he shut the door behind me.

I stood in front of the shower, debating how tonight was go-ing to go. I truly had no expectations, but something had changed between us. Bishop wasn't the gruff, brusque, and nearly mute broody guy who I had a crush on anymore. Now he was looking at me like I mattered. Like this might not be all one-sided and mostly in my head.

What was I supposed to do with that?

I didn't know how long I would be here, and I'd decided that was okay. Not knowing gave me some time to soak up all the adventures I could, but with it came a sense of urgen-cy so I didn't waste it.

The edges of my plan had frayed until it was in tatters. I wanted to stay. I wanted to be part of this little world I'd discovered. I liked the people and loved the city, even if I still got lost half the time.

And Bishop? What if this could be more than the dreams I had at night and the crush I nursed during the day? What if it could be real? I honestly didn't have a clue how to *have* a real relationship.

That was something to worry about some other time.

Like when I wasn't about to get naked in Bishop's apartment. *I'm getting naked in Bishop's apartment. Holy shit.*

34 *Bishop*

"**I** THINK I'M GONNA CALL IT A NIGHT, MAN. WE knew I'd need another session, so you cool with stopping now?"

My client's question was the best thing I could imagine him asking. "Your call."

He grinned. "What kind of guy would I be if I kept you down here working when you've got that sweet thing upstairs waiting for you? A shit guy, that's what kind."

I could try to pretend I hadn't been thinking about Eden since the second I'd walked back into the room. "It's up to you."

He lifted his arm. "Just wrap me up, and I'll give you my money and get out of your way."

"Sounds good. Let me make sure I've got you down for the second session and see if I need to block out more time."

I taped the wrap around the partially completed tattoo and snapped off my gloves again before tossing them in the trash.

After taking care of shit at the counter, I locked up the shop after he left and hustled back to my room to clean everything up faster than I'd ever done before.

My client was right that I'd never had quite the incentive like I did now.

Eden was upstairs, and I was still figuring out how I was going to let this play out. I'd never wanted a woman the way I wanted her, but I wasn't rushing things. Now that I'd let myself start considering the possibility of something that lasted beyond a night, everything had changed.

I flipped off the lights and opened the door to upstairs. I paused at the bottom of the stairs, listening for the sound of water, but heard nothing. Taking them two at a time, I reached the top and opened the door. Steam wafted from the open bathroom door, but I didn't see Eden when I looked inside.

I froze on the threshold of my bedroom. She faced away from me as she pulled a T-shirt over her head, covering her naked skin inch by inch.

Fuck.

When it dropped to cover her rounded ass, I wanted nothing more than to stride forward and lift it up again.

I wasn't sure if I'd breathed too loud or what, but Eden spun around.

"Uh . . . I borrowed a shirt." And she did. White, with the Voodoo Ink logo on the front. The water from her skin and hair was already making it see-through in spots.

I had to clear my throat to find my voice. "I see that. You hungry?"

"Yes." The glint in her dark eyes betrayed the fact that she wasn't just hungry for food, but something still held me back. I could stride across the threshold and have her under me in that bed, but it didn't feel right. I didn't want her to think that was the only reason I asked her to come up here. I'd never been in this situation, so I had to play it by ear.

"Then you're in luck because tonight you're gonna have killer shrimp stir-fry. You like seafood, right?"

Eden nodded, keeping the smile pinned to her face, but it didn't quite cover her disappointment.

Don't worry, cupcake. You're gonna get what you need. I don't have it in me to wait too much longer.

She followed me out of the bedroom and into the living area, and I nodded toward the old turntable on top of the entertainment system. "Go flip through the vinyl and pick something."

My collection was one of the things I'd always figured would suck to leave when I moved on, because I traveled light. Now that the possibility of staying in New Orleans was taking root, everything in me was lighter with a sense of relief.

I pulled open the fridge and grabbed the bowl of shrimp that had been thawing since noon, and a container of cooked rice. I was rinsing the shrimp when the sound of Louis Armstrong came on.

Footsteps padded into the kitchen, and I looked over my shoulder. "Nice choice. A favorite of mine."

"I figured since it looked like it was near the top of the stack. I've always liked Louis too."

"You want to help? It's not required, but if you're in the mood to chop vegetables, I could use a hand."

A flash of uncertainty crossed her face. "I'm a terrible cook. Like honestly terrible. So if you don't care what the vegetables look like, then I'm happy to help. If you care what they look like, you might not want my knife-wielding skills."

"Grab the celery and carrots out of the fridge and go to town. They don't have to be pretty."

"Aye aye, captain."

We worked in companionable silence for several minutes before Eden spoke.

"You don't have a New Orleans accent. Where are you from?"

I kept my focus on deveining the shrimp as I rinsed each one. "A little bit of everywhere. I started out in the east and ended up down south."

"What kept you moving?"

"A whole lot of things. Long story, not always pretty. Guess you could call me a wanderer."

Eden paused in her chopping for a moment before saying, "Most stories aren't always pretty. That's what gives them true beauty. I've always wanted to wander."

"Then why didn't you?"

"I didn't exactly have the option."

"Why not?"

She shrugged. "Another long story. Not so pretty. Mostly, my father wouldn't allow it."

I finished up the shrimp and grabbed a big pan from the cupboard. "And did you always do what your father said?"

Eden's voice quieted. "I couldn't ignore his orders and get away with it."

"Tough guy?"

"When he was around. The rest of the time my aunt raised me, or I was by myself."

"What was she like?"

"Fine. She was my father's half sister and didn't seem to have a whole lot of love for him. But he paid for her life, so it wasn't like she could do anything but be passive-aggressive about it when he wasn't around. Which was most of the time."

With each piece she revealed, I got a clearer idea of why Eden seemed so sheltered and yet wanted to see the world and be a part of it.

"Anyway, that's all boring. Tell me about you."

I poured oil in the skillet before moving across the kitchen to rest a palm on the counter on either side of Eden. "How are the vegetables coming?"

I glanced down at the pile on the cutting board and leaned closer. The veggies looked like they'd been hacked to pieces, but that wasn't what caught my attention. No, it was the scent of my shampoo on Eden's hair. I leaned closer and breathed it in. I liked it. A whole fucking lot.

"It was a massacre," she said with a laugh, laying the knife on the counter and turning around to face me. In the circle of my arms, Eden smiled up at me. "No survivors."

Eden

I WANTED HIM TO KISS ME. WHEN HE FIRST WALKED INTO the apartment, I'd wanted him to rush into the bedroom and pick me up and kiss the hell out of me before throwing me down on the bed and climbing on top, or even better, letting me climb on top so I could finally explore him. But something had stopped Bishop, and I didn't know how to change it.

Was I really so bad at sending signals that he wasn't getting the *all clear for forward movement* sign? I wasn't afraid to move this along. I was more afraid that he wouldn't.

His head lowered until his lips were an inch from mine. "You seem to have survived just fine, cupcake."

I wasn't leaving it to chance this time. Pushing up on my tiptoes, I wrapped my hands around his shoulders before pressing my lips to his.

Instead of pulling back like I'd feared, Bishop cupped a hand around my cheek and tilted my head for a better angle before his tongue dived into my mouth. It was like he was starving—for me.

I wrapped a leg around his hip, and his free hand caught it and held me closer so I could press my center against the hardening bulge in his jeans. The T-shirt I wore rode up with each movement. Within moments, his palm was touching my bare skin, and I was in danger of leaving a wet spot on his jeans.

With a boldness I'd never felt before, I released my grip on one shoulder and reached down between us. Shifting my hips a few inches, I palmed his cock and squeezed.

Bishop's sexy groan was my reward.

He pulled his lips away, but didn't release my face. His gaze burned into mine as he spoke.

"You make me want a hell of a lot more than your hand on my cock, cupcake."

I swallowed. "Maybe that's exactly what I want."

"Not yet."

"But—"

He released my face and lowered his hand to where mine was gripping him, and peeled my fingers away.

"First, I need to know."

"Know what?"

"How bad you want me."

He shifted his hand to cup my center. The heat already blooming between my legs rushed a dozen degrees hotter as he used one finger to stroke up and down the slick heat. My hips surged forward, grinding against his palm. I needed more pressure, more everything. My moaning sigh filled the kitchen, and I didn't care how I sounded.

"So fucking sweet. You want to come on my hand? Fuck my fingers until you scream?"

189

His coarse words pushed me harder because I wanted that and more.

When one thick finger slid inside me, I moaned even louder.

"Fuck, you're tight. You're gonna strangle my cock when I finally get inside you."

If I still had any grip on my rational self, I might have found the energy to be embarrassed, but he increased the pressure on my clit as a second finger slid inside.

Oh my God.

That's when he finally started to move, thrusting his fingers in and out as I bucked against them. Both my hands wrapped around his shoulders again, my nails digging in to keep me upright.

"You're gonna come for me, aren't you, cupcake?"

Words weren't possible. My response was a moan and a clench of my inner muscles as the climax drew closer. I could almost reach it. He pressed harder on my clit, and it sent me over the edge.

I buried my face in his shoulder so the scream wouldn't wake the neighbors. Over and over, my muscles clenched as he kept up the pressure and the thrust of his fingers.

When I finally came down, he withdrew his hand and lifted his fingers to his mouth, and sucked them clean.

My eyes bugged wide.

"Jesus fucking Christ, cupcake. You're even sweeter than I thought you would be."

The words should have burned my cheeks with embarrassment, but instead they made me bold.

"And how sweet are you?" They were the words of someone who knew what she was doing, not the words of a girl who'd never had a penis in her mouth.

His gaze heated, and I knew my inexperience didn't matter. I was going to make him explode the way I had.

Letting the T-shirt fall to cover me, I lowered myself to my knees and reached for his belt.

His big hands gripped my shoulders as he pulled me to my feet before I could get any further. "Not here. If you're gonna wrap that sweet mouth around my cock, I want us both to be comfortable."

Bishop lifted me into his arms and carried me toward the bedroom.

When he lowered me to the bed, he came down on top of me. "But first, I want you to kiss me. Hard. Like I've been wanting your lips on mine since the day I met you."

He flipped us over and my T-shirt flew up in the back again, but that didn't stop Bishop from wrapping a hand around my ass and sliding me up his body. He kept one palm covering my bare ass as he pulled my face down to his, and the other hand he tangled in my hair.

My attention was divided. The aftermath of orgasm. His clever tongue and amazing kiss.

Against my lips, he murmured, "You're fucking perfect, Eden. Fucking perfect."

I thought he was just as perfect, and the proof was slicking across his belly and the waistband of his jeans where I sat.

Screw it.

My boldness grew, and I pulled back and inched my way down his legs.

"It's my turn."

Bishop caught the ends of my hair in his palm and gripped tightly, stopping my movement. "Have you ever had a cock between those lips, cupcake?"

"Does it matter?" I refused to let my inexperience get in the way of what I wanted.

"Not at all, but I can't lie and say that teaching you to suck my dick the way I like it hasn't been on my mind."

"Teach me?"

He released my hair and skimmed a hand along my jaw as he nodded. "Teach you to swallow me down and let it go deep? How to suck hard as you pull away? How to totally fucking wreck me for life?"

None of these sounded like bad things.

"Yes."

Bishop's lids grew heavy even as excitement lit his eyes. "Unbutton my jeans. See how fucking hard I am for you."

I followed his directions and wrapped my hand around his solid shaft. I'd already seen how big he was, had felt his length against me, but pulsing against the palm of my hand, his cock seemed even bigger.

Instinct ruled, and I gripped him harder and stroked.

"You don't need me to teach you anything, do you?"

I lowered my head to circle the crown with my tongue. "Just tell me if I do something wrong," I whispered.

Where this inner temptress was coming from, I had no idea, but I was rolling with it.

Bishop groaned as I sucked the head into my mouth and teased.

"Your mouth might kill me, but I'll die a happy man."

He shoved his jeans further down his hips, lifting his ass so he could free himself.

I wasted no time taking him deeper, varying my suction and speed, trying to see what would wring another moan from him. Each noise acted like an incentive, and I wanted to make him come apart the same way I had.

"Grip the base and take me deeper."

I followed his directions and was rewarded with another groan. His orders fell away as I did what came naturally. Bishop's hands buried in my hair and lightly guided each movement when I would falter.

"Fuck, baby. I'm gonna come."

I wasn't sure if that meant he was going to pull out or if he was staying put. Either way, I kept going, sucking deeper, smiling inside as I felt his cock jerk, and hot, salty cream spilled into my mouth.

Was I not supposed to feel victorious? Because I felt like I'd just won a damn medal here.

When I finally lifted my head, Bishop hauled me up the bed and curled me into his side. I didn't know what exactly I was supposed to say after a blow job.

"You didn't need any instructions, did you, baby? Fucking destroyed me like it was nothing."

A smile tugged at my lips, but a shaft of uncertainty still sneaked inside. "Umm . . . did you want me to go?"

He turned his head to stare into my eyes. "No way in hell. You try to leave this bed, and I'll carry you right back. Besides, I want dessert before we have dinner."

"Dessert?"

His green eyes flashed with heat. "One little taste wasn't nearly enough. I'm gonna eat you until you scream."

My thighs squeezed together instinctively.

"Now, put that sweet little pussy on my face."

"What?"

"You're gonna ride my beard until I tell you to stop."

Holy. Hell.

When I didn't move quickly enough, Bishop wrapped a hand around each of my hips and lifted me up.

"Spread your legs, cupcake. I've been thinking about doing this since the first time I saw you."

"You have?" Even I could hear the shock in my voice.

"Fuck yes."

I moved up to straddle his face, and the first touch of his lips to my clit erased any self-consciousness at my position.

"Grab the headboard."

I followed orders, and his tongue lashed me from top to bottom as the pressure from his hands on my ass ground me down against his face.

Within moments, I was rocking against him of my own accord as his moans sent vibrations through every nerve ending.

It might have been the fastest orgasm in the history of orgasms. Maybe that was the magic of the beard?

I'd certainly never look at it the same again.

"Bishop!" I screamed his name, my fingers going numb as I squeezed the top of the headboard.

He didn't stop until I'd come a second time. My head fell forward, hanging between my limp arms.

Bishop shifted me off his face. "We're definitely adding that to the regular menu. The way you rode my face, so fucking sexy."

I flopped to the side and heaved in a breath and released it, hoping more oxygen would slow my rapid heartbeat.

"You okay?"

I tilted my head sideways just far enough to see his face. "I'll let you know in a few minutes."

His chuckle filled the room.

After several long minutes, my heart rate and breathing approached normal, and Bishop rolled out of bed and stood.

"I'm going to clean up, and then it's time to feed you."

"I could be on board with that," I replied just as my stomach growled.

When he returned from the bathroom, he came around the bed and lifted me into his arms. Once in the kitchen, he deposited me on a stool.

"You sit. I'll cook."

"I was that terrible of a kitchen assistant, huh?"

"You weren't terrible at all. But I've got it from here." Bishop turned to the stove and fired up the burner before pouring oil into the pan.

"How did you learn to cook?" I asked, mostly because it stopped me from asking the question I really wanted to voice. *How did you get so good at whatever the hell you just did to me?*

Bishop shrugged as he let the oil coat the surface. "Probably like anyone. I need to eat, so I cook."

I couldn't imagine that there weren't a lot of women who'd happily cook for him. "I bet you could've gotten all the girls throwing themselves at you in the tattoo shop to do it for you. Like a casserole schedule when someone's sick? Everyone could have had their allotted day and they'd show up with food."

Bishop turned and held up a spatula. "Oh, so now you're a comedian? I'll turn that tight little ass of yours red with this if you even think about suggesting that again."

The heat that raged through my body at his response shocked me. Maybe I wouldn't mind that kind of thing? One of Bishop's eyebrows went up, and I knew he didn't miss my reaction. Curiosity and a hint of daring invaded his grin.

When he moved back to the pan and tossed the veggies in, I couldn't help but continue. Maybe it was my insecurity that I'd never be enough for a guy like Bishop? I'd seen the girls who threw themselves at him, and I didn't exactly have a whole lot in common with them. Basically, my boobs were real, my ass wasn't perky, and I covered a lot more skin when I went out in public.

"They'd probably put all sorts of voodoo in those dishes, anyway. Love potions so you'd succumb to them."

Bishop grunted as he stirred the vegetables in the pan. "More likely aphrodisiacs over love potions. They don't want love. They just want a ride."

I begged to differ, although he had to be right about wanting a ride. Just the thought of him giving some other woman a *ride* made my stomach twist into knots. But before I skipped off down the green jealousy brick road, I considered his words. They said a lot more than he probably intended. How could this man—this kind, sweet, and thoughtful man—think that's all he was good for? He was wrong.

"I'm sure they'd rather keep you."

Bishop fit the lid onto the pan before turning around to face me. "You want anything to drink? Water? Beer? Liquor? I don't have any wine or shit like that."

"Water would be great. I'm thinking I'll give it a few more days before I go back to drinking. My tolerance isn't exactly the greatest, anyway. I rarely drank at home. Maybe a glass of wine when I took a bath, but nothing extreme."

He snagged a bottle of water from the fridge and set it on the counter in front of me.

See? Thoughtful.

"There's nothing wrong with laying off the alcohol, especially if you're alone."

"You getting sick of rescuing me, Bishop?" I tried for flirty, but his face lost all traces of humor.

"Never."

The word hung between us as I met his green gaze.

I wished it could be true, but there was definitely a time limit on whatever was happening here.

I had to keep reminding myself of that while I watched Bishop cook and tried to figure him out. He didn't fit into any of the boxes I stuck him in. He was the epitome of tatted-up badass, and yet he was making us food and it sounded like he thought the women who were after him only wanted him for sex.

Was he insane? The man—whose hair was still tied up in a knot on the back of his head while I was dying to get my hands in it—didn't understand his appeal went far beyond the physical. Given his ripped body, drool-worthy hair and beard, and epic cool factor, I would have expected him to be cocky and convinced that he was God's gift to women. But that wasn't it at all. Bottom line, he was a good man who didn't seem to be aware of his worth.

I opened my mouth to ask him a question about his background, but he beat me to it.

"Have you made a list of all the things you want to do in New Orleans? You seem like a list kind of girl."

If he only knew how many lists of things I'd left hanging on my bulletin board in New York, he'd laugh. But I couldn't tell him about that.

Instead, I thought about what was typed on the paper folded up in my purse.

Eat crawfish

Learn to say something in Cajun

Drink a hurricane at Pat O'Brien's

Catch beads on Bourbon Street (without showing my boobs)

Play a hand of blackjack at Harrah's
~~Watch a Mardi Gras parade~~
~~See Lafayette Cemetery~~
~~Eat beignets at Café du Monde~~

At least I'd crossed off a couple things on the list. Every time I'd been on Bourbon Street, I'd been more worried about getting where I was going, or following Bishop, so I'd forgotten to try to get beads.

I wondered what he'd say if I told him that . . .

He stirred the veggies in the pan and came toward me to lean on the counter. "You do have a list."

"Maybe."

"Come on, cupcake, you gotta share."

"Okay, fine." I rattled off the whole thing, minus the items I'd already ticked off.

Bishop's eyebrows were nearly to his hairline when I was done. "You've put a little thought into this, haven't you?"

I shrugged. "I've wanted to come here for a long time."

"So now that you're here, you've gotta check off the rest of the list, don't you?"

"I may never get another chance."

His eyebrows lowered into a furrow. "Why do you say that?"

"It's complicated."

He crossed his arms over his chest. "You really don't have a plan for how long you're staying here, do you?"

I shook my head. "It's . . . fluid at the moment. I'm going to stay as long as I can, though. I don't want to leave."

"Then don't."

"It doesn't work like that."

"This is your life, Eden. You get to choose."

If only he knew how very wrong he was about that. I

could only imagine what would happen if I didn't obey the summons to come running back to New York. If Dom had to send someone to drag me back, they'd probably do it by my hair.

"What I get to do is make the most of it. So, you want to help me?"

I immediately wanted to snatch my question back, but it was too late. What if he didn't want to help me? What if he didn't ever want to see me again after tonight? He was a one-night kind of guy, so what made me think it would be any different with me?

Bishop turned back to the pan on the stove and lifted the lid. Steam escaped, and he spooned the vegetables into a bowl before dumping the colander of shrimp in. He seasoned them, but didn't answer my question.

I felt like an idiot. "Never mind. I know you're way too busy with work and everything to have time to—"

He looked over his shoulder at me. "Eden, shut up. If you think you're going to knock that list out without me, you're in for a hell of a surprise. Now, let me work my magic on this stir-fry and then we'll eat and figure out what we're going to tackle first."

Eden

MY EYES FLICKED OPEN BUT THE REST OF MY body stilled. Heat radiated against my back, and a heavy arm rested on my side.

Oh my God, I'm in Bishop's bed. I repeat— In. Bishop's. Bed.

I scanned the room for a clock but saw nothing that could give me a hint as to the time. Last night, we'd eaten stir-fry off of mismatched plates and talked about my list until I could barely keep my eyes open. At one point, I was a little concerned I'd fall asleep midsentence and face-plant in my food.

I don't have a problem with carrying you home, Bishop had started to say, but I didn't remember anything after that.

He must have tucked me into his bed and called it a night.

I'm in Bishop's bed.

If I had to guess whether Bishop made a habit of letting

women spend the night, my answer would be an unequivocal no.

So, what was this?

He shifted, and a thick, hard ridge pressed into the crack of my ass.

Oh my God. His morning wood felt just as big as I remembered from last night.

"Mornin.'" Bishop's voice was rough from sleep, and sounded even more delicious than it did normally.

"Good morning," I replied before clamping my mouth shut. I had to have horrible morning breath.

"You passed out after dinner last night. I decided you were sleeping in my bed."

I opened my mouth to reply, but shut it again.

"You okay?"

My response was a nod.

Bishop's eyes clouded with confusion for a beat before clearing. "Ah, I'm killing you with my breath." He picked his arm up and rolled to the side. "Sorry 'bout that."

I didn't speak until he was firmly out of my bad-breath trajectory. "Not you, me. Do you have an extra toothbrush?"

All thoughts of brushing my teeth died when he pulled an elastic from his hair. The golden-brown waves fell around his shoulders, and he shook them out.

Holy. Fucking. Hell.

Everything in me screamed to throw myself at him and climb him like a tree. *That* was the guy who'd given me the best non-self-induced orgasms of my life. *That* was the guy who said he'd help me check the items off my list. *That* was the guy who'd spooned me last night.

"You're beautiful." My voice was quiet, almost reverent.

Bishop froze. "What?"

"You're beautiful. I just thought you should know."

"Guys aren't beautiful, cupcake."

"That's not true, because some definitely are. You're one of them."

He shook his head. "Goofball. You want to shower here again? I did throw your clothes in the wash before I climbed in bed. They shouldn't take too long to dry. I'll run down and grab donuts and coffee, and you can wait up here."

"You're . . . not going to tell Fabienne I spent the night, are you?"

A hard mask slipped over his features. "Why would I tell her?"

"I don't know. I just . . . She's my new boss and I'm still working on making a good impression. I don't want her to think I took the job just so I would see you. Never mind. I'm not making any sense. Forget I said anything."

Confusion flashed in his expression before it softened. "I wouldn't say anything to your boss you didn't want me to say. For the record, Fabienne wouldn't care about anything other than the fact that I'll be coming into the shop even more now, anyway."

Because he wants to see me?

The implication hung there, but I didn't ask to confirm.

Bishop didn't stick around to offer a confirmation either. He turned and walked toward the dresser, and it finally dawned on me that he was wearing boxer briefs.

But . . . "You don't wear underwear normally."

He swung his head around to look at me. "Is that right?"

"Well, at least not the night you came in the pool, or last night."

His gaze never left mine. "You making a study of my habits?"

I shrugged. "Not on purpose."

He winked. "Don't worry, cupcake. I remember every damn thing I learn about you too."

Mardi Gras was a blur of lattes, cappuccinos, double and quadruple shots of espresso, and thousands of donuts. Basically, a second-day trial by fire. Thankfully, Voodoo Ink was closing early tonight, and so was Your Favorite Hole.

Every time the door chimed, my gaze cut to it, wondering if Bishop would finally come in. Fabienne had mentioned offhand that he'd been in for his morning fix, which meant if he stayed with his routine, he'd also be coming in for his afternoon caffeine pick-me-up.

For the first time in my life, I was going to ask a guy out. Did it matter that we'd already technically spent the night together? No. That actually made it harder and more awkward in my opinion.

Another rush of costumed people filled the shop. Orders for donuts were shouted to Fabienne and Ellie, and they marked coffee orders on cups and lined them up near me. If things got too backed up, Fabienne would jump in and help, but I was busting my butt to keep up by making three drinks at a time.

My anxiety rose with each hour that slipped by without him making an appearance. I wanted to do this in person, not via text. My eyes scanned the next cup in line and I froze.

Quadruple-shot non-fat latte with cinnamon on top.

Delilah's regular.

My gaze immediately jumped to customers waiting in front of the espresso bar, and I found him watching me. His lips curved just the slightest bit, and mine did the same.

"Hi." My tone was quiet but cheerful as I refilled porta-filters and snapped them into place to make the espresso. He already held his tall coffee, so I assumed he was just waiting for Delilah's.

He nodded and watched me make the drink. I forced a shot of confidence into my veins so I didn't screw it up somehow.

When I was finished sprinkling on the cinnamon, I snapped the lid on top and slid it across the counter.

With a deep breath, I went for it. "So, I was thinking maybe tonight you might want to, if you weren't already busy—"

He interrupted my already botched attempt at asking him out. "I'll be here at seven to walk you home."

My hopes plummeted because I didn't want to go home while Mardi Gras raged on outside my windows. This entire town was celebrating tonight, and I wanted to be part of it.

"But—"

"You're gonna shower and change into a dress, and then we're gonna work on your list tonight."

My protests died on my lips, and I smiled.

"We are?"

He nodded.

"And that requires me wearing a dress?"

The barely there smile widened infinitesimally and his eyes flashed with heat. "That's for me. Skip the panties. I'll see you at seven."

He wrapped a big hand around Delilah's coffee cup before giving me a chin lift and walking out of the crowded shop with a bag of donuts under his arm.

Seven o'clock. Bishop was going to walk me home, and

I was going to shower and change into a dress and we were going to work on my list.

And I wasn't going to be wearing any panties.

Holy. Shit.

37

Bishop

EVEN IN HER POLO SHIRT AND JEANS, EDEN attracted looks on the walk back to her place from Your Favorite Hole. She stood out like a beacon in the crowd of women dressed for attention without even trying.

As usual, she was completely oblivious to the fact that she was gorgeous. It wasn't just her blond hair, pulled up in a messy bun, or her shining brown eyes or fucking kissable lips. No, it was the energy that surrounded her. Happy, positive, and practically vibrating with excitement about life. People were drawn to her as we walked by them.

And then there was me, following her like a big, hulking shadow with a look that said *keep the fuck back if you want to live*. More than one guy had opened his mouth or reached out only to shut up or snatch a hand back. I gave them a hard stare and kept moving. Eden didn't even notice what was happening.

The crowds thinned out as we turned the corner onto her street.

"That is just *crazy*. I've never seen so many people packed on that street."

"It's like this every year, from what I'm told."

We stopped in front of the gate and Eden pulled the keys from her purse. "Haven't you ever come down here on Mardi Gras before?"

"I've only been here a few years, and I've never been much for crowds, so I stayed away."

She fit the key into the lock and turned it, and I pushed open the gate.

"You never wanted to toss beads on Bourbon?" she asked as we stepped inside.

I shut the gate behind us. "Some guys don't need beads to see tits."

She swung her head around as we walked down the brick path leading into the courtyard. "Oh yeah, I forgot I'm talking to the guy who can't beat the girls away fast enough as they throw themselves at you."

"What you forgot is that I've never cared to see any of them."

"Riiiight." Eden stretched out the word as she climbed the spiral staircase in front of me before unlocking the door and stepping into her small apartment.

That's when I pounced, following her inside, shutting the door, and pinning her to the back of it.

Eden's lips parted and her eyes went wide as she stared up at me.

"You were the first one to walk into Voodoo who I didn't want to see walk out. If I could've, I would've dragged you up to my apartment and stripped you naked and tossed you onto my bed."

"Then why did you wait so long to touch me?" Her words came out breathy.

"Because some things are worth waiting for, and you're one of them."

"Why are you still waiting?"

"I'm not. I'm savoring." My lips lowered to hers and I covered her mouth before she could reply. When my tongue traced the seam, she let me in, and I took advantage. "You taste so fucking sweet. Sweeter than I should be allowed to have in this life."

"Shut up and kiss me." Eden's hands found their way into my hair, and she tugged my face down closer so she could kiss me back.

As much as I wanted to lift her into my arms and carry her to her bed, I wanted to give her more than just that. I wanted her to have everything she'd ever wanted, which meant everything on her list.

When I pulled away, her eyes were clouded and hazy. "Why are you stopping?"

"Because you're putting on a dress and we're working on your list."

"But—"

"Don't worry, cupcake. I'm going to taste you every chance I get tonight, and my cock will be buried inside you before the sun comes up tomorrow."

With that promise hanging in the air, I took another step back, and her gaze dropped to the fly of my jeans.

"I could—"

The thought of her mouth on my cock had it surging against the zipper so hard, I thought it might bust free.

"I know you could wreck me again with that sweet

mouth, but not right now. Go get in the shower. Don't touch yourself either. I want you just as needy as you are right now, because I just decided we're adding a new spin to your list. Everywhere we go to check something off, we're going to give you a whole different sort of experience too."

"What do you mean?" Even though her question was quiet, I knew she was intrigued.

"It means that if we're sliding into a booth to eat, I might finger that tight little pussy and play with your clit until you come. Or if we're getting a drink at Pat O'Brien's, I might drag you off to a supply closet, and you can wrap those sweet lips around my cock."

I didn't think her eyes could get any bigger as I explained.

"You down with that? You wanna get dirty in NOLA, cupcake?"

"Yes." The shock faded and daring took its place.

That's my girl, I thought. And I realized that's exactly how I thought of her—as mine.

Except I had no idea whether I'd get to keep her or not.

But tonight, I'd do my best to make her as addicted to me as I was to her.

Eden

I COULD SWEAR EVEN MY SKIN VIBRATED AS I STEPPED into the shower and hurried through my routine. I'd never been so turned on in my life than I was when Bishop was telling me about this new aspect he was weaving into my list.

You wanna get dirty in NOLA, cupcake?

With him? Absolutely. I wanted it more than anything. I was already dying to know how he was going to feel inside me, and now he promised I wouldn't have to wait long.

Tonight was the night.

I shaved every inch of skin that could possibly need to be shaved, and scrubbed the scent of donuts and coffee from my body and hair. When my fingers dragged over my pussy to make sure I hadn't missed any stray hairs, my clit flared to life and I stifled a moan. I was tempted to keep circling it until I came.

What would he do? Come in and spank me for being a

naughty girl and getting myself off in the shower?

"You better not be playing with that pussy in there, cupcake. I'll see it on your face when you come out."

Really? How could he possibly know that? His timing was unfairly ridiculous and accurate.

"I don't know what you could possibly be talking about," I yelled from the shower, although it was unnecessary. With an apartment as tiny as mine, you barely had to breathe to be heard in the next room.

"Yeah, you do."

"I'll be out in a second."

When I stepped out of the shower and wrapped a towel around myself, I peeked out of the bathroom door and Bishop was there watching me.

"Are you wet, cupcake?"

"Well, I just got out of the—"

"No, your pussy. The one you were touching while you were in the shower after I told you not to."

Heat bloomed on my cheeks, but I wanted him to know the truth. "Yes, but I only bumped my clit. I didn't even make myself come."

"I'm gonna have to check for myself, I think."

He reached under my towel and skimmed the back of his knuckle along my slit.

"Fucking soaked." He groaned as he pressed just hard enough to slide his finger between my pussy lips.

My legs trembled, and I reached out a hand to press against his chest to brace myself. I don't know what to call the sound I made, but it was somewhere between a moan and a cry for more.

Bishop kept stroking.

"You make yourself come a lot in the shower?"

My voice shook when I answered. "Sometimes . . ."

He straightened his finger and circled my clit. "Do you picture me while you do it? Say my name when you come?"

I leaned into his touch, wanting more pressure, but Bishop pulled away as I pressed closer.

"Answer me, cupcake."

On a moan, I replied, "Maybe."

Bishop pressed hard against my clit, and I could feel the orgasm rising. But he didn't let me have it. He pulled his hand away and sucked his finger clean.

"But—"

"Greedy girl with your wet little pussy. Get dressed before I change my mind and never let you out of your bed for the next twenty-four hours."

I stared at him. "How is that a threat?"

Bishop chuckled darkly. "Go, now."

When we stepped out of my apartment, anticipation thrummed through me, along with need that wouldn't quiet. It had taken everything I had not to get myself off in the bedroom after he'd brought me so close. But I had a feeling he'd make me pay for that somehow.

The sounds of a city partying its hardest came from every direction in the French Quarter, and it seemed every balcony was full. I'd opted for the teal dress and black ballet flats, and had dried my hair and applied makeup faster than I ever had before.

Bishop's appreciative gaze told me I'd done just fine. His words confirmed it.

"You're a class act, cupcake. And you're all fucking mine

tonight."

As much as I loved that, a feeling of disappointment threaded through the excitement. Tonight was all well and good, but what if I wanted more than just tonight?

I pushed away the thought and decided to focus on having fun and checking off as many items on my *Must Do* list as I could. I was here to live in the moment, not worry about what was going to happen tomorrow. For all I knew, I could get a message telling me to get my ass back to New York.

I pinned a bright smile to my face and followed Bishop. "Where are we going?"

I expected him to say something about crawfish for dinner or maybe the casino for blackjack, but instead he shocked me.

"First, we're gonna get you some beads."

"We're *what*?"

Bishop threaded his hand through mine and pulled me toward the corner. "Going to Bourbon Street."

"It's a madhouse out there."

"And you've got your own personal security, so don't worry. Besides, you wanted a hurricane at Pat O'Brien's and we're gonna knock that one off too."

"On Mardi Gras? Are you crazy?" After a few days in New Orleans, I realized how ridiculous it would be to try to knock off any of my list during Mardi Gras. It was the busiest time of the year, and we'd have to wait hours to even try to get into the bar.

"Let me worry about that." He glanced down at me with a grin. "You forget, I might not be the most social guy on the planet, but I know a fuck-ton of people. Who do you think Con turned over all his clients to when he stepped away from the business? Who do you think they keep coming back to?"

"You, I'm assuming."

"Which means I know a big chunk of the Quarter. So you let me worry about making things happen."

"Okay, big guy. Whatever you say."

He looked down at me. "Don't believe me?"

I shrugged playfully. "Maybe. Maybe not. We'll see if you can deliver."

I spun in a circle, and the skirt of my dress flared.

Bishop grabbed my hand and pulled me against him. "You better watch it. No one gets to see that sweet little ass but me."

One hand covered my left cheek and squeezed. I bit my lip, and he shook his head.

"Naughty little thing. You'll pay for that. And, cupcake? I always deliver."

He released me with another squeeze and I shivered with excitement.

I stayed beside Bishop until we reached the police barricades that barely held in the partiers on Bourbon, and then he released my hand and wrapped an arm around my waist loosely.

"You're gonna walk ahead of me, and I'll tell you where we're going."

"Wouldn't it be easier for me to follow you?" I yelled over the din.

"I can't see you if you're behind me. If someone grabs you or you get pulled away, my reaction time is slower. If you're in front of me, no one is going to touch you because they're gonna see me and know I'm what they'll have to deal with. And if someone does, they won't be able to do much before I grab 'em by the throat and take care of them."

His explanation made sense, and I walked as he directed me through the crowd. I was concentrating on the ground and the people right in front of where I was walking, but Bishop spoke into my ear.

"Look up, cupcake. This is what you wanted to experience."

I looked up as he turned me in a circle in the middle of the heart of Bourbon Street. I soaked up every sound, smell, and sight, tucking them away to remember someday soon. Bishop pointed up, and I followed his arm to see a woman in a purple, green, and gold tutu standing on a balcony with her gold bra barely concealing her large boobs. She threw beads every which way.

"That's where you're getting your beads."

"How—"

But I should have known Bishop already had a plan. He grabbed both of my hands and lifted them into the air and let out the loudest wolf whistle I'd ever heard. It got the woman's attention and she bounced on the balcony, hands full of beads waving back and forth.

"Do you know her?" I yelled.

"Nope."

But it didn't matter because she flung a handful of beads right toward us, and I pushed up onto my tiptoes and caught two strands as they flew our way.

Bishop caught four more, and turned me to face him in the middle of the street before lowering each necklace over my head. As he released each one, he pressed a kiss to my cheeks, nose, forehead, and finally my lips.

I wrapped a hand around his neck and pulled him closer

to take the kiss deeper.

Cheers and shouts dulled around us. Every one of my senses was focused on Bishop and the giddiness roaring through my senses.

This is living.

When I finally released him, he dropped another kiss on my temple and spun me around. "You see that corner? We're headed there and then we're taking a left. Next stop, Pat O'Brien's."

Eden

BISHOP DIRECTED ME TOWARD THE FAMOUS RED building of Pat O'Brien's, and once we broke through the crowd, the line I expected wrapped all the way around the corner.

We didn't slow or even try to find the end of it, though. Bishop walked us right to the front door where the bouncer checked IDs. The high from catching the beads began to fade as I worried about whether we could actually get in. It's not like we couldn't come back and do this another day, but I had to admit there was something incredibly cool about the idea of doing this on the most famous day of the city's entire year.

We stopped in front of the solidly built man as he handed a woman's ID back to her. The fierce frown dominating his face disappeared as soon as he saw Bishop.

"Hey, man. Never would've expected to see you here on fucking Mardi Gras. What the hell are you doin'?"

Bishop lifted his arm to wrap around the top of my chest. "My girl wanted one of Pat O's famous hurricanes on Mardi Gras. It wasn't like I could say no."

The bouncer's attention landed on me for the first time. "Hey there, Bishop's girl. You must not be from around here."

For a moment I thought I must still stand out like a tourist from his comment, but he continued.

"If you were, you wouldn't even attempt it. Just know, your man is making quite the sacrifice taking you to this zoo today. Enjoy it." He stamped our hands and jerked his head to the side, and Bishop propelled me forward through the darkened doorway.

Relief slid through me that he didn't ask for my ID. With Bishop standing right beside me, I wasn't sure how I could possibly explain why the name on it didn't match the one I'd given him. An icy trickle of guilt slid down my spine, but I pushed the feeling away. Tonight wasn't the night to worry about that. Besides, it wasn't like I'd lied to him about who I was. It would have been different if I'd given him the name on my ID, or so I convinced myself.

When we squeezed through the entry out into the courtyard, I realized why Pat O'Brien's was such a legendary tourist spot. The inner courtyard was totally New Orleans, at least from what I could see with the crowd of people. There wasn't any hope of getting a table, but Bishop got the attention of one of the servers passing by.

"Two hurricanes."

"Of course. I'll be right back with those."

Bishop guided me to the edge of a fountain where he sat down and pulled me onto his lap. My skirt spread out over us, covering the top of our legs and bunching up between us.

My butt rested directly on Bishop's hard thighs, without

anything between my skin and his jeans. He was completely aware of this because his hand slipped under the fabric and his palm skimmed along my thigh.

His promise from earlier rose up with the goose bumps rising on my skin.

"You think you can be quiet, cupcake?" His tone wavered between playful and seductive.

I nodded, wondering how quickly the server was going to return with our drinks, and what kind of panting, writhing mess I'd be by then.

"Good girl. Would it make you feel better if you knew we weren't the only ones doing this right now? I see at least two couples who are being a hell of a lot more obvious about it than we are."

"Where?" I scanned the courtyard.

"Red-and-black dress at three o'clock."

The only reason I knew three o'clock meant to my right was because I'd spent plenty of time watching *NCIS* reruns at night when I couldn't get into one of my books. Who knew it would ever come in handy?

I glanced in the direction he'd indicated and found the red-and-black dress and, *oh my God,* I could see her skirt riding up as the guy she was with slid his hand beneath it.

Even as shocking as it was, I couldn't deny my body reacted by pushing all the heat south, not that I wasn't already primed from my shower incident.

"Watch what he does to her." Bishop's voice was a husky whisper sending shivers down my spine as he tucked my hair behind my ear and skimmed his lips along it.

The man pulled up the back of the skirt, exposing the rounded curve of the woman's ass.

"Scandalous, what you'll see if you're looking for it."

My nipples tightened into hard points against the bodice of my dress as Bishop's fingers stroked my inner thigh.

I turned my head toward him, but he nipped my ear. "Keep watching them. I want to see if he's going to do what I'd do if that were us up there."

With every word, his fingertips edged closer to my center, and every sensation seemed heightened without panties acting as a barrier.

The man at three o'clock pulled the thong from between the woman's cheeks and tore it free.

I released a pent-up breath.

"He just ripped her panties off. Did you like that?"

But somehow, I couldn't find the right words to tell him just how much I liked it.

"Come on, cupcake. You can tell me how wet it makes you." He paused. "Or I could just find out myself."

His voice had dropped to seriously husky, and I nodded ever so slightly. I wanted him to touch me as I watched the other man yank the woman's skirt down over his hand as she threw her head back.

As soon as the pad of his finger slicked along my wet slit, I bit my lip to keep from moaning just like the other woman must be.

"Fuck, I love that you're soaked."

He didn't have to tell me because I could feel just how wet I was as he stroked and circled around my clit without touching it.

I opened my mouth, ready to beg him, when the server rounded the side of the fountain with our drinks.

Bishop's hand is up my skirt and there's a guy less than two feet away. But apparently the server hadn't noticed or just didn't care.

"That'll be fifteen," he said as he balanced the tray with two ornate glasses filled to the top with red cocktails.

I expected Bishop to slip his left hand out from under my skirt when he reached for his wallet, but he didn't. He pulled a twenty from his pocket and handed it to the server before accepting one cocktail and placing it in my hands. The second, he set on the edge of the fountain.

"Keep the change." The statement was a clear dismissal, and the server thanked him before walking away.

I slid the straw between my lips, desperate to look like we weren't doing what we were actually doing.

"Don't spill," Bishop whispered as his finger pushed inside me.

Oh my God.

My first taste of a hurricane at Pat O'Brien's happened with me a minute from orgasm, courtesy of the sexiest man I'd ever met.

With each drink I took, Bishop's fingers became cleverer and bolder. His thumb found my clit as warmth from the alcohol hit me.

He didn't let me come until I was almost finished with my drink, and then pulled it from my hand and covered my lips with his to hide the sound of the half scream, half moan I couldn't hold back.

The aftermath of the climax washed over me as Bishop pulled his hand from beneath my dress. To cover the tremor in my hand, I reached to pick up my drink and sucked down the final inch. When I lowered it, I turned on his lap to meet his gaze.

"Well, that might not have been what I'd expected when I made my list, but it was a million times more memorable."

One side of Bishop's mouth quirked up. "That's what I'm

here for, to make this memorable for you. Now, you want to remind me what else was on that list?"

Eden

WE LEFT THE CRAZINESS OF BOURBON STREET behind and headed down streets I hadn't yet walked. With Bishop beside me, his fingers twined in mine and the heat from a good buzz and an even better orgasm thrumming through my veins, I felt like I could take on the world. If one of Dom's goons showed up tonight and told me to come home, I'd squeeze Bishop's hand tighter and tell him to go to hell. It could have been my overactive imagination, but I thought that Bishop would tell him to go to hell right along with me. Possibly even fight to keep me here.

Maybe it was the alcohol, but every time he looked at me, there was something more in his eyes than I'd seen before.

He wanted me.

Well, no shit, E. He had his fingers inside you.

But more than that, he *liked* me. I could tell. Well, at

least I thought I could tell. I hoped I could tell.

But what was I going to do with that?

Grab on to him and ride this ride for all it's worth. Take this opportunity and live, came the bold voice from inside me.

Buoyed by good spirits and even better booze, I decided that's exactly what I was going to do.

When we slowed in front of a building I'd never seen and Bishop pulled me toward an old wooden doorway, the amazing scent of Cajun food wafted toward my nostrils.

The girl waiting at the hostess stand just inside lit up at the sight of Bishop. "Hey, Bish. I've been wondering when you'd come see me again."

Her tone was more than flirty, bordering on suggestive. Scratch that—to be accurate, I'd have to say she was eye-fucking the hell out of him.

Of course, because I was female and human and feeling all warm and fuzzy about the guy who'd just given me the most memorable orgasm of my life, I had to do a full once-over. Okay, maybe twice-over.

Her hair had to have been dyed that red because there's no way the color was real, and her purple eyes were so vivid they had to be fake, and why, if you were picking out fake contacts, would you let them clash with your hair so badly? She was curvy in all the right places, with cleavage for days visible in the low V-cut of her shirt. And, oh my God, she couldn't have been wearing a bra because I could see what looked like nipple rings through it.

Is that what Bishop likes? Nipple rings and gravity-defying boobs? Because I clearly didn't have either of those. Then I reminded myself of the most important thing—*He's with me. Not with her.*

"Hey, Jules. We'll take a table for two."

It wasn't until Bishop lifted his arm from around my waist to rest it over my shoulders that *Jules* noticed I existed.

Her bright smile instantly turned from genuine to *I'm going to keep smiling if it kills me.*

"Oh, I didn't even see you there. Of course, I'm assuming that means you won't want your normal seat at the bar." She gave me a cursory inspection and seemed to write me off.

Really? Dammit, I looked good. My dress was adorable, my makeup didn't scream *I raided the MAC counter and tried every single thing they had, including twenty sets of fake eyelashes* like Jules, but then again, I didn't know if I could look that trashy if I tried.

Okay, so maybe I was getting a little catty, but still, who wouldn't after being brushed off like that? What happened to sisterhood?

"No, we'll take a table in the corner. Something out of the way."

Her gaze came back to me, and this time she gave me a long, slow study. "Not your usual style, Bish."

I didn't know if she was talking about me or the table, but I had a feeling she was talking about both.

"Change is good for the soul," was all Bishop said in reply, along with pulling me closer to his side.

Non-alcohol-induced warmth rushed through me, but I tried not to read into his words. Maybe it was only a temporary change for him. Then again, from what I gathered, whatever was happening between us didn't seem to be his normal at all. That had to mean something.

The hostess grabbed sets of silverware from a bucket, and spun. "Come right this way. I've got the perfect table for you."

She led us to the very back of the restaurant, right near the door where servers slammed in and out of the kitchen. The table didn't even look like it was used regularly for dining. From the way Bishop's body stiffened against my back, I could tell he wasn't impressed.

"Here you—"

"This one isn't gonna work for us."

She turned around, her face the picture of innocence. "What do you mean? This is the most secluded—"

Bishop grabbed my hand and pulled me toward the front of the restaurant, and for a moment, I thought he was going to lead me right out the door. But he didn't. Instead, he stopped next to a table in the corner that hadn't yet been cleared.

"We'll take this one. I'd appreciate you sending someone over to bus it." He pulled out a chair and waited for me to sit before looking at Jules.

"You don't date. That's what you told me. Sorry if I'm a little shocked."

Still standing behind me as he pushed my chair in, Bishop's hands landed on my shoulders and he squeezed. "I didn't then. But sometimes a man has to change to go after what he wants."

Another rush of warmth filled me along with a realization. It didn't matter if Jules was skinnier than me, had better makeup contouring skills, or bigger boobs with blingy hardware—I was the one who inspired Bishop to change. I was enough for him, and that was all that mattered.

A silent Jules gathered the plates in her arms and mumbled an apology before taking them away.

Bishop grabbed the menus from a holder between the

condiments and set one in front of me.

"You'll be able to find crawfish every which way you could possibly want it here."

"Are we going to pretend that didn't just happen?" If not for the hurricane courage, I might not have said anything.

He looked up at me from where he was already checking out the menu. "There's not much to say. I want to be with you. No one else. End of story. I don't give a shit what Jules or the fuckin' pope thinks about it. I won't let anything stop me from making this night the best it can be for you."

I want to be with you. I'd already rationalized that myself, but hearing Bishop say it made all the difference.

"Thank you."

"You don't need to thank me. Tonight is already the best night I've ever had. You make everything I've walked past a hundred times seem new again. It's like I'm seeing it through your eyes, and the world is a hell of a lot brighter that way. You make me happy, Eden."

It was the best compliment I'd ever been given. The simplicity. The sincerity. The meaning behind it.

"You make me happy too. I can't imagine how differently this last week would've gone if I hadn't met you."

"I don't even want to think about you out there on your own. That's enough to give me nightmares, and I'm a pretty tough motherfucker."

"I would've survived. I just wouldn't have gotten a chance to experience all this." I gestured to the restaurant around us, but we both knew I was referring to so much more.

"Stick with me and I'll make sure you get all the experiences you could possibly want."

My smile widened as the server came to the table to welcome us and take our drink order.

"Another hurricane?" Bishop asked, an eyebrow raised.

"Why not?" I was feeling bold and alive and like nothing could possibly bring me down.

Bishop ordered a bourbon and let me taste the smoky liquor when the server brought it to the table. I wasn't a fan, and washed it down with my hurricane.

The second cocktail hit me a little harder, and I was laughing as Bishop told me stories about tattoo cover-ups he had done. From the run-of-the-mill ex's names, wedding dates, and wedding rings, to penises, vaginas, and things that couldn't actually be identified.

"Don't you get tired of covering up people's mistakes?" I asked.

He shook his head, his expression thoughtful before he answered. "I don't consider it a mistake. It's a new beginning. A second chance. Why should we be stuck with something we don't want when it can be fixed?"

The words hit home. *A new beginning. A second chance.* Wasn't that what I really wanted? Not just an experience or an adventure? Something permanent. Like ink.

It suddenly occurred to me that Bishop might have an ex's name hiding under one of his many tattoos. Did he have a second chance or a new beginning on his skin?

"Have you ever had a tattoo covered up?"

Bishop nodded, and I held my breath waiting for his answer. "Absolutely. Who do you think had the tattoo that couldn't be identified?"

I blinked as a rush of relief blasted away the momentary gut twisting. "What do you mean, it couldn't be identified? How do you get tattooed and not know what it is?"

Bishop shrugged. "I was young and stupid and it was a friend. He sucked, and I should never have let him near me with a tattoo machine. I had my uncle cover it up."

"Your uncle?"

Bishop's posture stiffened, and his easy mood seemed to evaporate. "Yeah, he's the one who taught me the trade. He raised me, most of the time in the tattoo shop. He's the reason I do this."

"Is that how Delilah learned too?" Part of me wanted to drop the subject because something about it clearly made Bishop uncomfortable, but I wasn't sure if I'd get another opportunity to ask.

He shook his head. "No. Our parents were killed in a car wreck and they didn't have a will. My mom's sister didn't want to take us both, so she took Delilah, and my dad's brother stepped up to take me. He already had a kid of his own and a struggling business, so he couldn't handle adding two more mouths to feed either. Just one extra was a struggle. I think Delilah became an artist just to piss off our straight-laced aunt, if you want to know the truth."

My heart clenched as I imagined how horrible it would have been to lose your entire family in one fell swoop the way he had. "I bet that was hard, especially being separated from your sister."

Bishop shrugged. "It was better than ending up in foster care. We were lucky, really."

"Do you still get to see your uncle? Does he still have his shop?"

Bishop's gaze dropped to the table as his shoulders tensed again. "He passed away. My cousin too."

Kicking myself for probing what was obviously a painful subject, I apologized. "I'm so sorry for your loss. I didn't know. I wouldn't have brought it up otherwise."

He held up a hand. "Don't worry about it. It's been a

long time, but you know some things just take a hell of a lot longer to fade."

I thought of the flashes of memories I had of my mother that weren't even fully formed. I was four when she died. I still missed her, even though I'd never had a chance to actually know her.

"I understand."

Our conversation trailed off as the food began to arrive. Crawfish four different ways, and I loved every single one of them. I steered the conversation back into lighter territory, and the easy, fun Bishop I'd had all night surged back to the surface.

"Did you save room for dessert?" the server asked as he cleared away our plates. "We've got a phenomenal crème brûlée and a fabulous apple dumpling."

Bishop shot a look at me before answering. "I'll let the lady decide if she wants anything, but I know what I'm having for dessert, and it's not on the menu here."

A shiver ripped through me at the heat in his gaze, and I knew exactly what he was talking about.

"I'm good. No dessert for me."

"We'll take the check," Bishop said, his tone husky.

Bishop

THE WALK BACK TO VOODOO INK AND MY APARTMENT seemed to take forever as we dodged the people clogging the streets. No one was ready to call it quits on Mardi Gras, and I knew the party would last until the sun came up, just like it did every year.

After three hurricanes, Eden's steps were more measured and deliberate as the buzz hit her harder.

"Come on, cupcake." I swept her up into my arms as she shrieked.

"You can't carry me all the way back! I'm too heavy."

"Watch me."

She wrapped an arm around the back of my neck and with her other hand, stroked my beard. "I like the beard. A lot."

Immediately, an image of how she'd ridden it popped into my head. I fucking liked my beard too. "Is that right?"

"Yep. You should probably think about taking up

lumberjacking as a second career if tattooing ever falls through. Is that a thing?"

"Lumberjacking or tattooing falling through?"

"Either."

I shook my head. "No way am I gonna go somewhere cold and dress up in flannel in order to chop down trees. If you've got a lumberjack fantasy, you'll have to lock it away for a while."

She looked up at me, her eyes shining as I turned the down the alley that led to the back of Voodoo, and the crowd thinned out. "Nah, I'd rather have you than a lumberjack."

"What a coincidence. That can be easily arranged." I set her on her feet, and she held on to my arm.

"You make me feel like I've been waiting my whole life to meet you. Like everything was in a holding pattern until I got here, and now I'm finally getting a chance to live."

Her words hit me somewhere deep and resonated. I'd been existing, never letting anything go beyond superficial. Eden had plowed through my walls without trying, and from the moment I'd met her, everything had become more vivid. She was the turning point. She was a wild card.

What I didn't know was if this could ever be more than an adventure for her. More than one of the experiences she wanted to have. She still hadn't figured out how long she was staying, and as much as I wanted to tell her she wasn't leaving, it wasn't my choice.

All I could do was wait and see. And give her a reason to stay.

"Meeting you has been just as much of a revelation for me as it has been for you."

"Really?" Her dark gaze filled with longing.

"Yeah, cupcake. Really." I leaned down, cradled her face

in my hands, and poured all the crazy shit I was feeling into a kiss.

Even though I was consumed by Eden, a noise grabbed my attention. Yanking my lips away, I shoved Eden behind me as movement came from the shadows of the alley.

"Who the fuck is there?"

The light on the back of the building that should have been shining over this section of the alley was out, but it hadn't been the night before. No one answered my demand.

All my senses jammed into high alert as I reached into my pocket and pulled out the keys. I held them out behind me to Eden.

"Open the door. Get inside. Single key on the big ring."

Eden's hand shook as she picked them out of my palm, but she didn't say a word.

I heard the door open and said, "Hit the light inside." I couldn't make out whoever was in the alley, but I heard footsteps as someone ran for the street.

When the light from inside the tattoo shop flooded a small section of the darkness, I caught a glimpse of the back of a dark hoodie as a guy turned the corner.

I stepped inside the shop. "Go upstairs. I'll be right there."

"Are you going after him?" Eden asked quietly.

"Just checking shit out as soon as I can get a flashlight from the break room. I'll be right up. I promise."

With a small, uncertain nod, Eden opened the door to my apartment and climbed the stairs as I stepped into the break room and retrieved a flashlight.

The first place I pointed it was up at the light fixture Con had added to the back of the building for security. Power ran up the back in a piece of conduit rather than through the brick.

Crouching down, I checked the wire. *Cut.*

I locked the door before stepping farther out into the alley. If someone took me out, there was no way in hell I was letting them get to Eden.

The first noise I'd heard had come from near the Dumpster on the opposite side. Scanning the area, I found three cigarette butts in a pile. Someone had been watching. Waiting.

Anger and unease pooled in my gut.

Was my past finally catching up with me? Had they finally decided to collect? *Fuck.*

I knew I should have taken them out first, but that was like attacking a snake that would regrow three heads when you chopped off one. What was that Hercules shit called? The hydra?

If it wasn't them, then who? The question gnawed at me as I headed back inside. Fuck whoever that asshole was for screwing with our night. I wasn't going to let them wreck a goddamned thing.

I'd made promises to Eden, and I was keeping them.

Eden

I SHOULD HAVE BEEN FREAKED. I SHOULD HAVE BEEN terrified. But instead, the adrenaline pumping through my veins manifested in a completely different fashion. When Bishop cleared the stairs, I was ready for him.

"I want more. Tonight. I want everything you promised me, and I'm not going to let anything get in the way." I wasn't sure I'd ever spoken bolder words that were more true.

His neutral expression changed in an instant.

"Fuck, I'm glad you said that. Because I'm dying for you, cupcake." Bishop crossed the floor and lifted me into his arms. "Fuck the world. I don't care if it burns to the ground. I need to be inside you."

His lips crushed to mine, and I wrapped my legs around his waist. He carried me to the bedroom and lowered me onto the bed. Ever since I'd come in the middle of the court-yard at Pat O'Brien's, I'd been wet and ready for more.

Before the bitchy hostess incident, I'd been teasing

myself with the thought of Bishop dragging me off to the ladies' room and taking me against the wall. I made a mental note to add that to my list for later.

It seemed the man had quite the talent for checking things off my lists.

When he pulled back, my gaze zeroed in on the bulge beneath his zipper. I already knew what I was getting, but that didn't mean I wasn't just as excited to get my hands on it.

But Bishop had other plans. He tossed my dress up and buried his face between my legs.

"Fuck, baby. I wanted to feel you coming on my tongue earlier. I'm gonna eat this pretty pussy for dessert, and then I'm going to make you scream."

My hips lifted toward him, sending an undeniable message that I wanted this just as bad as he did.

"Please."

Bishop splayed his hand out over my center. "If you were wearing panties, I'd rip them off you like the guy did at Pat O'Brien's. But you're such a naughty fucking girl that I don't have that option."

He dragged his fingers over my most sensitive skin. "You know how fucking hot it was to watch you walk through the streets knowing I could reach under your dress and touch nothing but bare skin? Do you know how many times I had to talk myself out of dragging you into an alley and finding out how tight this little pussy would feel around my cock?"

"I want it. I want it all."

His lips twisted into a smile. "You want to be my bad girl, don't you? My naughty girl? If you only knew all the things I wanted to do to you."

I started to reply, but whatever words I meant to speak

died as Bishop moved his hand and bent between my legs. His tongue stroked me from top to bottom before spearing inside. He moaned against me, like he was truly enjoying every lick and suck as much as he might his favorite dessert.

The feeling was decadent, and heat radiated from my pussy outward.

"So fucking sweet." He lifted a hand and slid two fingers inside me, reviving all the nerves that had been so overwhelmed by my earlier orgasm. They were ready for more. I was ready for more.

And he gave me more.

Curling his fingers, he found that perfect spot at the same time his lips closed over my clit, unleashing an orgasm like a tsunami. I gripped the sheets of the bed with both hands as I writhed against his face, shameless as I took my pleasure. I didn't feel inexperienced with Bishop; I felt amazing. Desired. Wanton.

It was fabulous.

Slick with my wetness, he pulled a finger out and slid it lower, brushing over a part of me that I'd never expected him to touch.

My entire body jumped, not out of fear, but from surprise and a sensation overload.

"You've never tested this sweet little ass, have you, cupcake? Never had anyone play with it and get you off just from the thought of how dirty and bad and naughty you'd be if you let someone touch it?"

I shook my head.

"Sweet little virgin asshole." His eyes darkened. "It's sexy as fuck to know that I'm the only guy who's ever touched it."

He dropped his mouth back to my pussy and proceeded to tease my clit until I was screaming and pressing against the finger he hadn't moved. It breached the muscle and slipped inside, and I froze.

A riot of sensations rolled through me. Oh my God. He had his finger in my ass. I didn't even know how to process it, but Bishop had no such difficulties.

"Someday you could take my cock here, but I gotta work you up to fitting it in that tight little pussy of yours first."

His dirty words sent me over the edge into another orgasm, this one darker and more delicious than the last.

When Bishop rose above me again, he was tearing open a condom packet with his teeth. "You're so fucking soaked. I can't wait to slide every inch inside you."

Everything in my body felt like it was moving faster, down to the very blood pumping through my veins.

"Yes."

He rolled the condom on and pressed my legs open wider. "I wanted to take this slower, but you're killing me, cupcake. You're fucking killing me."

"I don't want slower. I want you. Now. Right now. Don't make me wait."

His gaze heated again, and he lined up his cock and notched it against my entrance.

"So fucking tight and so fucking wet. You're going to milk this orgasm right out of me. I'm not going to stand a chance."

He pressed inside inch by inch, and my nipples hardened as he filled me. Twinges of sensation, not quite pain, not quite pleasure, zinged through my body until his thumb landed on my clit and I screamed.

Screamed.

Everything was a blur after that. I bucked up against his cock as he began to move and groan and fuck.

The orgasm hit me so hard and so fast, I couldn't keep my eyes open. Stroke after stroke, I writhed beneath him and begged him not to stop.

It was a revelation. It was *everything*.

When Bishop's groan filled the room and he fell to his forearms above me, I knew I was screwed. Not just literally, but every way imaginable.

Everything I'd wanted, he'd delivered. And now I had absolutely no idea what to do next.

Bishop

THIS WAS THE PART I'D NEVER LIKED. THE PART where I rolled over and felt like it was just another empty fuck. But with Eden, everything was different. I never wanted to roll over. I wanted to stay buried inside her for as long as I possibly could.

I kept my weight braced on my forearms, not wanting to crush her. Her heart hammered against my chest almost as hard as mine did against hers.

I'd fucked up my plan, though. I knew she wasn't wildly experienced, and instead of taking things slow, I'd just barreled right through.

Jesus, I'd told her I wanted to fuck her ass.

Don't get me wrong, I *did* want to fuck her ass. What sane guy wouldn't? But she wasn't like any woman I'd ever been with, and I needed to tread more carefully so I didn't fuck this up.

From beneath me, Eden shifted, and I knew I had to

move off her whether I wanted to or not. I rolled over onto my back beside her, and still the only sound in the room was our pounding hearts and uneven breathing.

"Wow," Eden said, her voice hushed like she was praying.

A smile tugged at my lips.

"Definitely, wow."

I unrolled the condom from my dick, grabbed a handful of tissues from the nightstand, and wrapped it up before tossing it in the trash next to the nightstand.

Eden rolled over onto her side. "Do you want me to go?"

I pulled my head back so I could see her face. "You think I'd let you leave right now?"

A small smile tugged at the corners of her lips. "I hope not."

I wrapped an arm around her and pulled her into me. "No way in hell, cupcake. I like you in my bed, and I'm sure as hell not letting you out of it now."

Eden

FOR THE SECOND TIME IN MY LIFE, I WOKE UP WITH the heat of a man at my back and his morning wood pressed into my butt crack.

I liked it, for the record. But only because it was Bishop. Maybe it was proof of just how little experience I had, but it was hard to picture waking up like this with anyone but him.

He liked to spoon, keeping me tucked in close to his body all night, and I slept like a rock in his arms.

But now the light of morning spilled through the shades, and I had to force myself out of his bed before I overstayed my welcome. Yes, he'd told me he wasn't letting me leave last night, but that was then.

My body twinged in places that hadn't twinged in a long time. Bishop's chest rose and fell behind me, and I carefully lifted his arm to sneak out from under it.

Except my careful sneaking wasn't very careful.

"Where do you think you're going?" Bishop's

sleep-roughened voice broke the silence of the room.

"I'm getting up."

"That's a terrible idea." His arm tightened around me, and he pressed a kiss to the back of my head. "I think you should stay right here. Are you sore?"

The question sent a shaft of embarrassment through me that I shouldn't be feeling considering everything we'd done together, but I couldn't help it.

"A little."

"I'm sorry, cupcake. I should've taken it easier on you."

I twisted my body around so I could see his face. "Why would you have done a stupid thing like that? That would have been a terrible idea."

His concerned expression shifted to one of satisfaction. "Just trying to be a gentleman. Not sure I know how."

"Maybe you should just worry about being you." I shifted the rest of the way so I was facing him in the circle of his arms and pressed a kiss to his lips.

"I think I can handle that. Are you working today?"

I nodded. "Yeah, from twelve to six."

"That means we've got time to get breakfast before my first appointment." He pressed a kiss to my forehead. "Gotta feed my girl."

My girl. Two words that sent a shaft of belonging through me and made me never want to get out of this bed.

"But first, we should probably shower together. Just so I can make sure you get all those hard-to-reach places nice and clean—after I dirty them all up again."

Heat bloomed between my legs, but I kept my tone nonchalant. "I think I could manage getting out of bed to do that."

Two hours later, we left Bishop's to head to my apartment so I could change out of my dress. We ventured to a little hole-in-the-wall place Bishop preferred for breakfast and settled on a bench near the front while we waited for them to set up our table. Beside me sat a stack of newspapers people had left behind.

My father's picture, albeit small and in the dot style that particular paper was known for, stared back at me from a column on the front page. The headline read WILL THE CASSO EMPIRE CRUMBLE?

Bishop stood to hit the restroom, and I grabbed the paper.

Dominic Casso's seemingly untouchable empire has come under attack from all sides. Feds have crippled the economics, and rival families are attempting a power grab while he's investigated on several counts of racketeering and fraud. Through it all, Casso remains a stoic head to what is suspected to be one of the most profitable organized-crime families since the 1970s. A long, detailed history of my father's rise through the ranks followed, but no new information about what was happening.

If I knew anything about Dom, he wouldn't let a single charge stick. He'd been questioned many times in the last ten years, which was when I started to become aware of the nature of his business, and nothing had ever stuck.

There had been no trials, no sentences, and nothing else that could slow him down. But he had to believe that whatever was happening right now was different from those other times because he'd never sent me away before.

I reached the end of the article where there was speculation as to how many illegitimate children Dom had fathered, and the current count was two. Two sons, that was. Very few people within or outside the family knew that I was his daughter and not his niece. Maybe it made more sense since I was forgotten half the time anyway and had been raised by his half sister.

I was folding the paper up and setting it aside when Bishop came back. His gaze darted to the front of the paper as I added it back to the pile. I didn't expect him to snatch it off the stack.

His eyes scanned back and forth as he read the entire article that I'd just finished before shaking his head and dropping it back on the pile.

"Seems like they'll never take that bastard down." His words carried a harsh edge, like it was something he took personally.

"You follow this stuff?" I asked, not sure why I risked the question. Maybe because I wanted to get a feel for his knowledge if I was ever allowed to tell him who I was.

"As much as the next guy. You would think we were still in the '70s with how much that guy gets away with and the cops' inability to do jack shit about it."

The hostess came to tell us our table was ready, and I was glad I didn't have to come up with an answer. *Bishop knows who my father is.* It was a revelation I didn't want to consider. My past and my present were supposed to stay separated with a neat line, not collide while we were waiting for breakfast.

It wasn't until I was at work that night that the next reminder came.

45

Bishop

I HATED THAT I'D LET SEEING THAT FUCKER'S FACE IN the paper ruin my appetite, but my body didn't know any other way to react. It hadn't been long enough since I'd seen Dom Casso's face through the sight of my gun, and I hadn't been able to pull the trigger.

I had no doubt that if I'd killed him that day, I would have died in short order, and the power vacuum left in his organization would have been filled by someone just as ruthless.

But I hadn't, even though he'd deserved that bullet through his chest. What were the odds that he would have had some girl come running to him and ruin my shot? When his bodyguards had spotted me and started shooting, I'd run, leaving revenge for another day and choosing to live.

But I'd done a shitty job of living until just lately.

46

Eden

THE PHONE I'D CARRIED SINCE I LEFT NEW YORK vibrated in the front pocket of my apron as I handed a brown paper bag of donuts across the counter to an older couple. The vibration startled me so much, I lost my grip and dropped the bag before the man had a hold of it.

"So sorry." I snatched it off the counter and handed it to him again.

"No worries, darlin'. Ain't gonna hurt those donuts none." He winked. "But I hope she doesn't spill our coffee."

I glanced down the counter to where Asha, my coworker for the evening, filled two small cups with espresso.

"Of course not. Her hands are steady as they come."

The couple collected their coffee, and I stepped toward Asha. "I need to step out for a second to check this missed call. You mind?"

"Of course not. The rush is over. I can hold down the fort by myself for a few. Take your time."

I nodded and hustled out from behind the counter and down the back hallway. Pulling the phone from my apron pocket, I saw the number I'd memorized across the screen. MISSED CALL & VOICE MAIL.

My hand shook as I unlocked the phone and tapped the screen for it to play.

Instead of words, the message started as just static. Then something garbled and shouting. "Where the hell is she? Why isn't she at the safe house?" It was Dom's voice and he was *pissed*.

"You wanted her out of the way. I got her out of the way," a second voice said. It was much calmer and sounded like Vincent.

The called ended abruptly, and the rest of the conversation was cut off like someone had realized they'd accidentally made a call.

Dom wanted me in a safe house?

I listened to it three more times and was sure that Vincent hadn't intended to call. *One heck of a butt dial, Vin.* But nothing made sense, including the fact that Dom had sounded concerned about me. Not like the absentee father he'd always been.

But then Vincent's words brought home the reminder. *You wanted her out of the way. I got her out of the way.*

I turned and looked at the empty donut shop, and then to the back door that led into the alley.

I needed a minute and fresh air to gather my thoughts. "I'll be right back," I called to Asha.

"Told you to take your time, girl. I had seven shots of espresso to kick my hangover from last night, so I'm wired. I could handle a crowd all by myself."

With a weak smile on my face, I pushed open the back

door and stepped into the alley. The air wasn't the freshest, but it wasn't clogged with the sugary sweetness from inside.

What the hell is going on?

Vincent had told me Dom wanted me gone, and sold me that spiel about no one knowing where I was, which I didn't even question at the time. And now? Now, I had no idea what the hell to think.

I stared down at the phone, my thumb hovering over the CALL BACK button, but I remembered Vincent's warning. The number was to be a direct line to him, not Dom. And what good would that do me? I'd followed orders like the good little mobster's daughter that I was and had left my phone behind, which meant I didn't have anyone's contact information except for the few numbers I'd memorized.

I didn't have Dom's personal cell phone number memorized. No one had ever bothered to give me the number to the Hell's Kitchen brownstone. I could call my aunt . . . but there was no way she'd give me any information that would allow me to disturb Dom. She wouldn't take the chance of earning his displeasure.

Did I even want to get in touch with Dom? If he hadn't given the orders for me to leave New York on my own, then wouldn't his first order be for me to come back? I couldn't honestly say I *knew* my father, but my gut said yes. As soon as he figured out where I was or how to contact me, he'd have his guys here to collect me and put me on a jet back to New York before I could even pack my suitcase.

Back to the gilded cage.

No more New Orleans.

No more experiences.

No more Bishop.

No. I wasn't ready. I didn't want to go. But how long

would it take for Dom to find me? Vincent knew what credit card he'd given me, which meant he knew exactly where I was.

He's always known where I am. The realization swept over me.

From the second I'd booked my ticket with that credit card, he would have known where I'd gone. How could I have been so stupid to not even think about that?

There had been a few times I'd felt like I was being watched, but I'd brushed it off as my overactive imagination.

What the hell is going on?

Like the person in the alley last night. The one who'd been watching me and Bishop and then run.

Who was that? One of Dom's goons here to watch over me, even though I was supposed to be on my own? Or maybe the FBI had pulled the credit card records?

Too many questions and not enough answers.

The back door to Voodoo banged against the brick wall of the building, and Bishop stepped out with a ladder.

He stopped when he saw me leaning against the back of Your Favorite Hole.

"Hey. What are you doing?"

I shoved the phone into my apron pocket and crossed my arms over my chest. "Nothing. Just . . . needed some fresh air."

Bishop looked around the alley. "Not the freshest back here."

I shrugged. "It was the best I could do for the moment."

He leaned the ladder against the wall and came toward me. "Are you okay? You look upset."

"I'm fine. Just . . . tired."

A smile tugged at the edges of Bishop's mouth. "Some

of that is probably my fault." He pressed a palm to the wall on either side of my head. "I'm staying at your place tonight, cupcake. We're not done by a long shot."

The heat in his eyes and the husky tone of his voice pulled me from my mini meltdown.

"Is that so?"

"Damn right. And before we do that, we're checking a few more things off your list. Although I probably should make you slow it down, because I don't want you runnin' out of town as soon as you've hit them all."

The lightness that had begun to take over when he'd spoken was momentarily doused. More than likely, before I could check them all off, I'd be dragged out of town. But that also sent a shaft of urgency through me. I needed to soak up every moment. I didn't get to keep this man. I didn't get to keep this city. I didn't get to choose my future.

My face must have reflected my thoughts, because Bishop frowned. "Hey, what's that look for? You already making your plans to bolt?" His posture tensed as if waiting for me to deliver the hard truth.

I shook my head. "No. I don't want to leave."

"That doesn't exactly sound like you're planning on staying." The hands on either side of my head clenched into fists.

How honest was I going to be? He deserved more than my lies. "I might not have a choice."

"You've always got a choice. It all depends on how much you're willing to sacrifice to get what you want."

"I want to spend tonight with you."

His smile came back, but his posture didn't relax. "Good, because you're going to. Stop at the shop when you get off."

"Okay."

He leaned down and brushed his lips across mine. "So fucking sweet."

Eden

47

AFTER HOURS OF SERVING DONUTS AND MAKING coffee drinks, I'd come to a decision. I would focus on living every moment in New Orleans like it might be ripped away from me at any time. When I hung up my apron and walked toward Voodoo, I made an impulsive decision.

I wanted a tattoo, and I wanted Bishop to be the one to do it.

That way, when I was alone in my apartment in New York, watching the world pass me by, I would have a permanent, tangible reminder of the amazing memories I'd made here.

Shaking off the depressing thoughts of what would certainly be my future, I smiled as the chimes on the door tinkled to announce my entrance. Delilah leaned over a man, no doubt creating some awesome piece of art, but Bishop stood at the counter, his arms crossed over his chest while he talked to a woman I'd never seen before.

"I don't have the money right now. But I swear I'll pay you soon. Or we could trade . . ."

Why was someone always hitting on him? Seriously, it was getting old.

"I've got a woman. No trades."

A sense of déjà vu swept over me. How many times would this happen after I was gone? It pushed me to embrace the time I had even more.

With a burst of confidence and attitude, I walked toward the counter. "I bet I could get you to do mine for a trade."

Bishop's attention cut to me, and his lips twitched. "You're the exception to the rule, cupcake."

The woman turned and her gaze raked over me. I expected a snide comment, but perhaps her fear of what Bishop would say in response kept her quiet.

"I'll just go down to Magazine. Those guys will trade."

"Good luck with that."

She stalked away, and Bishop watched me come toward the counter still riding my wave of confidence.

"What if I really did want a tattoo?"

"You serious?"

"Maybe."

"I need more than a maybe before I'm going to ink that skin."

"Do you have time to do it tonight?"

He tilted his head to the side. "What brought this on?"

"Does it matter?"

"Everything does when it comes to you."

His words, so simple and sincere, hit me somewhere in the vicinity of my chest.

"Then don't let me forget any of this."

With his expression darkening, he called to Delilah. "I'm knocking off for tonight. You got a problem with that?"

She looked up from the room where she worked. "It's been slower than shit all day. Make a run for it. I'll lock up."

Bishop stepped out from behind the counter. "Let's go. We've got some shit to talk about."

He grabbed my hand and pulled me along behind him to the back door. Outside in the alley, he unlocked a small garage door built into the back of the building, and a motorcycle came into view as he pushed the door up.

After he threw a leg over, he backed it out and dropped the kickstand before heading back into the garage and emerging with two helmets.

Once the garage door was closed and locked again, he held out a helmet to me. "We're going back to your place."

I stared at the helmet for long moments before taking it from his hands. "We're riding this?"

"That gonna bother you?"

Riding a motorcycle hadn't been on my list, but I wasn't opposed to trying it out. "No, not at all."

"Good. Let's go."

The ride to my apartment was short, but the feeling of Bishop in front of me and the vibrations of the bike between my legs wasn't something I'd forget anytime soon. When he parked on the street and I stepped off, I wanted to climb him, and he read it on my face.

"You liked that, didn't you?"

"I had no idea . . ."

"That you'd feel like you had the world's best vibrator between your legs?"

I bit my lip to hide the grin stretching my cheeks. "Basically."

"Get your keys. I see I've got something to prove now."

"Oh really? What's that?"

"That I'm a better ride than my bike."

A laugh burst free of my lips and the easiness from earlier today came back. "I don't think you're going to have a hard time proving that."

I unlocked the gate leading into the courtyard, and Bishop followed me inside.

Harriet's back door opened just before we reached the spiral staircase leading up to my place. "Eden, dear. Were you expecting company this afternoon?"

I stopped so abruptly at her question, Bishop's hand landed on my hip to steady me. "Company?"

"Someone rang your buzzer at least a dozen times. I finally got sick of hearing it so I looked out front, but they were leaving."

"They?"

"Two men in suits. They looked official. You haven't gotten into any trouble, have you?"

"No," I answered in a rush. "No trouble. That's just . . . strange."

Suits? It had to be Dom's people. Or the men from the hotel? FBI?

"Yes, very strange." Harriet's gaze was appraising. "If I didn't know better, I'd think I had a second Charlie on my hands. On the run from the law." She laughed. "But of course that's just me being a little bit of a conspiracy theorist in my old age."

I smiled, hoping it didn't look as strained as it felt. "I'm definitely not on the run from the law." *I don't think*, I added silently.

"Damn. I was hoping for some excitement to spice up

the week. Unless they got the wrong buzzer and it was the IRS coming after me. Bastards."

Bishop and I traded glances at that before I thanked Harriet for the information. He followed me up to my apartment, and once he closed the door behind him, he asked the question I knew had to be coming.

"You gonna tell me what the hell you're running from? Or are you gonna make me keep guessing?"

I locked the door and turned around slowly to meet his gaze. "I'm not running from anyone."

"Why don't I believe that?"

"I don't know."

I moved toward him, wanting nothing more than to change the subject and forget about everything outside of this apartment for the rest of the night. The world could go to hell, but I wanted to savor whatever time I had left with Bishop. I pressed both hands to his abs.

He studied me under his hooded gaze. "You trying to distract me?"

"I'm trying to get you back on track with your earlier plan."

"Is that right?"

I nodded before pushing his shirt up. "Yes."

"I guess I'll just have to let you do that then."

And he did.

Eden

IF BISHOP WAS AN ADDICTION, THEN I NEVER WANTED A cure.

For the next couple of weeks, we bounced from his apartment to mine, losing ourselves in each other. When we weren't in bed, he showed me more than the city. He showed me a life I desperately wanted to claim as my own.

With each day, I fell harder. I was in so much damn trouble, because I didn't know how I was going to walk away from him when the order came. Every day I waited for the text, but it didn't come. No more cryptic and accidental voice mails either, which I tried not to let stab me in the heart. Dom didn't know where I was, and apparently he'd decided he didn't care.

I pushed down that familiar disappointment and focused on all the good around me.

Bishop had become an integral part of my happiness, and the simple life I was living here was more than enough for me. I'd even started helping out with the books at both Voodoo and Your Favorite Hole, putting my skills to work.

Everything felt so . . . right.

But that didn't mean it was perfect.

"No."

The word came out of Bishop's mouth with more force behind it than I expected, and his entire demeanor changed with it.

We were curled up on my bed, and the easy postcoital moment was broken. I pushed up on my elbow, my hand resting on his chest, and looked down at him.

"What do you mean, no?"

It wasn't like I'd never heard the word before. *No* had been a common concept in my life in New York. It just wasn't something I'd expected to hear Bishop say when it came to something so simple as finally going to the casino so I could learn to play blackjack at a real table.

"No, as in I don't fucking go to casinos. They're not a good place for me."

Without another word, he rolled to his side, dislodging my hand, and climbed out of bed. He reached for his jeans on the floor and yanked one pant leg on and then the other. He zipped and buttoned them and turned from the room before I could even figure out how to respond.

I scrambled out of my side of the bed, grabbing his T-shirt and pulling it on. Everything felt off. I'd seen Bishop shut down like this around other people, but never around me. I didn't know what to make of it. He had the fridge door open in the small kitchen, and I spoke to his back.

"I'm sorry; I didn't realize that was a touchy subject for you. I can . . . go by myself. It's no big deal."

He slammed the fridge door shut and turned. "And

who's going to teach you how to play blackjack? Some random guy who happens to see a sweet thing at the table and decides she's the one he wants to take home?"

The statement came out with sharp edges, and I jerked back. Was he . . . ? No way. I blurted it anyway.

"Are you jealous?"

Bishop's big hands landed on his hips and he drew up to his full height, dwarfing me in the tiny kitchen. If he were anyone else, I might have felt a shred of unease, but not with Bishop.

"Of course I'm fucking jealous, Eden. I know exactly what every man sees when he looks at you. You're totally oblivious to the fact that they'd trip all over themselves to get closer to you."

Now I was getting angry. "Of course I'm oblivious to all of that. I only see you!" I yelled the words across the kitchen with my own hands on my hips like some kind of shrew.

Bishop's face relaxed and the tension in his stance drained away. He crossed the small space between us and cupped my face in his hands.

"I know, cupcake. And I'm the luckiest guy in the goddamned world because of it. I just don't want to see anything happen to you. I couldn't handle it."

"Nothing's going to happen to me. There's security, and even if there wasn't, I'm not completely helpless."

I'd even walked home from work *all by myself* several times in the last couple of weeks. Never mind that I never walked home alone if I worked until dark. That was just being smart, I assured myself.

Something that approached a growl escaped from Bishop's throat. "Security at a casino isn't your friend. They have one purpose and one purpose only—protect the interests of the house at all costs. That's it."

"Well, I'm checking this off my damn list, and if you won't come with me, then what choice do I have?"

"And what is your goddamned hurry, Eden?"

I squeezed my eyes shut. This was a question I kept dodging, and Bishop was well aware I wasn't giving him a straight answer. "I thought we decided we weren't going to talk about that?"

"Like you never told me the real story behind why you skipped out on the hotel? You're going to have to talk about it sometime, unless you plan to just up and leave without telling me a damn thing."

I wanted to tell him everything. Every day that I kept my silence ate at me. I couldn't keep this from him any longer. It was time.

He dropped his hands away from my face and jammed them into his hair, then turned away to face the counter. "Of course you'd have to be this stubborn. Why would I fall for someone who was easy to get an answer from?"

Everything in the room seemed to come to a screeching halt, except for my heart, which hammered harder than ever before.

"You're falling for me?" My voice carried a tremble.

Bishop spun around to face me, his hair wild and his gaze intense. "How couldn't I? You're . . . everything."

My head jerked back at his admission, and warmth slammed into my chest.

You're everything.

The look in his eyes said it all. He meant it.

"You're everything too."

His arms closed around me and he pulled me against his chest, lifting me off my feet.

I soaked up his warmth, his scent, his *everything*. Even with 4.2 million men in New York, I knew I'd never find someone like Bishop. He was it.

And I can't keep him.

No. I refused to let that stand. I wasn't going to let this go and walk away from him. I'd figure out a way. There was no other option.

When he loosened his hold and lowered me back to the floor, determination flowed through me. I would figure this out.

"Let's get you fed so you can get ready for work."

I lifted up on my toes and pressed a kiss to his jaw. "Okay."

Bishop

49

I SAT UP ON MY STOOL AND STRETCHED MY BACK, AND my client readjusted his position in the chair. From his stiff movements, it seemed like a break might be welcome.

"You want to take a break before we keep going?"

He lit up at the suggestion. "Yeah, man. That'd be great. I need a smoke and some coffee. You think we can finish this piece tonight?"

"We can, if you want to push through. I don't have anything after you."

"I just want it done. No offense, but my old lady might kill me if I have to keep coming back for more sittings."

I set my machine on the counter. "I get that, man. I'm heading next door to grab coffee. You want one?"

"Yeah, black. None of that frappe frou-frou shit."

"Cool. I'll be back in a few."

I stood, snapped off my gloves, and stretched as my

client headed out the front door with a smoke in one hand and his phone in the other. The door chimed a second time as Con walked in. But he didn't look a whole hell of a lot like my boss the way I was used to seeing him. Instead, he was kitted out in black tie, and his hair was slicked back from his forehead.

"Did you get kidnapped by the guy on the fucking Men's Warehouse commercial?" I asked. "Do you *like the way you look*?"

"Shut the hell up. You work for me, fucker. I could fire you for that shit."

"Yeah? You got someone else to pick up the slack who isn't going to fuck up your shop's rep?"

"Shut up. I just came to pick up the bank deposit I forgot yesterday. I'm meeting Vanessa at a fundraiser, and she'll kick my ass if I'm late, so I don't have time to screw around."

"Raising more money for those boxing kids?"

Con nodded as he headed for the break room where the cash bag was locked in a drawer. "Yeah, we're working on expanding."

"Both of you, do-gooders."

"It's good to give back, man. You should try it sometime. Come down and let the kids take a few shots at you. It's a fun time."

"Maybe I will. So, where's this fundraiser at tonight?"

"Casino. Somehow Vanessa talked them into donating a portion of the house's share. I swear to God, that woman could talk anyone into anything."

At the mention of the casino, I thought of my earlier blowout with Eden.

"Is it like five grand a person to get in? Or can anyone show up?"

Con shook his head. "Nah, we'll take anyone's money. There's a silent auction, but that shit isn't required."

"If Eden shows up there, would you mind keeping an eye on her? She wants to learn to play blackjack, and that ain't my scene."

Con's brow furrowed, but he didn't ask questions. "Yeah, if she needs something, we'll be there."

"I'll let her know."

He grabbed the bank bag and headed toward the front. "You sure you don't want to put on a monkey suit and come too?"

"You think I've got a tux lying around? Hell no. And even if I did, me and casinos don't get along anymore."

I knew what Con would think, what everyone thought when I said that. Gambling addiction. It was probably part of the truth, but not the whole truth.

"I get you, man. Tell your girl we'll be there until at least midnight, but probably later. I'm hoping I can talk Titan into losing a million at the craps table. I already know Lord will lose miserably at poker because I've got Elle to distract him."

Knowing the whole crew would be there made my unease at having Eden go to the casino without me drop to lower levels.

"I'll let her know. Thanks, man."

Con pushed out the front door and I was only a few steps behind him to head over to Your Favorite Hole. My client paced the sidewalk, puffing on his smoke and talking into his phone, so I figured I had a few more minutes. Either that or he could wait. I'd be staying at least an hour past what I'd planned to in order to finish his piece, so he didn't have room to bitch.

The place was empty except for a kid with huge

headphones on in the back corner, and his fingers flew over the keys of a laptop. He looked up at me when I came in, but quickly dropped his gaze back to whatever the hell he was doing. He'd been taking up space in that corner all frigging afternoon. If he were anything but a skinny, nerdy-looking kid, I would have warned him off, but he didn't strike me as any kind of a threat.

"Hey there. What can I get for you?"

My attention cut to Eden and her purple apron and hat. She still looked delicious. "Hey, cupcake. I need two black coffees so I can push through and finish this piece I'm working on."

Her smile dimmed a few watts. "Does that mean you're working late?"

"Yeah, but I think I found a way to make amends for earlier today."

Confusion drew her brows together. "What do you mean?"

I didn't want to talk about our argument this morning, but I couldn't avoid it.

"If you want to go play blackjack, tonight is the night. Con, Lord, and Titan will all be there with their women. Charity thing. You lose at the game, you're going to be helping fund the nonprofit afterschool boxing program Con and Vanessa run."

"You want me to go with them?" She looked down at her uniform. "I'm off as soon as Asha gets here, but I'm not ready for any kind of charity thing."

"Take your time. They're already on their way. You show up when you can, take a cab, and find one of them to help you learn the rules of the game."

"You're not going to come, are you?" Eden asked.

"No. I told you, I don't do casinos. Take a cab back to Voodoo when you're done, and hopefully I'll be finished with this piece I'm working on."

She turned away and grabbed two coffee cups before filling them and popping the lids on. "I wouldn't want to intrude. I've already crashed one party. I don't need to crash another."

Eden's disappointment came through loud and clear as she set the cups on the counter in front of me. She kept her gaze on my shirt rather than lifting it so I could see her eyes.

"Hey. What's going on? Look at me."

She lifted her face, and disappointment was stamped on every feature.

"I don't like that you only want me to go because you know there'll be a whole crew of your friends there. It's like you think I'm not capable of doing it by myself."

I jerked back. "You want me to apologize for wanting to make sure you're not alone in a casino by yourself?"

"You don't have to manage me. I can handle myself."

There was something more going on here, but now wasn't the time to get into it. "I'm not managing you. But wanting to make sure my girl is safe while she gets to have all of her experiences isn't something I'm ever going to apologize for. Not a fucking chance. So are you going to go or not?"

"I don't know. Right now all I want is to get out of these clothes and into a hot shower. I'll decide once I get home."

"You're not walking by yourself at this time of night."

I could tell she wanted to roll her eyes, but she didn't. "I can't keep taking a cab six blocks every night that you can't walk me home. It's getting ridiculous."

"You want me to get someone down here to walk you

home? Because there's no way you need to be out on those streets alone. I'm not taking chances with you, Eden. You're too fucking important to me."

Frustration rolled off her in waves, but I wouldn't budge. "Fine. I'll take a cab."

"Good. Text me if you decide to go out tonight."

"Fine."

Her response was short, and I leaned across the counter. "I'm not trying to be a dick. I'm just trying to be a guy who cares about you."

"And I'm trying to prove to myself that I can do some things on my own, okay? You're going to have to let me, Bishop. I don't do clipped wings. Not anymore."

I leaned in and brushed my lips across hers. "I don't want to clip anything. Be smart, babe. Text me later."

She returned my kiss. "Your coffee's on the house. I'll talk to you later."

I dropped a ten on the counter anyway, and watched her grab a rag to wipe it down as soon as I was out the door.

Even though I'd expected to feel lighter when I came up with this solution, something about it left me off-balance.

Eden

I STOOD IN FRONT OF MY SMALL CLOSET, THE TOWEL from my shower wrapped around my body while I debated what I wanted to do. My gaze traveled back and forth between a little black dress and a T-shirt I'd stolen from Bishop and didn't have any plans to return.

Why did it bother me so much that he wanted me to go tonight when a bunch of his friends would be there?

If Bishop had said he would go and help me learn black-jack, I wouldn't have cared. But his aversion to casinos was obvious. It didn't take a genius to realize that he must have had some sort of gambling problem in the past and now didn't want to be close to temptation. I could respect that. After I'd figured that out, I felt awful about asking him to go in the first place. It was like offering up a shot to someone who had dropped hints about being in AA.

Idiot.

But instead of telling me to go and have fun, I felt like

he'd organized some kind of safe encounter for me. I should have appreciated it, but something about it had rubbed me the wrong way.

Black dress or T-shirt long enough to be a dress? That was the question.

Did I let my momentary annoyance stop me from experiencing more of New Orleans?

Screw it. I grabbed the black dress off the hanger and made my decision.

I was going, and I would have an amazing time. I might not know the finer points of playing blackjack, but I wasn't stupid. I could count to twenty-one. I understood the basic principles. I'd take fifty dollars and wouldn't let myself lose any more than that.

After spending what was probably a little too much time on my hair and makeup, I called a cab and headed down to the courtyard to wait. Harriet sat outside with a bottle of liquor and a giant cigar, puffing away like a pro.

"If I were fifty years younger and into women, I'd pick you up in a heartbeat. Way to go, girl. That man of yours is going to pin you to a wall when he sees you."

Hearing something like that come out of the mouth of a woman closing in on seventy was still jarring, but Harriet was truly one of a kind and only marginally batshit crazy. I loved her.

"I'm not going out with my man tonight, so he's going to miss out on all this." I gestured to my wildly curling hair.

"Oh really? You have a fight? That boy doesn't seem like the type to let you go out on the town without making sure he can keep his claim intact."

Her words fired up my annoyance from earlier. "He's working."

"His loss. You'll be the center of attention."

Immediately, I began to regret my decision to go all out with my primping. The center of attention was not something I needed to be.

She held out the cigar. "Want a puff? It's a good Cuban."

Of course it was. Because why would Harriet smoke anything but a Cuban cigar?

"I'm good, thanks. I don't smoke." I was actually considering going back up to my room and calling off the entire night when the sound of a horn honking came from out front.

"That'll be my cab. I should go."

"Have fun tonight, Eden. Don't do anything I wouldn't do."

I wondered what exactly that mandate would preclude me from doing, but decided not to think too hard about it. Harriet seemed like she'd done *a lot* of living in her years, and I couldn't imagine what she would consider off-limits.

When the cab pulled up in front of the casino, I paid the driver and climbed out. A big sign hung out front advertising the charity event for the evening—THE ONE NIGHT YOU CAN LOSE AND STILL CONSIDER IT A VICTORY.

That was an amazingly generous situation, and I was stunned any casino would agree to donate part of their take. I supposed it had a lot to say about the persuasiveness of the charity and its benefactors.

I took the steps one at a time, careful to make sure my dress stayed down with the breeze picking up off the river. I didn't want to have a Marilyn Monroe moment and flash an entire crowd of potential donors.

At the door, the man spent longer than normal staring at my ID, and I started to get nervous.

"Enjoy yourself, Ms. Madden," he finally said before handing it back to me.

I shook off the odd feeling that came with his smile, and headed to the floor. *It's just nerves because you don't like using a fake ID*, I told myself.

The floor was filled with machines that lit up and played music, along with tables, dealers, and plenty of players. More signs that announced the donations that would go to charity tonight hung from the ceiling and sat on the tops of machines. I had no doubt they'd encourage people to play deeper and lose more because they felt like they were losing for a good cause. It was actually a pretty brilliant fundraising idea.

Signs pointing to a silent auction room led in one direction, but I didn't follow them. I headed toward the tables to watch and teach myself how to play blackjack.

The annoyance and unease I'd felt earlier in the evening fell away as excitement bubbled up. I'd never been inside a casino before, so every part of this experience was new and different. I could see how people would be drawn to the lights and sounds of the slots. They seemed so cheerful and fun. I thought of the fifty dollars in my purse and wondered if I should just stop and try one . . .

No. I was going to the main event. I had a purpose.

Men in tuxes and women in evening gowns were scattered around the giant room in stark contrast to the little blue-haired ladies and people in jeans. I caught sight of Con and his brother, Lord, at a table on the opposite side of the slot machines, but didn't head in their direction.

I hadn't texted Bishop yet to tell him my decision, even though I knew it was a shitty thing to do. The last thing I wanted was for him to send his friends to find me and babysit me. I'd had enough babysitting to last a lifetime. Guilt rode me as I walked toward the tables, because I knew Bishop had to be wondering what I'd decided to do. Unless he was so into the tattoo he was finishing he hadn't noticed the time . . .

That was a cop-out and I knew it. I stopped next to a machine and unzipped my purse to find my phone.

"I remember you."

The deep, smooth voice came from beside me, startling me so much that everything tumbled out of my purse. I jerked my eyes up to see a familiar man in a tux beside me, and we both crouched to collect my lipstick, loose change, ID, the little cash I brought, keys, and other flotsam and jetsam.

"Shit. Sorry. I didn't mean to scare you."

I loaded my purse back up. "No worries. You just surprised me is all."

"My wife will never let me live down scaring people by just saying hello if you mention it. Actually, she'll probably say something that will have me carrying her out of here clawing and kicking. So, feel free to mention away."

"Umm . . . okay."

"Lucas Titan. We met at Dirty Dog and again at Valentina's party before Mardi Gras."

"I remember. It's good to see you again." It was one of those polite throwaway lines, and I immediately wondered if he'd been on the lookout for me at Bishop's request.

At least, until he spoke again.

"Is Bishop here with you?"

Any budding concern I might have had about him being

sent to babysit me fell away with his question. "No, he's working, but I wanted to . . . show my support and probably lose the entire fifty dollars I'm planning on gambling."

"What's your game?"

"It's about to be blackjack. After I watch a few hands and get the hang of it."

Titan studied me closely. "You've never played?"

"Nope. Never. But tonight I'm going to."

"You want a rundown on how it works? I'm due to lose some money, otherwise I'll never hear the end of it from those two."

He jerked his head toward Con and Lord, who were ordering cocktails from a circulating server.

"Are you sure you don't have something better to do?"

He glanced back toward the group. "My wife shooed me away so she could spend time with her girls, so I don't think I'll be missed quite yet."

"Okay, then I appreciate it."

Lucas Titan led the way to a blackjack table, and I scanned the felt to see what the minimum bet was. I got the feeling his idea of gambling and mine were worlds apart. His tux looked like it cost more than a nice used car.

Five-dollar minimum bet.

I could handle that. I had said I only planned to gamble fifty, so maybe he was being polite.

"I'll play a few hands and talk you through them. You can jump in whenever you're ready." He reached into his breast pocket and pulled out a money clip. He peeled off a hundred and slid it across the table to the dealer.

"Changing one hundred," the dealer said aloud, and a man stepped up behind him and nodded.

The pit boss? My guess was solely fueled by the

knowledge of casinos imparted to me by Hollywood.

The dealer sat out stacks of chips and spread out one stack on the table before pushing them toward Titan. Then he began to deal.

The two other players at the table received their cards first, and Titan kept a running commentary of what he was doing and why as I stood behind him.

I wondered if the dealer would get annoyed, or perhaps the pit boss, but neither said a word. Titan's stack of chips grew and then diminished before growing again. After about fifteen minutes, I felt like I was getting the hang of it. My hands were sweating where I gripped my wristlet, and equal parts of anticipation and anxiety spread through me.

What if I lost it all in five minutes? I guessed that didn't really matter, as long as I got to try.

A piece of bumper-sticker philosophy floated into my head. *It's not whether you win or lose; it's how you play the game.*

Well, I couldn't win if I didn't play at all, and this was what I had come to do.

"I'm ready," I said as I slid into the seat next to Titan.

He gave me an encouraging nod, and I pulled the fifty from my purse. I had an extra twenty stashed to make sure I could get home, but otherwise I was spending everything I had.

I slid the bill across the table, and the dealer repeated the process he'd done with Titan and pushed chips toward me.

The other two players stood and collected their chips. Apparently they didn't want to play at a table with a complete newbie.

Titan watched them leave and must have read the embarrassment on my face. "You've got as much right to play at this table as anyone. Don't worry about it."

I nodded and placed a five-dollar chip on the circle in front of my seat, and the dealer began to flip the cards in front of us. Titan talked me through the first four hands, and I lost two and won two.

"Not bad for a beginner. You're doing fine."

Two more hands went by, and I was down to thirty dollars in chips and getting a little nervous. I'd taken my chances splitting aces and lost both.

"You'll either come back or you won't. The thing you're doing that's smart is not betting more than you're willing to lose."

"And now you're a blackjack coach?"

A woman's voice came from behind us, and we both turned.

"Yve, the love of my life, you remember Eden?"

"Of course I do. I see you're not wearing one of my dresses." Her tone sounded playfully disapproving.

"I wasn't sure what would be considered appropriate for tonight so I fell back on the little-black-dress rule." I hoped she wasn't offended, but the smile that spread across her face told me she wasn't.

Her dress was some kind of vintage couture that hugged and flattered her every curve, and I was immediately envious.

"It was a good choice. Next time, I'll have to find you something like this. I'll keep an eye out."

The next hand was dealt, and I lost another five dollars while Titan won a stack of chips.

"Oh good, you're winning. Can I borrow you to go bid on a piece that Valentina donated to the silent auction? It matches the other pieces of hers we bought, and there's no way I'm letting someone else get it."

Titan stood. "Of course. But you know you can bid on whatever you want."

"If I'm going to bid enough to buy a car, I kind of need you there to do it for me. I think I'd puke otherwise."

"All right. I'm coming. Eden, would you like to join us?"

I looked at the dwindling pile of chips in front of me. "I think I'm going to finish this out and probably head home."

"I think you'll be playing a lot longer than you think. Good luck. We'll be around if you need anything."

The couple, gorgeous in their evening wear, moved in the direction of the silent auction, and I played one more hand before the red card popped out of the deck.

"New dealer," the current one said as he stepped back to make room for another man. Another player sat down at the table and shot a glance at me with a nod. Not wanting to seem rude, I smiled back at him.

The deck was reshuffled and play continued, but with one very important difference.

I started winning. Every time. It was crazy. I started to bet ten dollars on each hand, and my pile grew and grew. I'd lose once and think my streak was over, but then I'd win the next six in a row. The stacks of chips seemed to multiply, and a heady feeling swept over me.

This was *fun*.

Bishop

I FINISHED WRAPPING UP THE TATTOO, LOCKED UP THE shop, and checked my phone. It was almost one and I hadn't heard from Eden. I'd lost track of time as I'd put the finishing touches on the piece, so it hadn't even occurred to me until I was done.

I texted her.

BISHOP: *Did you decide to stay in?*

I hoped she hadn't. Tonight was the best night for her to check blackjack off her list. I just hoped she didn't get bit by the bug and want to go more often. It wasn't something I could do with her because showing my face in a casino was the fastest way to bring my past crashing down on me.

Now that I had something to lose, I wasn't taking any chances.

My phone buzzed with a text as I wiped down my

station. It wasn't from Eden.

CON: *Your girl is playing deep at the tables. She a card shark?*

BISHOP: *Never played before in her life.*

CON: *Something seems off. Pit boss is watching her close, but it's not my place to step in.*

An uneasy feeling twisted in my gut. Fuck. What the hell was going on?

BISHOP: *Beginner's luck?*

CON: *More like card-counter's luck.*

My stomach twisted and fell to my feet. Eden wasn't a fucking card counter. No fucking way. I grabbed the keys to my bike off the counter and headed out the back.

When I parked my bike in the lot closest to the casino, I hurried up the stairs. My phone had two more texts from Con. The last one was from two minutes ago.

CON: *I'm going over there. I think the pit boss is about to call security.*

I flashed my ID for the guy at the door and rushed past him. If he ran my ID, there was a good chance it would pop up in the system.

"Hey, I need to see that closer." He stood to follow me, but I wasn't stopping for anything.

I scanned the tables, looking for Eden. I'd get her and get the hell out before security caught up with me.

I returned a text to Con.

BISHOP: *I'm here.*

But before I could find Eden, I saw two men in suits closing in on a blackjack table. Con's blond head stood out above the crowd as they stopped.

Fuck.

"She's done. She's leaving. It's a simple case of beginner's luck," Con told the men as he stood between them and Eden. Lord, Titan, and Simon were headed over as well.

"I didn't do anything. Mr. Titan showed me the ropes and I started playing. This dealer just gave me good cards."

"We need you to come with us, miss. We just have a few questions for you and your associate, and we'll need your ID."

"Associate? I don't have an associate."

One of the security guys had a man in a white shirt and brown pants by the arm. "We've been watching both of you. You're clearly working together. You both need to come with us."

I stepped up to the other side of Eden. "Not fucking happening. She's leaving with me."

Her head whipped around and shock flashed over her face at my appearance. I didn't fucking care if she was pissed because there was no fucking way I was letting casino security take my girl any goddamned place.

"Gentlemen, I think you're getting worked up over nothing. She'd never played before we sat down tonight. She also doesn't know this man." This came from Titan. "To assume anything else is simply ludicrous."

The pit boss recognized Titan. "Mr. Titan, we appreciate

you vouching for her, but we need to handle this internally." To the dealer, he said, "Take her chips."

The dealer reached for them.

"Seriously? You're gonna go there?" Con interjected.

"I won those myself," Eden said, protesting as the dealer pulled them away.

Another man in a suit joined the group. "Do we have an issue here? All we ask is for your cooperation. Please come with us."

"Fine, but I didn't do anything wrong." Eden stepped toward them in a move that seemed like she planned to follow them.

I grabbed her arm. "No way. She's leaving. Keep the fucking chips. We're done here."

"Sir, that's not your call."

Eden whipped around to look at me. "It's fine. I'll explain, and they'll understand this is all a big misunderstanding."

Did she seriously think I was going to let her go? I kept a firm hold on her arm and pulled her behind me. "You gonna back me up here, guys?"

Titan, Lord, Con, and Simon formed a wall between me and Eden and the casino security personnel.

"It would be in your best interest for you to let them leave," Titan said, his tone daring them to try to do anything else.

"Mr. Titan, we're not looking for trouble."

"Then you should get back to work. There's a fundraiser happening tonight, and you're attracting the wrong kind of attention from your patrons."

A crowd was gathering around us, including Yve, Vanessa, Charlie, and Elle. The entire place felt like a powder keg about to blow if the security crew took one wrong step.

I took advantage of the moment of stillness and turned to hustle Eden out the nearest fire exit. The alarm blared, but I didn't give a shit.

"What the hell are you doing? Stop. They're not going to do anything to me."

"You don't know a goddamned thing about what happens in the back rooms and basements of casinos, cupcake, and you're not going to fucking find out while I'm breathing."

She struggled against my hold, so I lifted her up and tossed her over my shoulder. Her scream barely roused any strange looks, not that I cared about that or how she beat against my back with her hand and small purse. When I reached my bike, I lowered her to her feet, and an enraged Eden, the likes of which I'd never seen before, greeted me.

"You fucking caveman! What the hell is your problem?"

I grabbed the helmet off the back and strapped it onto her head, avoiding her slapping hands. "Get on the bike, and we'll talk about this at your place."

Three men in suits were running toward us down the sidewalk as I started the bike.

"Oh my God, are they coming after us?"

"And the cops are probably next."

One man had a phone to his ear, and when Eden finally regained some of her common sense and hopped on, I tore out into the street.

No one would catch up to us on a bike, but I still took turn after turn just in case someone was trying to follow us. When I finally pulled up in front of Harriet's house, Eden flew off the bike and ran toward the gate to unlock it. I pushed the front tire up over the curb and followed her through with my bike, hoping like hell the passageway was wide enough. It was, but barely.

When I dropped the kickstand and stood it up on the cement pad, Eden ran back and slammed the gate shut.

"What the hell just happened?"

My entire body buzzed with the rush of adrenaline, and I stalked in circles around the courtyard.

"Go upstairs. Inside. I'll be up when I've cooled the fuck down so I don't say anything I'm going to regret."

Eden's face paled in the moonlight, but her mouth flattened into a thin line. She didn't say anything before she stalked up the spiral stairs and unlocked the apartment door.

I would have bet money on the fact that Eden wanted to slam it, but was too worried about waking Harriet to do it.

My phone buzzed, and I pulled it out of my pocket as I paced.

CON: *That was fucking crazy. They ran out of here after her. Asked for both your names. I didn't give them.*

BISHOP: *Thanks, man. I'm at her place. I appreciate you coming to her rescue. I don't know what the fuck happened tonight, but it's not fucking happening again.*

CON: *I think it's safe to say that neither of you should be coming back anytime soon.*

BISHOP: *Not a fucking problem. Sorry to interrupt your fundraiser.*

I shoved my phone back in my pocket and sucked in a few deep breaths.

Visions of what could have happened to Eden had flashed through my head the entire way to the casino and all the way home. I knew better than to think they'd give her the benefit of the doubt because she was a woman.

Guilt and pain from everything I'd fucked up before battered me. I hadn't been able to stop them when they had dragged my cousin Abby into a back room along with me. There was no fucking way I'd ever let that happen to Eden, regardless of her need for independence.

Eden

I SHUT THE DOOR AND PACED BACK AND FORTH ACROSS
my tiny living area. A whirlpool of emotions spun in
dizzying circles inside me. Anger. Guilt. Annoyance.
Frustration. Helplessness.

Bishop finally came upstairs and let himself inside. I
stared at him for long moments while neither of us spoke.
Whatever he was feeling was bubbling close to the surface.

"What the fuck did you think you were doing?"
Apparently he hadn't cooled down.

"What the hell were *you* doing?" I shot back. "You were
the one who didn't want to step foot inside a casino and then
bam, there you are. I was fine. You didn't need to come to my
rescue again."

His green gaze seemed to shoot fire as it locked onto
mine, and everything but the rise and fall of his chest stilled.
"You think you were *fine*? They thought you were a fucking
card counter, Eden, working with a partner. Do you know

what casinos do with card counters? Do you think they really just wanted to take you into some little back office to *chat*? They could've killed you."

"This isn't a freaking movie. No one was going to do anything to me." To myself, I added, *especially once I dropped my father's name*. Only someone with a death wish would dare touch me.

"Yeah, you're right. No one was going to do a god-damned thing to you because I wouldn't let them."

Frustration overwhelmed the other emotions fighting for precedence. "I don't need you to save me every time, Bishop! How the hell am I ever supposed to learn to stand on my own two feet and save myself if you're always going to rush to the rescue? I don't need a babysitter. I need to learn to be self-sufficient, and if no one in my entire freaking life will give me the chance, then how am I ever going to get there?"

Bishop jerked back like I'd slapped him. "What the hell kind of man would I be if I didn't step in when shit goes sideways? You want me to back away and let you put yourself at risk? No fucking way. I can't do that. I won't do that."

"Then you're going to suffocate me." My words fell like heavy boulders between us.

"Is that what you think I'm doing? Trying to suffocate you? Fuck, Eden. All I want is to keep you safe so I don't lose you like I've lost damn near every other person in my life who fucking mattered!"

He stalked closer to me, and I backed away instinctively until my butt pressed against the cabinets in the tiny kitchen.

"I get that you need to prove that you can handle yourself. I get it. I really fucking do. But tonight was not the night to try. Those people aren't a joke. They don't believe in a slap on the wrist. They break fingers. Hands. Arms. Kneecaps. Legs. They fucking kill people who try to steal from them."

Intellectually, I knew that he was right. But what he didn't understand was that in *that* world, I was untouchable. I wanted to explain. I wanted to tell him exactly why he didn't need to worry about me tonight. The words were there on my tongue, but I couldn't get them out because he kept going.

His palms pressed down on either side of the countertop and he leaned over me. "I would die before I'd let them hurt you. Don't take that away from me, Eden. Don't tell me I can't protect you."

The anger and frustration that had been roiling within me drained away. How could I possibly stay mad at the man when he wasn't trying to cage me?

"You have to know that sometimes I can handle myself, even if you don't believe me. I promise I'm not a fragile little princess. I'm not going to break."

The intensity burning in his eyes turned molten. "I know you're not a fragile little princess. You're fucking resilient. I see it every time I look at you. If I thought you were going to break, I wouldn't do this."

His hand came off the counter and buried in my hair, tugging my head back before his lips crashed down onto mine. Every bit of emotion that had been flying between us burst into heat. I grabbed his shoulders, giving back as good as I got. I wanted his kiss, wanted him to take me right here, against my counter.

Bishop must have read my mind, because he dropped his hand from my hair and reached for my thigh, lifting it and wrapping it around his waist before shoving my dress up.

"You want me to prove that I don't think I'll break you? I'll take what I want and make you scream for me."

"Yes, yes." I moaned against his lips, tugging his shirt away from his shoulders, and his hand slid between my legs. He tugged my panties aside.

"Fuck, cupcake. You're so goddamned wet. Fighting with me makes you want to fuck, doesn't it?"

The heat of a blush burned over my cheeks, but I wasn't about to deny it. "Everything about you makes me want to fuck."

The words felt foreign coming out of my mouth, even though they were the absolute truth.

"Naughty little girl. You fucking love when I tell you what I'm going to do to you, don't you?"

I moaned a response and it spurred him on.

"Shouldn't have worn panties tonight. I'm gonna rip them off and turn you around and bend you over the counter. You're not going to move your hands while I drop to my knees and eat this sweet pussy until you scream. I'm not going to fuck you until you're begging for my cock with every breath. When I take you, I'm not holding back. You're going to feel me tomorrow with every step. If you're a really fucking good girl, I'm going to play with that virgin asshole so you're one step closer to taking my cock there. Because you're mine, Eden. I'm going to own every fucking inch of you."

My entire body went up in flames, and he did exactly what he promised.

The elastic of my panties snapped, and Bishop pulled my leg from his hip and spun me around.

I grasped for any kind of purchase, but my palms found nothing on the countertop to anchor me against the waves of anticipation rolling through me. My skirt was flipped up over my ass, and the cooler air of the room provided a counterpoint to the heat of my body. Bishop's big hands covered my ass as he lowered himself to his knees.

I only had a fraction of a moment to feel a shred of embarrassment that he must have been staring right at my ass as he spread my legs, but given his promises about what he'd do if I were *a really fucking good girl*, I couldn't help but shiver.

His mouth covered me from behind as he pressed his face between my legs, his tongue thrusting into me. My clit throbbed and ached for more until he slipped a hand around to circle it and tease me.

Moans slipped from my mouth, and Bishop growled his approval between my legs in a way that I felt all the way to the pleasure centers in my brain. They were blaring with color, and I swear whatever he did next had black spots invading my vision.

"Bishop!"

His name was ripped from my throat on a hoarse cry, but he didn't slow. He pushed harder, finally making contact with my clit as an orgasm barreled down on me and shoved me toward the edge.

"Please, please." I didn't care that I was begging, and when the orgasm hit, I dropped my forehead to the counter and screamed.

Still, he didn't slow. His movements sped up, and Bishop dragged another orgasm from my body until I was shaking and doubted the ability of my legs to hold me up.

"You ready to beg for my cock, cupcake? You want me to give you more?"

I nodded.

"I need the words, Eden. I want to hear it. I want you to

tell me just how fucking bad you need it."

"Please, I need it. I want it."

"Not good enough, baby."

Desperation rode me and I would have said anything, but words eluded me. "Please, I want you."

"What do you want?"

"Your cock," I said on a moan.

He pressed two thick fingers into me, and my body wept with the temporary relief.

"Yes!"

"In this tight little cunt?"

"Yes!"

"You gonna let me have it any way I want it?"

It seemed my vocabulary had diminished to only one word. The only one that mattered.

"Yes!"

"You gonna let me protect it and keep it safe so I can make you scream like this every night?"

Again, only one answer would work. "Yes."

"Good, because you don't have a fucking choice anymore, Eden. You're mine. I don't have much, but what's mine I keep. I protect. I don't ever let it go."

"Please."

"You on the pill? I want you bare. Nothing between us anymore."

"IUD. I'm covered. Hurry."

My words were pleas, but I knew I wouldn't have to wait much longer because Bishop stood behind me and the hiss of his zipper was the best sound I'd ever heard.

"I've never fucked anyone without protection. I've never wanted to. But you crashed into my life and changed every goddamned thing."

Bishop notched the thick head of his cock against my opening and then leaned over me, covering my hands and interlocking our fingers.

He pushed inside with one solid stroke. I expected him to pull out and slide in again and again, but he stilled. "I've been waiting for you my whole fucking life, and I didn't have a clue."

"I know. I know."

"I don't want to let you go, but I know you want my fingers on the hungry clit of yours, don't you?"

I nodded. "I just want you."

"And I want you to scream and squeeze the fuck out of my cock when you come."

He released one hand and swept my hair over my shoulder and pressed his lips to the curve of my neck before trading it for his teeth. His fingers found my clit as the sharp sensation registered in my brain, and he began to move.

Decadent pain and overwhelming pleasure warred within me as he thrust and retreated, slamming against my G-spot. I screamed his name as my inner muscles spasmed.

Over and over, he fucked into me, delivering more pleasure than I thought possible.

"Fucking perfect," Bishop growled into my ear, finally slowing. "So fucking perfect."

He readjusted his grip, one hand coming around my hip to glide his fingers over my clit as the other thumb slid between my legs, gathering up my slickness. My overwhelmed brain tried to keep up with his movements, but didn't compute.

Not until I felt that same thumb reposition itself right over my ass. All the nerve endings blared to life, and if it was even possible at this point, my pussy got wetter.

"Fuck, baby. You like that. My sweet naughty little cup-cake wants my finger in her ass."

He pressed against me, and another orgasm burst just before Bishop's roar filled the kitchen.

He continued to thrust, to press, to devastate, for a few more moments before he collapsed over my back, his arm holding us both up.

For long minutes, neither of us moved.

Before he pulled out of me, Bishop growled one more word into my ear. "Mine."

Bishop

I'D NEVER COME SO FUCKING HARD IN MY ENTIRE LIFE. Bare. Inside Eden. The feeling was primal, and I wanted to end every night buried inside her before I tucked her into my side and we both passed out from exhaustion.

I wanted to wake up every morning by slipping inside that sweet pussy so the first thing she felt in the morning was how hard I could make her come.

Before, that was just a fantasy. Now, I wanted to make it a reality. I carried Eden to her bed and laid her down before heading into her bathroom to find a washcloth to clean her up. She tried to sit up when I returned, but I pressed her back down.

"I'm taking care of you. Let me."

She didn't protest, and I wondered how embarrassed she must be. She'd have to get used to it. Besides, I loved seeing the hot pink color rise in her cheeks. The dim light shining from the bathroom spilled onto her, and I wondered how far

I could get that color to spread.

"You like when I play with your ass, don't you?"

There it went. Almost immediately, rising higher and diving lower. Her gaze darted away before returning to mine.

"Maybe."

"You like it. You want it. Makes you feel naughty, doesn't it? That forbidden thrill? Knowing I'm going to take you there and you're gonna beg for it?"

The blush kept going.

"You gotta know it makes me harder than a fucking rock to even think about it. Knowing that no one has ever touched you there, and I'm the one who's going to corrupt you?"

I could tell she fought the urge to look away, but my girl was tougher than that.

"You can admit it. You can like it."

"I can't help it. I like everything you do to me."

The smile that crossed my face had to be the epitome of *smug son of a bitch*. "I'll never give you anything but pleasure. Fucking promise." I returned to the bathroom and finished my own cleanup before turning off the light and coming back to her bed.

Wrapping myself around her, I tucked my cock between her ass cheeks. Perfect fucking place to sleep. She shifted back against me, and I wrapped an arm around her and pressed a kiss to her hair.

"Goodnight, cupcake."

Her breathing had already evened out, and I knew she was under. It didn't stop me from saying the words.

"Fucking love you, Eden."

Eden

THE NEXT MORNING, I WOKE UP WITH A MOAN AS Bishop's hard cock pressed into me from behind.

Full.

So fucking full.

His fingers played over my clit like he knew every move that would take me higher and higher until I screamed.

"Need more. Deeper." He pulled us both up so I was on my knees, my ass in the air, and he pounded into me, never letting up on my clit.

My pillow muffled the screams as I came.

Bishop climaxed with a yell and his cock pulsed as he poured into me.

Morning sex was a revelation. Even after I collapsed back onto the bed in an ungraceful pile, Bishop cleaned me up again, and this time I couldn't summon the energy to be embarrassed. My body had apparently decided that it was his and he could do whatever he wanted with it. I couldn't find any rational reason to disagree with this new development.

When he returned, he pressed a kiss to my shoulder. "We slept in, babe. What time do you have to work today?"

This yanked me from my happy post-orgasm state, and I rolled out of bed. "It's Saturday, right? Which means noon. What time is it?"

"Eleven fifteen. You got time."

"Shit!" All relaxation evaporated. "I need to shower and get dressed."

"I'll take you. We can shower together."

I turned around and looked at him. "Oh no. If we're going to shower together, I'm definitely going to be late. I've never had shower sex, so I'm not rushing through the first time."

Bishop's laugh, something I didn't hear nearly enough, echoed off the walls of my bedroom.

"Deal. I'll shower at home. You do your thing."

Forty minutes later, I walked in the door of Your Favorite Hole after standing on the sidewalk and kissing Bishop for a solid five minutes. I think three people told us to get a room.

Fabienne was behind the counter, and Asha pumped her fist in the air when she saw me. "Thank Christ. I need to go home and sleep. This shift has been killer." She covered her mouth with a yawn.

Fabienne shook her head at the girl. "You've been dragging ass all day, so don't pretend like you worked all that hard."

"I'm here; you can get back to bed."

Both women looked at me, and Fabienne jerked her

head toward the front window.

"You totally got laid this morning, didn't you? I thought you were going for a second round the way he was about to eat you alive on the sidewalk."

Eden pre-last night would have been embarrassed, but the Eden of this morning who had discovered the joys of morning sex, just answered, "Sure did. And it was fabulous."

Asha frowned. "Dammit, I want morning sex. I need to get a man who looks at me like that."

"Don't we all," Fabienne drawled before looking at Asha. "Get out of here. I don't want you dragging ass again tomorrow. You screwed up three orders."

Asha waved her fingers and bolted for the back room to hang up her apron before she slipped out the back door.

After she was gone, Fabienne looked at me. "You know what you're doing with that guy?"

"Probably not, but does anyone ever really know what they're doing with a guy like that?"

"Touché."

Whatever else Fabienne wanted to say about it was forgotten as the door chimed and customers descended.

Six hours later, Fabienne had left and I had two hours on my own before my relief for the night shift showed. Bishop had come in during an unexpected rush, and I'd barely had a second to smile and say hi as I handed him his coffee.

The door chimed again before I could get lost in my thoughts about what was going to happen when my two lives collided, and a familiar face popped in the door.

Delilah.

She looked incredibly amused.

"I don't know what kind of mojo you worked on Bishop, but he actually smiled at customers today." She strolled toward the counter, the petticoats swishing under her dress. "I don't actually want to know, because *eww*, but I wanted to let you know that there's something different about him."

"Can I plead the Fifth? Because I can't . . . I just can't talk about that with you."

The door chimed again and more familiar faces walked in. Charlie, Elle, Yve, Vanessa, and Valentina.

Delilah smiled. "Then it's a good thing I'm getting coffee and bailing so they can get the scoop."

"Are you okay?" Vanessa came toward the counter, ahead of the others. "Because Con and the guys were telling us about last night, and *holy hell*, I would've been freaking out."

Delilah's smile vanished. "What happened?"

Yve filled her in on the details. "Some guy at the casino might've set Eden up and made it look like she was counting cards. Security wanted to drag her off, but the guys wouldn't let her. Bishop busted in and yanked her out of there, and security ran after them."

Delilah blanched. "Bishop went into a casino? On purpose?"

The guilt I'd felt last night about putting him in that position came back with a vengeance. "He didn't need to come to my rescue. I would've been fine. Really, I'm not completely helpless."

"Do you realize what they do to people who they think are counting cards? They will fuck you right up and not ask questions." Delilah's concern sounded a lot like Bishop's, except quieter.

"I wasn't counting cards, so nothing would've happened. I don't even know how. I wouldn't have a clue what to do."

"I hate to say it," Vanessa chimed in, "but I don't think it would've mattered. They were adamant, from what Con told me."

"You could've walked out of there with broken or missing freaking fingers! This is serious shit."

"They wouldn't have dared."

Charlie watched me, and even though the other five looked like they thought I was living in Denial Land, Charlie seemed to notice more.

"Have you figured out how long you're staying in town?" she asked.

I shrugged. "As long as I can. I don't have a solid plan."

"Why is that?" Delilah's tone was skeptical. "Because if you're going to jet out of here and break Bishop's freaking heart, we're going to have a serious bone to pick."

Did she really think I had the power to do that? I needed to turn this conversation away to something else before I ended up telling them everything. The need to tell the truth was so heavy on my conscience that I could barely hold it back anymore.

"I doubt Bishop would let her go anywhere," Yve drawled. "I know what *possessive man in overdrive* looks like, and he's got it stamped all over him."

Considering she was married to the very powerful, very notorious billionaire Lucas Titan, I assumed Yve probably knew what she was talking about.

Vanessa nodded her agreement. "Caveman mode has been activated. She's screwed."

This wasn't news to me, and the feelings I'd been wrestling with for the last eighteen hours came to the surface again.

"How do you deal with that? I'm not fragile. I need to be able to stand on my own two feet. I don't always need him coming to my rescue and then getting pissed when I tell him I can take care of myself."

All the women laughed at me, except for Delilah, who just smiled and shook her head.

"Good luck with that one," Valentina offered. "Rix would've killed anyone who tried to hurt me. Actually, he did, but that's a long story. That kind of alpha instinct isn't something you can turn off."

Elle pointed at her. "You were the one who didn't want an alpha. I believe I remember you saying that you wanted a beta. Someone to watch *Masterpiece Theatre* with and drink wine." Elle's laughing eyes cut to me. "And she ended up with a crazy badass motherfucker who wouldn't drink wine if Jesus himself made it from water."

Valentina rolled her eyes at Elle. "I was drunk and clearly misguided." She turned her attention back to me. "This is what I learned, and you can take it or leave it. But if you want the guy, you get the whole package. There's no picking and choosing between the parts you like and the parts that make you want to rip your hair out. If he's alpha, he's always going to be alpha. You can't turn that off. You can't tell him not to protect you, because it would be going against every instinct he's got."

"She speaks the truth," Yve said. "But if you've got demons you need to fight on your own, that's something you need to come out with and tell him. Men, despite our every wish and hope, can't read our minds. That said, even if you want to prove that you can handle yourself, there are times when it's okay to break. You can lean on someone and not be weak. Believe me when I tell you that I didn't need any man to take care of me, and it took me a hell of a lot to realize accepting help when it was offered didn't make me less. It just meant I had more in my life."

I soaked up Yve's words. *It just meant I had more . . .*

"But you were a badass bitch from day one. The fact that Lucas got through your walls was a freaking miracle." This came from Charlie.

"I've never been a badass bitch," I said without thinking. "I've never had the chance. I've been shielded from everything, and this was my one chance to experience life without watching it go by while someone stood in front of me to protect me from it." As soon as the words were out, I knew they were a mistake. All the women looked at me.

"You want to elaborate on that?" Delilah asked.

Charlie shook her head. "You don't have to."

I chose my next words much more carefully. "Do you know what it's like to live in a protective bubble?"

Charlie, Vanessa, and Valentina all nodded.

"Then you get that when you're in the bubble, all you want is to get out. I can't go back in the bubble. I need freedom."

"Then tell him," Valentina said. "Tell him exactly what you need, and if he can't give it to you, then you know you've got a choice."

Delilah kept quiet through this exchange, until she said, "He wants to keep you safe, and he's got reasons, but there's no way he'd want you to be unhappy. There's gotta be balance."

She was right. Balance was what I needed and hadn't found.

"So, what do I do?"

"Talk to him." This came as a chorus from the women.

"But before that, we all need coffee," Yve said.

I laughed and nodded. "Deal. Give me your orders and I'll get them going."

Bishop

ON CAME OUT OF THE BACK ROOM AS I SENT MY client on his way. "Van come back with my coffee yet?"

"She was here?"

"Nah, she went next door with the women to talk to Eden, but she was supposed to bring me back coffee when they were done."

"What do you mean, they went next door to talk to Eden?"

"They were worried about her after last night. Wanted to make sure she wasn't freaking about what happened."

"I took care of it."

Con shrugged. "You know women. They gotta do things their own way. Your girl has been adopted into the crew whether you like it or not."

I did like it, actually. The more ties Eden had holding her here, the less likely she was to leave. Even though I hadn't

303

pushed it lately, it drove me fucking nuts that she didn't have any kind of long-term plan. I had lived that life. Staying in a place for as long as it worked, and then moving on when it didn't.

With no ties, it was easy. I didn't want leaving to be easy for Eden.

"So, basically, they're over there meddling."

"Basically. On the upside, you might learn something from it."

"Oh yeah, like what?"

"Like why she was so fucking unconcerned about the idea of being dragged off into a back room at a casino. I know she's naive and shit, but that should've scared the hell out of her."

I'd been stewing over that all day. Eden wasn't stupid. She could recognize when she was in over her head, even if she was hell-bent on pretending she could get out of it herself.

"I don't have an answer for that."

"You want me to call my people and start digging around to see what we can find out about her?"

The offer hung between us, and even though I wanted to say yes, I was waiting for Eden to come clean with whatever it was she was running from by herself. I wanted that. I needed that from her.

"Not yet. I'm gonna give it some more time."

Con shrugged. "Offer's on the table if you want it."

"Thanks, man."

The front door whooshed open and Delilah and Vanessa came inside, each carrying two cups of coffee. "Charlie said hi, but she was catching a ride with Elle, Yve, and Valentina, so she couldn't deliver that herself."

"You really did interrogate her with the whole crew, huh?" I asked, my gaze on Vanessa and Delilah, wondering who was the instigator behind this.

"We just wanted to make sure she was okay. She is."

"And?"

"And nothing."

"Bullshit, princess. We all know you got way more than that out of her." Con raised an eyebrow at his woman, and I turned the same look on my sister.

"You're gonna have to talk to her."

"Thanks for the inside scoop, ladies."

Con laughed. "Stubborn, both of you." He accepted the coffee that Vanessa finally handed over and sipped. "But you got me the good shit, so I'm not complaining right now."

"You better not complain. You like me stubborn." She smiled up at him, and I wanted the easiness they shared.

Someday, I'd have that with Eden, but we had a hell of a lot to air out before we got there. It was kind of hard to push forward when we were both keeping so many fucking secrets.

I almost told her everything last night. I came close. But my secrets were tied up with the shame I carried. I hated that I'd been such a fucking selfish punk kid who thought he knew every goddamned thing. And then the fact that I'd run from it? Not exactly something I was proud of.

It occurred to me, while Vanessa and Con and Delilah shot the shit, that maybe whatever Eden wasn't saying was the shit she wasn't proud of. I wandered back to my room and pulled out equipment to sterilize before my next appointment.

Before Con and Vanessa left, Vanessa stuck her head in. "I'm not saying anything you probably don't already know, but I think Eden's dying to stretch her wings, and if you don't give her that chance, she's going to be miserable."

"I got that from her last night."

"I'm not trying to get in the middle of it, but I get where she's coming from. You can give her a world she never knew existed and still keep her safe while you do it."

I nodded. "She say anything else I need to know?"

Vanessa smiled. "You'll figure it out."

"Come on, princess," Con called. "Let's get out of here before the rain comes and we both get soaked on that bike."

"See you around, Bish. Good luck." She winked at me.

Delilah stepped into the doorway as soon as the back door closed. "You sure you know what you're doing with her?"

"Figuring it out as I go."

"You might want to figure it out faster."

Eden

THE MAN CAME IN YOUR FAVORITE HOLE twenty minutes before the end of my shift, his dark hoodie pulled up and his hands in his pockets.

Every instinct I had said something wasn't right with him. I fingered my phone in the pocket of my apron, the urge to call Bishop screaming at me.

But I was the one determined to stand my ground and take care of myself.

"Can I get you something?"

He looked up at me, and I could have sworn I'd seen him before. Somewhere. But before I could figure out where, he charged toward the counter.

"Give me all the money. Every fucking dime."

Fear. Honest-to-God fear ripped through me. It multiplied when he pulled out a gun.

Oh my God. Who the hell holds up a donut shop?

I raised my hands in the air like any normal person

would who had a gun pointed at them. "Okay. Okay. You can have it."

"Open the fucking drawer."

I lowered my shaking hands and turned the key, then pressed the button to release the cash drawer. The gun wavered in the air as I pulled each stack of cash from its slot and piled it on the counter.

"Don't put it on the fucking counter, put it in a god-damned bag. What the fuck is your problem, bitch!"

I wanted to yell that I'd never freaking been robbed before so I had no idea what the protocol was, but I kept it in. After yanking a bag from underneath the counter, I stuffed the money inside.

The chime on the door sounded, and both our heads whipped toward the door.

Oh shit. Oh shit. Oh shit. A visibly pregnant woman walked inside holding the hand of a toddler.

"I want all the chocolate ones," the little boy said.

The woman looked up and saw the man and the gun and froze for a split second before turning to drop to her knees and shield the boy with her body. A uniformed cop walked by the front window, and the woman screamed for help.

The cop froze and tilted his head to see inside. The moment he saw the gun, he spoke into the radio on his shoulder and drew his weapon.

"Fuck. Fuck. Fuck," the man bit out as he grabbed the bag. "Not fucking supposed to go like this." He turned the gun on me. "Where's the back door?"

I pointed to the hallway as the wail of police sirens became audible from outside and the cop pushed open the front door. The man with the gun shoved the paper bag of money inside his coat and fired off three shots at the front windows. Glass shattered everywhere, and the woman screamed before shoving her son toward the wall and curling her body around him.

The man ran to the back hallway and disappeared out the door as the front flew open again and the cop charged inside.

"He went out the back," I yelled. The cop nodded and gave chase.

The front door slammed open again and I expected more cops, or even Bishop coming from next door, but instead I saw Angelo.

Angelo?

"Come on, E, we gotta get out of here. Now. Hurry. More cops are coming, and they're going to have all sorts of fucking questions for you that you can't answer. They'll arrest you, and I can't let that happen."

What the hell is he doing here? Confused, I stared at him. The normal suit I was used to seeing him wear had been traded for jeans and a leather jacket.

"How—"

"Come on, we ain't got time for questions. We gotta go."

My brain tried to make sense of what he was saying, but between being robbed at gunpoint and having my past show up, I stood frozen behind the counter.

"Eden, now! Your dad would fucking kill you if you talked to the cops."

The sirens grew louder as Angelo hustled behind the counter to grab me by the arm and drag me toward the back door where the man and the cop had run.

"I have to make sure she's okay!" I tugged at his arm, worry for the pregnant woman struggling to her feet shooting through me.

"You need to worry about your fucking self. We're going."

"No, I'm not going anywhere. You go. I'll be fine."

"Don't make me hurt you, Eden. I don't want to hurt you."

I dragged my attention away from the woman to Angelo.
Hurt me? Why would he . . .

I saw something different in Angelo's eyes. The easy camaraderie I remembered was gone, and in its place was crazy desperation.

"Let me go!"

Angelo's fist shot out and slammed into my jaw. The pain didn't even have a chance to register before everything went black.

Bishop

GUNSHOTS. BREAKING GLASS. SCREAMS. I COULD hear everything through the wall of Voodoo Ink, and it was coming from Your Favorite Hole. I was out of my seat, tossing my tattoo machine on the counter and gone without saying a word to my client.

I pushed through the door in time to catch a glimpse of a man carrying someone out the back. A woman hunched over a little boy in the front, and sirens grew louder and louder. Scanning the store, I saw no sign of Eden.

The woman rose on shaky legs, gathering the boy against her chest. She pointed to the back door.

"A man took the girl who worked here. Out the back."

Fuck.

I ran for the back door and shoved it open just in time to see a man carrying Eden round the corner and leave the alley. Her arm flopped lifelessly, and her head lolled backward in his hold.

"Stop right fucking there!"

I ran toward the man, my adrenaline pumping overtime. I reached the end of the alley and raced left. He was shoving her into the backseat of a Lincoln. She was clearly unconscious.

"Do not fucking move!"

He looked up at me for only a beat before slamming the back door and jumping in the front. I was twenty feet away when he gunned the engine and tore out into the street, narrowly missing sideswiping a cab.

I gotta get my bike. Follow them. I memorized the license plate number and grabbed my phone as I ran back to the alley.

"What up, man?" Con asked.

Between heaving breaths, I told him. "Find everything you can on Eden. And get your people to run this plate." I rattled off the number before I could forget it. "Someone just grabbed her out of the donut shop and shoved her in a car. She didn't look conscious."

"You're fucking kidding me."

"No. Hurry. I'm grabbing my bike. I'm going to try to follow them. Call me when you get anything."

I pushed open the back door to Voodoo and Delilah was standing at the front. "What the hell just happened? Cops just swarmed Your Favorite Hole. They wouldn't let me go in."

"Eden's gone. Someone took her. I'm going after him." I ducked into the break room and grabbed my keys off the desk, not giving a single shit about the person still sitting in my chair. Delilah could deal with them.

I ran out into the alley, intent on getting on my bike as fast as fucking possible, but three cops with drawn weapons stopped me in my tracks.

"Stop right there!" one officer yelled. "Who the fuck are you?"

"I work at the tattoo shop, and some asshole just grabbed my girlfriend and shoved her in a car. Get the hell out of my way so I can go after them."

"No way, man. We're questioning everyone. You're staying right here."

Rage roiled in my gut. "Did you not fucking hear me? Someone just grabbed my girlfriend and shoved her in the back of a car and took off. If you're not going to go after him, I sure as shit am."

"Come with us. Inside."

Gritting my teeth at every second I was losing, I realized I didn't have much choice unless I wanted to ruin my ink with the new addition of bullet holes.

The woman with the toddler was sitting in one of the chairs, rocking the boy back and forth. She looked up when she saw me.

"Did you get her?"

I shook my head, and the cop started asking her questions.

"Can you confirm what this man is telling us? His girlfriend was abducted?"

"Yes. Yes, he tried to get her to go with him and she wouldn't, so he knocked her out and carried her away."

"Now can I fucking go?"

The cop made notes on his little cop notepad as Delilah stepped into the doorway.

"Ma'am, step back," another officer said to her.

"You can use the tattoo shop if you want to clear people out of here. We have room."

The woman stood with her little boy and looked at the officer. "I want to get out of here."

"Fine. We'll move this next door." He looked at me. "Everyone can move next door."

I wanted to knock that fucking look off his face. Every second that slipped by made it less and less likely that I'd find Eden.

"Where is she?" Delilah demanded as I followed the cop out front. "Where the hell is Eden?"

The woman replied before I could. "He said she had to go. She couldn't talk to the cops. Her dad would be mad."

What the hell?

"Ma'am, if you could hold on until we're ready to get your full statement, that'd be helpful."

Delilah led the way into Voodoo, and the cop gave the woman the go-ahead to give her statement, but wouldn't let me out of his sight.

By the time the woman was done, I was more confused than ever, but that didn't change a fucking thing about needing to go after Eden.

"So you're sure she knew him?"

"It seemed like it."

"But he still hit her and carried her out anyway?"

She nodded.

"Something doesn't seem right," the cop said.

"No shit," I interrupted. "I've got the plate number. Call in a BOLO. Get every cop in this city looking for her."

He glared at me, but I rattled the number off anyway and he wrote it down.

The door to Voodoo swung open and another cop came in holding a plastic bag with a purse inside. Eden's purse. I went toward him.

"Can you confirm this belongs to your girlfriend?" he asked me.

"Yes. It's hers."

"Elisha Madden, right? I'll run it and see if we get anything."

I frowned and shook my head. "Eden Madden. Not Elisha."

The officer's brows furrowed. "That's not what the ID says."

"Let me see it."

Rather than telling me to fuck off, the cop slipped on a rubber glove and pulled it from the bag, holding it in front of my face.

"This her?"

The picture was Eden. The last name was right. The first name was not.

What the hell? I pulled out my phone and snapped a picture of it before he realized what I was doing.

"Hey—"

"Like you really fucking care."

"So this isn't her?"

"It's her. But that isn't her first name. It's Eden."

"You sure about that?"

I didn't know what to say in response. Apparently I was fucking wrong about my girlfriend's name.

The cops finished questioning the woman as Fabienne showed up and started making demands about what the hell had happened to her shop.

During the distraction, I called Con. Without a greeting, I launched into what I needed. "I need you to run a different name. Cops found Eden's ID and it's her picture, but the first name is Elisha. I got a picture. I'll send it."

"I'll get him this ASAP, and I'll call you back. You find any trail?"

"Cops wouldn't let me go. They're putting a BOLO on the car. Hoping like fuck they find it."

"Good. That's actually better than you roaming the streets hoping to catch a glimpse. I'll call Rix, and hopefully he can give us the inside word from the cops. We'll find her, Bish."

58

Bishop

I'D CRUISED FOR AN HOUR ON MY BIKE LOOKING FOR any sign of the Lincoln and had found nothing. According to Rix, the cops were getting hits on the BOLO, but none of them were the right car. Something had to break soon.

My phone rang and I grabbed it. *Con.*

"You got answers?" I demanded.

"Not all of them. But I can tell you one thing for sure. My guy ran the license, and even though it's a good fake, it's definitely a fake. He can't find an Elisha Madden or an Eden Madden. He's digging further. Going to see if we can figure out where it came from."

"New York City. That's where she came from."

"That's what I told him, but there are a lot of people who make fake IDs in that city."

"What about the Lincoln?"

"Rented by one Angelo Francetti over a week ago. For all

317

we know, he could've stolen it."

"Did you give the name to your guy?"

"Still waiting to hear back on him. I'll let you know as soon as I hear."

I hung up, and Delilah watched me lower my phone back to the counter. "Something's not right here. Something's really not fucking right."

"I know."

I rode the streets again for another hour and came back to Voodoo when I didn't have a fucking clue where else to go.

She was gone.

What the hell is her real name? Fake ID? Why?

It seemed the woman I'd fallen for was a hell of a lot better at keeping secrets than I was. I'd gone round and round with my emotions. Anger that she hadn't told me. Concern that whatever she was running from caught up with her. Disappointment with every corner I turned that I didn't see her.

I called in every marker I had to find the car, and no one had a clue. Con's contacts were better than mine, so I hoped he'd find out something really fucking soon. Before I lost my goddamned mind.

We closed Voodoo, and Delilah made coffee up in my apartment. She and I sat across the table from each other, both staring at the phone between us, waiting for it to ring.

The pounding of someone running up the stairs from the downstairs shop to my apartment had me whipping my head toward the door.

Only Con had a key besides me or Delilah, so it was no surprise when he threw the door open. In his hand was a pile of papers.

"What do you have?" I demanded.

"More than I expected, that's for fucking sure."

He tossed the stack of papers on the counter, and I grabbed the top one.

Angelo Francetti had a mugshot and a rap sheet. One part stood out more than anything else.

Soldier for the Casso crime family.

Everything inside me went cold. Fucking frozen.

The Casso crime family. Dominic Casso. The head of the fucking mob. The reason I had no uncle, no cousin, and had been running for ten years.

"What the fuck?"

"Your girl . . . her name is Eden. Eden Mathews. But that's only because she doesn't have her father's name."

I remembered what the lady in the donut shop had told us the guy who took Eden said. That her dad would be mad. I looked up at Con's solemn features and tried to put it together.

"Who the fuck is her father?"

"Dominic Casso."

Ice froze my chest as realization slammed into me.

Delilah sucked in a breath. "Holy fucking shit. Was she here spying on you?"

The possibility hadn't even crossed my mind until the words came out of Delilah's mouth.

"No fucking way."

"Knew you were running from something, but didn't have a clue that was it. Fuck, man. Do we need to get you out of here?" Con asked. "This family is no joke. Even if they're in a tailspin right now because of the Feds, Casso is still as dangerous as ever, according to my contact."

Delilah pushed up from the table. "Con's right. You need

to pack your shit and go. What if they come for you?" Her tone took on a hysterical edge. "This could all be a setup."

I looked at Delilah. "No. No fucking way." I refused to believe it. *How can she be a Casso?* The odds were ridiculous. It couldn't be true.

She put her hands on her hips. "How do you know? Isn't it a little convenient that she ended up here?"

I thought of the sidewalk where I originally found Eden about to be assaulted. "I just know. There's no fucking way. You're sure that's who she is?" I asked Con.

"Yes. No doubt at all. This shit is straight from the FBI database. Casso kept her under wraps, but my guy has a comprehensive file on the whole damn family. Fuck, she has a half brother who's a movie star and one who's a fucking billionaire. You've heard their names before too. Guaranteed. Report says she has no contact with them at all."

I didn't care about her siblings. "So, what the hell happened? Soldier from the family comes to drag her home, but she won't go, so she struggles and he knocks her out and takes her anyway?"

"That would be the best guess I have."

"What else do you have on him? Where would he take her?"

"Not sure. But my guy pulled credit card records, so that should tell us where he was staying. They're in here somewhere. I just printed out the whole pile and came."

All three of us flipped through the pages and scanned for the information.

In my head, I couldn't stop thinking about how Eden had looked as he'd shoved her in the car. So fucking helpless while she was unconscious. The fact that she fought him and didn't want to go with him gave me some hope.

"Where's Casso now? Do we know?"

Con shook his head. "He's under grand-jury investigation. The news has been all over the place, but he's still walking free. Not sure exactly where he's holed up, but the Feds are saying there's been a power struggle and two of the other families are trying to wrestle control."

Was that why Eden was in New Orleans? Out of the way to keep her safe? Fuck, I hated having this many questions and no answers. More than anything, I hated that she hadn't trusted me enough to tell me.

"He was at the Sonesta." Con held up a piece of paper. "Checked in under his real name and everything. He's been there since before Mardi Gras."

While Eden was there.

"What the fuck?" I grabbed my phone and pulled up Leon's contact.

"What up, Bish?"

"You have a guy staying there named Angelo Francetti?"

"Why? What's up?"

"Just check for me, would you?"

I heard clicking computer keys in the background. "Okay. Okay, yeah, I got him. He's still checked in."

"I'm on my way. Get me a key to his room."

"Man, I can't—"

"I'll do your next piece for free. Just get me a fucking key to the guy's room and don't fucking tell anyone."

"Okay. Okay. But if I lose my job over this—"

"We'll worry about that later."

I hung up and looked to Con. "You coming?"

"Fuck, yes."

***

When we got to the Royal Sonesta ten minutes later, Leon slipped a key across the desk in a little cardboard jacket.

"He's in 208. You better not make a fucking racket. I'll lose my job and then you'll be doing all my shit for free."

I grabbed the key. "We'll be quiet." It might be a lie, but it was what Leon needed to hear right now.

Con followed me to the elevator and I punched the button. "We got a plan?" he asked as we stepped into the elevator and the doors closed.

I looked at him. "This ain't no special-forces op. This is smash-and-grab and get my girl."

I'd grabbed my .45 before we left Voodoo, and if I knew Con, he was armed too.

"You carrying?"

"Of course."

"Then we go in quiet and grab her."

With both of us in agreement, we stepped out of the elevator and walked down to room 208. A Do Not Disturb sign hung on the knob. I pulled out the keycard and listened at the door for any noise.

Nothing.

I inserted it into the reader and waited for the light to turn green before moving the handle slowly. When I was ready to push it open, I looked to Con, and he nodded. I shoved the door open and we both drew on the room.

The empty room.

"Bathroom."

I rushed to the open door and checked inside while Con cleared the closet and under the bed.

"Fuck."

"Doesn't look like he planned on leaving."

It wasn't until that moment that I looked around and

took in the contents of the room. Clothes were tossed over the armchair and the bed was unmade. A small printer was set up on the desk connected to a laptop, and photos were spread out across it.

Eden by herself. With Vanessa. With Delilah.

"He had her under surveillance." It was obvious, but I had to say something.

There were pictures of Eden with me, but in every one, my face was blacked out.

"That ain't normal surveillance technique," Con said, pointing at it.

He flipped through the stack of pictures, some where my face had been cut out. It was eerie, seeing that shit. It also told me that the guy didn't seem to be the most balanced.

"This guy doesn't like you much, does he?"

"Fuck him. Let's search the rest of the room."

A ten-minute search turned up a burner phone, three pairs of women's underwear that in my gut I had to guess were Eden's, and a stack of papers that had been shoved into the bottom drawer of the nightstand.

I was thinking of all the ways I wanted to break this fucker into pieces for touching my girl when Con's phone rang. He answered and immediately put it on speaker.

"BOLO turned up the car. It was left at Lakefront Airport. Rent-a-cop called it in. Officers are headed out there now, but chances are if he had a jet, they're long gone."

"Can you get the flight plans for every plane that has left?"

"Might take me a few, but yeah, I can."

"Thanks, man."

"Anything I can do to help, just let me know."

Con hung up and looked to me. "What do you want to

do now?"

"Let's take the laptop, the burner phone, the papers and photos. Anything that could give us something to go on."

"Got it."

Con and I gathered it all up, stuffed it in a dry-cleaning bag, and headed back to Voodoo. My brain was sifting through all the possibilities. If they had a jet, she was long gone. The only place that made sense for them to take her was New York.

But if he was acting under orders, why would he knock her out? I couldn't imagine Daddy would be too fucking happy to have his girl manhandled like that.

When we got back to Voodoo, Delilah had questions too.

"How do we know if he's acting under orders or if he's on his own?"

"That's a good fucking question, but without calling Dom Casso himself or someone in his organization to confirm, there's no way we can know."

I grabbed my phone and kept calling Eden's number. It went straight to voice mail.

Unease laced the blood in my veins. If this was Eden's family coming to collect her, what the hell could I do?

But something about it felt all wrong. The woman from the donut shop said she hadn't wanted to go, which meant I wasn't going to rest until I was sure Eden was safe and happy.

I hadn't come this far only to lose her.

Eden

MY JAW ACHED AND MY HEAD THROBBED. I opened my eyes as someone lowered me into a chair.

I blinked. Not a chair. A seat. On a jet?

Angelo?

"Sorry about that, E. Didn't want to have to hurt you, but you didn't want to cooperate. You should know better. When I tell you to do something, you have to do it. It's for your own safety."

"Where are we?"

"Going home."

"Where did you come from?"

"You should know I wouldn't let you go without making sure you're safe. Now, buckle up. We're leaving."

Even in my pounding head, none of this seemed right. Angelo shouldn't be here. Why did he have a jet on standby? This didn't make sense.

"I can't leave yet. Not like this. I have a life here."

Angelo's normally affable features were hard as he reached down and buckled my belt himself. "You weren't supposed to *have a life* anywhere but New York. This was always temporary. And you don't have a choice. You're leaving."

I was sick of other people making decisions for me. Calling the shots. Telling me what to do.

"No. I'm not going." I grabbed the latch to unbuckle it, but Angelo wrapped a meaty hand around my arm and stopped me.

"You're not going anywhere but exactly where I tell you. That's how it's gonna go from now on."

This wasn't the kind, easygoing Angelo I'd always known. This was someone completely different. All my instincts shouted that I needed to get away from him. I forced myself not to panic.

"Okay. I'll do what you say."

He released his grip on me and stood. "Good. That's how it's gonna go. Nice and easy. You want something to drink? We're taking off in a minute."

I nodded. "Sure."

He turned to the bar and removed a bottle of Fiji water, just like what he always stocked for me in the SUV. Handing it to me, he said, "Drink. Don't want you to get dehydrated on our flight."

I uncapped the water and took a sip. *Does it taste funny? Or am I paranoid?*

I waited for Angelo to turn back to the bar to get himself a drink, and I slipped the latch from my buckle and bolted for the door.

I made it three steps before he tackled me.

"Eden, Eden, Eden. You know better than that." Angelo's words took on a chiding tone. "You're gonna have to take a nice long nap on the way home if you can't behave like a good girl."

He leaned up, but didn't move off me.

My cheek pressed into the carpet, I waited for another chance to move when I felt a sting on my neck and my vision blurred. Angelo stood and I rolled over onto my back, blinking up at him and trying to focus.

"What—"

"Sleep. It'll all make sense soon."

Everything went black just after I realized I'd been drugged.

60 *Bishop*

"WE GOT A FLIGHT PLAN. JET LEFT AT 2030 hours, headed for Teterboro airfield in New Jersey. Manifest lists two passengers, Angelo Francetti and Eden Mathews." Rix delivered the information via Con's phone on speaker.

"At least now I know where the fuck I'm going." It had been the longest four hours of my life waiting for confirmation.

"You can't take on the mob by yourself, man," Rix said, and Con nodded in agreement.

"No way in hell," Delilah chimed in.

"I'm not taking opinions right now."

"Well, that's too fucking bad because we've all got them." Con looked at me from across the table where we'd spread out the pictures and shit from the hotel room. "Titan has a jet, and I'm guessing he'll let us take it, but he's going to want to go with. He's like that. Lord'll want in. Simon will fucking fly the thing if we can't get Titan's regular pilot. You've got a crew whether you want one or not."

"I'm going." This came from Rix. "If Hennessy is sober, we might be able to get him on board."

"I'll call Titan. Plan to meet at the airstrip in sixty minutes unless you hear otherwise."

Con hung up the phone and looked at me. "There's no way in hell we're sending you into this without backup. Besides, if Dom Casso tries to kill you, we'll just use Titan as a human shield. No one would dare shoot that cocky son of a bitch because he's got more money than God. Definitely more money than the mob."

"What about me?" Delilah stood, her arms crossed.

"No fucking way. I'm not taking a chance that I could lose you too. You're staying. Hold down the fort."

"You know I don't like it."

I wrapped an arm around her and pulled her into my chest. "But you'll deal because you're the best fucking sister a guy could ask for."

"You're such a dick sometimes."

"Most of the time."

"If you two are done with sibling-bonding time, I'm calling the cavalry and we're going in armed to the teeth."

It might not have been the plan I intended, but that was the plan we were going with.

An hour later, Titan led the way up the stairs to his jet, and I followed behind with Con, Lord, and Rix. Simon was already in the cockpit finishing the preflight check. Hennessy was MIA, which wasn't anything new since he'd turned in his badge and left the NOPD.

Lord, Con, and Rix dropped their duffel bags on the floor of the cabin and Titan laughed. "You'd think we were going to stage a coup. Anyone feel like becoming the new leader of Cuba?"

"Only you, Titan. Only you."

Con looked to me. "You want to give your girl one more call before we take off? Try her cell?"

I'd been trying it every five minutes for the last hour and hadn't gotten an answer. I tried it one more time.

Straight to voice mail.

"Let's go."

Titan studied us. "Then buckle your fucking seat belts, boys, because this flight is taking off."

Eden

WHEN I WOKE, MY HEAD THROBBED AND MY mouth felt like I'd swallowed a bag of cotton balls. I wasn't in the jet anymore; instead, I was in a small room I didn't recognize. I rolled over and swung my legs over the side of the bed and stood, holding the edge of the mattress until the urge to puke passed.

Where am I?

The furniture was dark wood and the linens were gray and navy, masculine colors. The shades were drawn, and the only light in the room came from a small lamp on the bureau. The glow cast a circle of light on framed pictures, and I moved toward them, hoping they'd give me a clue about where I was.

But all they did was confuse me more.

They were all pictures of me. In one, I recognized a dress I hadn't worn since dinner after my college graduation. I remembered because Dom had taken me out to celebrate, one of the rare times we'd had a father-daughter moment in the last decade. Another picture was from only a few days before I left New York as I was leaving work. Finally, it was the last one that scared the ever-loving crap out of me. I was naked. In my bed. My vibrator in my hand and my eyes squeezed closed as I orgasmed.

I wanted to throw up, and it had nothing to do with my aching head.

Angelo.

How? And why? He'd always been more kind and personable than any of my other babysitters, but everything seemed to point to it being a front for something much scarier.

He kidnapped me. Hit me. Drugged me.

None of that seemed like the guy I thought I knew.

And now he has a picture of me at my most intimate moment? Shivers of revulsion tore through me. Any sense of security and privacy I had was destroyed.

But why?

I knocked the frame facedown on the bureau so I didn't have to look at the picture. I wanted to take it out and tear it up, but I had to focus. I had to escape. It was up to me now.

I rushed to the door and yanked on the handle.

Locked.

I spun and headed for the window, but didn't make it more than a few steps before the door swung open.

"I saw you were awake. You like our room? I thought you might. You don't need all that girly shit like you have at home. That's not who you really are." A smug smile stretched across Angelo's face.

"Where am I? Where's my father?"

"You don't need to worry about anything, Eden. I got

you covered. This is our new place. No one's going to bother us here. You slept longer than I thought, though. It's almost time for breakfast."

"You said you were bringing me home. I want to go home!" I was trying to hold on to my sanity and not lose it in hysterics, but Angelo's crazy talk was making it hard.

"You are home." He emphasized every word. "This is where you're going to be from now on. I've been working up to this for a long time. All your favorite stuff is in the bathroom. I bought you new clothes too."

Working up to this for a long time?

I studied Angelo's expression, trying to pinpoint what the difference was. Instead of deferential, he was cocky and assertive.

I gestured to the dresser and demanded, "How did you get that picture?"

He didn't even ask which one I was talking about. "From the cameras," he said as though it were obvious. There wasn't a hint of remorse either.

"Cameras?" My brain was having trouble computing.

"Yeah. How did you expect me to keep you safe when I wasn't around if I didn't know what was happening? You never had to worry about anything, Eden. I was always there for you. You were never alone."

Disgust blew through me. "You watched me?"

He nodded. "You can't pretend you didn't know. You put on shows just for me. I know you did."

I wanted to throw up at the thought of him watching that, of seeing me so exposed. My stomach twisted and threatened to rebel.

"How could you?"

Angelo shrugged. "I just wanted to keep you safe. I had

to be able to see everything. But now we can be together all the time, and I'll never let anyone get to you."

"What are you talking about?"

He was crazy. I'd never seen it before, but I could see it now.

His swarthy skin creased around his dark eyes as a smile spread over his face. "We're gonna be together. Forever."

I knew I had to be careful when dealing with someone this unbalanced, but it wasn't like I had any clue how that worked. I wanted to scream that I was with Bishop and I loved him, but I was afraid it might push Angelo over the edge.

But apparently I didn't have to bring up Bishop because Angelo was way ahead of me.

"I know you think that guy was the one for you, because he kept saving you. But that was supposed to be me. I didn't make that shit happen so someone else could rush in and save the day. That wasn't how it was supposed to work. You were supposed to realize how much you needed me. How only I can keep you safe. He doesn't know anything about you. He can't take care of you and love you like I do."

Love? I barely held back the bile in my throat. Angelo didn't love me; he was a freaking paid stalker.

"What shit are you talking about?"

"In New Orleans. The guy I paid to drug you at the bar. The tour guide I told to leave you at the cemetery. My buddies at the casino. You were supposed to realize you needed me, but you let that son of a bitch help you instead. He'll never love you like I do."

An icy-cold chill engulfed me when Angelo's words sank in. Those things weren't accidents. It wasn't just me not being able to handle myself. I'd been set up. *And dammit, I'd survived and thrived against the deck he'd stacked.* It wasn't my naïveté; it was Angelo the whole time.

He was fucking crazy.

"Where's Dom? Does he know I'm here? Did you tell him I'm back?" I had to assume I was in New York, because I didn't have any other guesses.

"Dom is busy taking care of Dom like he always does. He's never had time for you, but I do."

Another direct strike to the heart. It made me think of all the times that Angelo had hammered home how much Dom didn't care about me. Was that classic behavior of a crazy person? Trying to isolate me from my family?

"What about Vincent? He told me I couldn't come back until I got word from that number. I never got word."

"Vincent let me decide. Dom didn't have anything to say about it."

"I need to talk to Dom."

Angelo's features hardened. "You don't need Dom. You only need me."

"I need to talk to Dom," I repeated.

"I said *no*. You're going to have to learn to follow my directions, Eden. That's the only way we're going to be happy and keep you safe. No one loves you like I do. It's going to be fine as soon as you see that."

Nothing about this situation was fine. Angelo was unhinged, and I was all alone unless I could reason with him.

I decided to try a different angle. "But my dad will be happy that you've kept me safe, so don't you think you should tell him?"

"He'll be mad because he wanted you in a safe house and Vincent didn't follow orders. He sent you away so I could watch out for you. I needed you to get your adventure out of your system before we settled down."

Then what I'd gathered from the accidental voice mail made sense. Dom had been mad that Vincent had taken liberty with his orders. That meant Dom didn't want me out of the city. But the rest of what Angelo was saying didn't make sense either.

"Out of my system?"

"Yeah, I knew you wouldn't be happy until you got a chance to see some of the world. But you had to learn that it wasn't safe. You don't listen so good, so I had to show you. But that dick kept getting in the way. It worked out in the end, because now you know that he can't keep you safe like I can. Only me."

Which meant the robbery hadn't been random either. Angelo had set me up on every level. Made me doubt myself and my ability to take care of myself. As soon as I talked my way out of this, I had a lot to think about. But first, I had to get away from Angelo.

"I'm safe now, so there's no reason for me to stay here, right?"

"You're not leaving until I say you can. That's how this goes now. Are you hungry? I'm gonna get us some breakfast. You'll feel better after you've had food. Take a shower and get dressed in something pretty for me."

My heart hammered as he came closer. His overpowering spicy cologne filled my nostrils as he leaned down to brush his lips across my temple. My skin crawled where he came into contact.

"I can't wait to watch you come with my cock buried inside you. I'll show you what it means to be with a real man. Your man." He stood tall, his six-foot height dwarfing me. "I'm gonna give it to you so good you forget you've ever had another dick. I'm gonna blow my load all over your tits so you'll remember who you belong to. We'll call the doctor and get that IUD out so we can start our family. I can't wait to see you fat with my kid. Knowing I put it in your belly will keep my cock hard all the time. Just wait, Eden. Life is gonna be so fucking good."

Chills rippled over me because he meant every single word. He pressed another kiss to my head before he turned and left the room.

Oh my God. I had to get out of there. There was no way in hell I was going to let Angelo have the chance to rape me. And it would be rape, because I'd never let him touch me willingly.

I wanted a chance to save myself? Well, I guess the universe decided to make it count.

I tore through the room, searching for a phone. A laptop. Anything.

Of course, there was nothing. Why would there be? That would be too damn easy.

I rushed to the windows and shoved open the curtains. The glass was frosted, and beyond I could see the shadows of bars.

The connected bathroom didn't turn up anything useful either—except for a tiny window with more frosted glass. It wouldn't budge. I jammed all my weight into it, but it held firm.

Did I dare break it? Even if I did, there was no way I'd squeeze myself through the window frame. My hips would never fit. I just wished I could see out and get some idea of where I was.

I needed a plan.

I wasn't helpless or a liability.

I didn't need to be rescued. I could rescue myself.
I hoped.

Bishop

62

TEN YEARS AGO, I'D LEFT NEW YORK IN A CAR I'D stolen in Queens. I dropped it in Pennsylvania and stole another one to get me to Cleveland. With every mile I'd driven, I plotted my revenge, rage and despair tearing through me.

I'd been so fucking cocky, thinking I could win enough counting cards to pay off the loan shark and set us up so we wouldn't have to worry. When security had come, I'd told Abby to run, but neither of us made it. They'd beaten the fuck out of us both, making it clear that they'd hunt us both until they'd been repaid double. Then they left us in an alley like trash, and Abby was dead by the time I came to. I'd carried her home, tears streaming down my face, as the acrid smell of smoke grew stronger and stronger. The tattoo shop and our apartment above it had both burned with my uncle inside.

Abby's body had joined my uncle's in the van to the

morgue, and I'd made my plan. I knew they'd be back for their first payment. And I knew I had no way to get it to them.

I had nothing to lose.

So I bought a gun off the street and went looking for the man who'd ordered it all. He took what mattered to me, so I'd take his life.

His offices weren't far from the shop, and I went looking for him there. Standing in front of a brownstone in Hell's Kitchen, I'd leveled the gun at his chest as he'd stepped out of the front door, my finger on the trigger.

Until a blond girl had come rushing out of an SUV, raced up the steps, and thrown herself into his arms.

Surprised, I'd jerked, and my shot went wide. Casso's thugs had swarmed him and rushed the girl into the building.

Now I knew the blond girl I'd almost shot.

Eden.

And now I was going back, ready to trade my life for hers. I didn't have any false hopes that I'd be making a return flight on the Titan Industries jet.

No, this was coming full circle and ending here.

I was a dead man walking when I stepped off that jet, and I didn't give a fuck. All that mattered was making sure she was safe. I just didn't expect everything to come full circle quite like this.

When Simon brought the jet to a stop on the tarmac just before sunrise, we all rose, armed to the teeth and with duffels slung over our shoulders as we waited for Titan to open the door.

"I never have to do this shit myself," he grumbled as he pushed it open and lowered the steps.

Another jet was parked under giant spotlights a hundred feet away, and Rix stopped short on the tarmac as he studied it. "Same tail numbers as the one that left NOLA. That's Casso's jet."

We all froze.

"Why is it still on the tarmac? Looks like it's getting ready to fly again," Con said.

I ran back up the steps to the cockpit as Simon was removing his headset. "Can you check with the tower, ask if that jet is leaving?"

He looked at me and pulled the headset back down. "They might not tell me, but I can try."

I stood behind him as he radioed and asked for information.

"Roger that." He lifted the headset off again. "It's set for takeoff as soon as the passengers are aboard. No more than fifteen minutes."

Con stood behind me in the doorway. "You think it's him? Taking your girl somewhere else?"

"Don't fucking know, but I'm not leaving until we see who's getting on it."

Con called the other guys back inside, and I explained.

"Change of plans," I said. "That might be them. We're not leaving until I know my girl isn't here."

Lord leaned against the cabin wall. "Want to set up a couple sniper positions? Me and Con can take 'em. That way, if shit goes down we can take them out."

I thought of the airstrip. "Where the hell are you going to do that?"

Lord laughed. "Let us worry about that."

"We got less than fifteen minutes, so we're going now." Con unzipped the duffel and pulled out two rifles. "I'll keep it low so we don't get any interest from the tower."

Con and Lord exited the plane.

"Simon and I can cover you from here. There's no point in not being totally prepared." This came from Rix.

"And what about me?" Titan asked.

"You're with Bish. Don't let him die."

"Thanks," Titan drawled.

We headed down the stairs and Con and Lord were nowhere in sight, already having disappeared to God only knew where. It was easy to forget the brothers had been lethal in the military in their day. Simon and Rix stood like sentries at the stairs, sidearms out of sight.

"Here comes someone," Rix said as headlights cut through the darkness.

A blacked-out Escalade pulled to a stop next to the jet, and the driver jumped out to open the back door. A man stepped out that I recognized all too well. It had been a long fucking time, but Dominic Casso wasn't someone you forgot.

A flunky in the front passenger seat had circled around to open the other back door, revealing a second man. Both doors were shut after the two men exited, and it was clear there was no one else inside.

"No Eden."

"But you've got the boss man, and you've got questions to be answered about where the fuck his goon took his girl. I say, no time like the present to ask them."

I inhaled and slipped my gun into the back of my jeans. *Dead man walking.*

The two bodyguards carried suitcases up into the plane,

and Dom and the other man stood on the tarmac.

It was time. Fuck it.

"Where the fuck is Angelo Francetti?"

Both men spun around to face me as I stepped into the light, and one bodyguard came back to the stairs and drew a weapon.

"Who the fuck are you?" Dom demanded.

He looked exactly the same as I remembered. It was like the man hadn't aged a day, despite running an empire that should have aged him years ahead of his time.

"Doesn't fucking matter who I am. What matters is he's got your daughter, and I'm not leaving until I find them both."

Dom's face pinched with confusion. "My daughter? What the fuck do you know about my daughter?"

"You don't tell us who you are, you're gonna catch a bullet to the skull in five seconds." This came from the other man.

"You really don't care where she is? Or that Angelo Francetti knocked her unconscious and dragged her out of a shop in New Orleans and put her on this same plane?"

Dom's head jerked back and he looked at the other man. "What the fuck is he talking about, Vin? New Orleans? You told me she was safe. Why the fuck would Angelo dare lay a hand on her?"

"Get on the plane. I'll take care of this fuck. He's stirring up shit he has no business stirrin.'"

"I'm not going any fucking place until you answer my question. Where the fuck is my daughter? You've been puttin' me off for days."

"She's safe. She's fine. No one will bother her."

"She's not safe," I said. "She sure as shit didn't ask to be knocked out or kidnapped. And neither of you is going anywhere until I have my answers."

Dom turned to Vin. "You've got sixty fucking seconds to get Eden on the phone or I'm gonna put a bullet in your brain. I don't give a fuck how long I've known you."

Vincent bristled. "All due respect, Dom, but you've got a lot more to be worried about right now than where your daughter is. You need to get on this plane and get the hell out of the country before the Feds catch up with you."

"You're not hearing me. Why the fuck aren't you hearing me?" Quiet, yet lethal, anger edged Dom's tone.

"Yeah, answer the fucking question, *Vin*."

"Shoot this guy," Vincent yelled to the bodyguard, his arm flung out toward me, but Dom held up a hand.

"Don't fucking shoot anyone until I give the word." He looked at me. "Now, tell me why I shouldn't leave you bleeding out on this tarmac right now?"

"Because I'm here to find your daughter. Because apparently I'm the only fucking person who's worried about her."

Dom looked at Vincent. "New Orleans? I told you I wanted her in a safe house, and you said it was taken care of. What the fuck is your problem? Are you deaf?"

"She was taken care of. You wanted her out of the way; I told you, I got her out of the way."

"In fucking New Orleans? Where the fuck is Angelo now?"

Vincent shrugged. "Busy doing what he's told."

Dom's voice dropped into a harsh whisper. "You give me a fucking straight answer, Vin, or I will shoot you myself. Where the fuck is your kid, and where the fuck is my daughter?"

Kid?

Vincent looked at me closer, and recognition finally hit me. Ten years ago, he hadn't been the number-two guy. He'd been climbing the ranks and carrying out orders.

He recognized me at the same time. "I remember you. You're the one who ran like a fucking coward and never stopped. You've got balls of brass, boy, to come back here. You didn't have so many fucking tats or as much hair then, but I remember you." He leveled the pistol at my head. "Time for you to pay in blood."

Two red dots popped up on his chest.

"That would be a really poor idea on your part," Titan said, stepping up next to me. "Two ex-Special Forces snipers will take you out before you can pull the trigger."

I looked at Dom. "And if you let your guys shoot me, I won't be able to tell you about the burner phone we found in Vin's kid's hotel room and all the interesting numbers it has on it. Like the Feds."

I'd been saving that piece for leverage, and it worked.

Dom held an arm out in front of Vin. "Put the fucking gun down." To me, he added, "What the fuck are you talking about? You trying to tell me Angelo is a rat who kidnapped my daughter?"

Before takeoff, I'd tried every number on the burner phone we found in Angelo's room, and had two conversations with very special agents who were ready for the information Angelo had promised to deliver.

Vincent didn't notice, but from behind him, both bodyguards leveled their weapons on his back.

"This fuck doesn't know jack shit."

"All I want is to know that Eden is safe, and you can have everything we found and do your own investigation, Mr. Casso."

Dom looked at Vin. "Get Eden on the phone, now. No more fucking excuses, or I will end you. I don't fucking care who you are. And you." He raised his gun at my head, and one of the little red dots jumped to his chest. "You're going to tell me why the fuck you're so interested in my daughter."

"Can't you tell the guy's in love with her? Jesus, why else would he face down the mob boss who had his family killed ten years ago?" Titan's drawl was thicker now. "That's storybook shit right there."

"He telling the truth?" Dom asked.

"Fucking right, he is," Titan replied.

"You've got to be fucking kidding me." Vincent laughed. "What the fuck is it about that girl?"

"You better start from the beginning, boy," Dom told me.

"Don't have the luxury of that kind of time, Mr. Casso. Right now, Angelo Francetti has your daughter."

"Angelo isn't going to hurt her," Vincent said. "He's protected Eden for years."

"Where the fuck did he take her, Vin? I want answers. *Now*."

"He's got a place in Jersey. He wanted some time alone with her."

Dom turned to Vincent, his gun held loosely in his hand. "Wait. You knew your boy took my girl? What the fuck else did you know? That she was kidnapped? What about the Feds on your kid's phone? You got explanations for all of that, my friend?"

"You're gonna believe this guy over someone you've known for years?"

"This kid that walked up to us with the balls of a fucking elephant to make sure my daughter was safe? What motive does he have? Because the fact that you've been giving me the runaround for fucking days tells me that you're the one I've got to worry about right now. Get her on the phone or my bullet goes in your brain."

Eden

"I want to talk to my father," I told Angelo when he opened the door to my newest cage.

His features hardened into a scowl. "I told you to shower before breakfast."

I knew I had to walk a delicate line. "I'm not feeling well, so I decided not to."

Angelo rushed inside the room, and I had to curb my gag reflex when he reached for my hands and squeezed them.

"I didn't want to drug you, but I didn't have a choice. You need to learn to follow my orders, Eden. That's the way this works."

I forced a weak smile. "I really need to talk to my father."

"You will when I say you're ready."

"And when will that be?"

Angelo didn't answer, but instead dropped his grip on my hands and turned toward the door. "Come eat. It'll make you feel better. And then you can shower after. We need to wash that city off you. Gotta make sure my girl is clean before I give her my cock."

I shuddered and stopped just short of gagging at the thought. Schooling my expression so he wouldn't read my disgust and decide not to bother waiting, I followed him into the living area of what appeared to be an apartment. But where?

"Where are we?"

"Doesn't matter as long as we're together, baby." Angelo reached for the takeout containers he'd left on the kitchen counter with his wallet. "Got you eggs Benedict and an extra side of bacon. Your favorites."

They actually were my favorites, but right now, the thought of eating either was enough to make me want to run for the toilet.

But I didn't have to say anything because Angelo's phone rang.

"Sir?"

At his greeting, I hoped like hell it was my father.

"He wants to speak to Eden? That's not possible right now. She's sleeping." Angelo's response was clearly a lie, and I had to assume the call was from Vin.

"No, I'm not sleeping! He's holding me here against my will!" I screamed as loud as I could.

Angelo's hand lashed out and he backhanded me across the face. "Don't listen to her. She's still doped up. She was doing all kinds of bad shit in New Orleans."

My cheek burned where he'd struck me, but I didn't care. "Fucking liar!"

He held the phone away from his ear. "You're going to—"

"Daddy! Help!"

"I'll call you back."

Angelo hung up and turned to me. "What the fuck is wrong with you? You don't get it yet, do you? Your life only matters as long as I say it matters. My pop is steppin' into the number-one role, and he don't like you much."

"What the hell are you talking about?"

"Dom is going down. Feds are all over him, and we've given them everything they need to move in. The only way you're not going down is to stick with me."

I shook my head, unable to believe him.

"You think it was a coincidence when your credit card got canceled for fraud? I did that. Your bank account frozen? I did that too. The Feds eat up whatever info we give them, and they're going to put Dom away for life. Now sit the fuck down, eat your breakfast, and I'll be back after I've talked to my dad."

He walked toward the bedroom, his phone already lifted to his ear. As soon as he shut the door, I ran toward it.

While Angelo might be crazy, a mental giant he was not. I guessed he'd forgotten that he'd set up the bedroom door to be locked from the outside. I threw the dead bolt before Angelo realized his mistake and began pounding on the door.

"Let me out of here, Eden. You're not safe without me!"

"Fuck you!" I yelled.

I grabbed his wallet off the counter and ran for the door. Adrenaline and giddiness rolled through my veins as I unlocked it and threw it open.

Freedom. *I can save myself. I'm the hero of this freaking story.* Fuck Angelo and his whacked-out plans. I didn't need him to keep me safe. I just needed to get away from him.

I ran down the stairs, four floors, until I hit the lobby of what appeared to be a less-than-posh building. Slowing my pace, I walked out to the curb, hoping I'd be able to catch a cab this early in the morning.

I had to be in Jersey somewhere, because this definitely wasn't Manhattan. A cab turned the corner, and I waved it down. As I slid into the backseat, I heard someone calling my name.

From four stories up, Angelo yelled down at me. "Someone stop her!"

The cabbie looked up and then looked at me. "You okay, kid?"

I glanced into the rearview mirror to meet his gaze and winced at the red mark it revealed on my face.

"I've been better. Can you take me to Hell's Kitchen?" I gave him the cross streets of the brownstone. I didn't know where else to go, and my apartment didn't seem like the best choice. I needed to get to Dom.

"Sure, hon."

I did it. I really freaking did it.

I straightened my shoulders and held my head high.

I rescued my own damned self.

64
Bishop

VINCENT HUNG UP THE PHONE AND LOOKED AT Dom. "He's going to call back when she's awake. She's sleeping right now. It's still early."

Dom tilted his head, suspicion clear in his gaze. "I don't fucking care what time it is. You call him right now and tell him to bring her to the brownstone. We'll all have a little come-to-Jesus meeting."

Vincent bristled. "You need to get on this fucking plane, Dom, or the Feds are going to be all over your ass."

I expected the crime boss to reconsider and act to save himself, but instead, he shook his head.

"Not getting on any fucking plane until I know my daughter is safe. If any of what these gentlemen say is true, I've put way too much trust in your family, and it's time to clean house. After all, wouldn't that be why the Feds are gonna come down on my ass?"

Vincent looked from me to Dom. "You're gonna believe

some kid who wants you dead over me?"

"He's got no other motive. You have plenty." Dom called to the bodyguards. "We're going back to the city. Keep the jet on standby." He nodded at me. "You're coming with us. Your crew can follow, but if they take one shot, you're dead."

"Fine."

"We're right behind you, Bish," Titan said.

I gave him a chin jerk and climbed in the SUV with Dom Casso.

Something wasn't right. The last time I was on this block, there were SUVs parked along the curb with armed men inside and a man posted at the door. Today, there were empty parking spots and no one else in sight. There had to be more to it than just the early-morning hours. Mobsters didn't exactly work nine to five.

"Where the fuck is everyone?" Casso asked Vincent as we circled the block.

"Why would I know?"

"Because you're in charge of security."

"Boss, I think we should keep driving," the bodyguard in the passenger seat said as we pulled up across the street from the front of the building.

"Park here and keep it running. We're not leaving until Angelo shows up with my daughter."

Vincent lifted his phone. "He said he's on his way."

We'd only heard Vincent's side of the conversation, but I had a hard time believing anything that came out of that slick fucker's mouth. Another SUV parked behind us, and I spotted Lord in the driver's seat.

Now, we waited.

Or at least, that was the plan until a taxi pulled up along-side us and Eden jumped out of the backseat.

I threw open the door, and Vincent's gun pressed against the back of my head. "Don't you fucking move."

Dom saw Eden right after I did. "There she is. Where the fuck is your kid?"

Eden raced toward the building, only to be grabbed by a guy who darted out between two cars.

"He's right there."

A man in a leather jacket, who I had to assume was Angelo, held a gun to her head, and Dom twisted in his seat to raise his pistol at Vincent's head.

Vincent laughed. "This right here is a predicament. You can't shoot me without killing her. I'm definitely going to kill this guy because he just fucking pisses me off. You ready for all that, Dom?"

"What the fuck do you think you're doing, Vin? Drop your fucking gun or I'll rip your goddamned throat out with my bare hands. And Angelo better drop his, or he's gonna choke on his own fucking cock while he bleeds out."

"I don't think so. You're gonna be in handcuffs in a mat-ter of minutes, and I'll be taking over the family. If you want your daughter to outlive you, you're gonna go quietly."

While he spoke, Angelo dragged Eden toward the car.

"Did you hear that, Eden? Your dad gets to decide whether you die or whether he goes to jail. What do you think he's going to choose?" Angelo's words were a taunt. "You've never mattered to him like you matter to me. And every time you run, I'm going to find you."

Eden's face fell . . . until she saw me and froze. "Bishop," she whispered. "Oh my God. You're here."

Dom spoke next. "You shouldn't have come here, Eden."

His words might as well have crushed her. "I'm sorry."

"This life was always too dangerous for you. You deserved better. I was selfish, though, wanting to keep you close instead of sending you farther away. Forgive me."

Everything stilled for a moment, and I took advantage of the lull. Reaching behind my head, I grabbed the barrel of Vincent's gun and jammed it up into the ceiling of the car. He pulled the trigger instinctively, and bullets ripped through the roof.

Chaos ensued.

I swung my elbow hard enough to break Vincent's nose and dived out of the car. One of the bodyguards turned and fired.

I ran toward Eden but Angelo raised his gun, aiming it at my head. I didn't slow, didn't stop. The heat of bullets ripping through my body never came because Angelo's body jerked as he fell.

I didn't hear the report of the rifle until after he hit the ground. I lunged for Eden, catching her around the waist and throwing us both to the ground and using my body to cushion us. Bullets flew as I rolled us under a car for protection, happy to hear the steady beat of her heart.

I kept her head covered until the shots died and sirens wailed in the distance. Pulling her face away from my chest, I looked down at her.

"You okay, cupcake?"

"You came for me."

"You saved yourself."

Eden's eyes filled with tears. "My dad? Is he—"

"Come on, man. Let's get you both out from under there."

I recognized Con's tattooed wrist, and let him pull Eden out from under the car. I followed right behind her. "Casso? Is he—"

The black SUV disappeared down the street, squealing around a corner. Vincent's body lay unmoving on the sidewalk, as did Angelo's.

Eden lifted a hand to cover her mouth. "He left me. He left me." The words were mumbled from beneath her fingers.

"Let's get the fuck out of here," Con said as he and Titan hustled us into the other SUV, and Lord roared down the street.

No one else said a word as we hauled ass back to the airport. We all knew we'd have confirmation as soon as we got there. Casso's jet was waiting on standby. The Feds were coming down on him. He had every reason to run—and only one reason to stay.

Lord called Simon as we made the last turn, and he had the jet ready to move. Part of me hoped Casso at least waited to tell his daughter good-bye, but my chest clenched when I saw his jet was gone.

No one told Eden.

Eden

MY FATHER HAD APOLOGIZED. I WAS TRYING TO take comfort in that as Bishop half carried me up the stairs of the jet and settled me on his lap in a big comfy seat. I didn't want to cry tears for a man who'd basically abandoned me, but I couldn't stop myself.

I clung to Bishop as Titan gave the orders for takeoff. It didn't once occur to me to stay in New York. There was nothing for me there.

We were almost to cruising altitude when the bathroom door at the back of the jet opened, and every head swung in that direction.

"What the fuck?" Bishop said.

Con reached for his gun. "How the hell—"

My father stood in front of the bathroom door as though this were any normal flight for him.

"How did you . . . I don't understand . . ."

"It appears you and I have a lot to catch up on, and I

couldn't very well do that from Costa Rica. Now, I believe some proper introductions are in order." He looked at Bishop. "I'm Dominic Casso, and I want to know why exactly my daughter is sitting in your lap."

Eden

I STOOD ON THE TARMAC AND WATCHED MY FATHER FLY away. Apparently, his jet had tailed us all the way from Teterboro, ready to pick him up and take him to some undisclosed location.

Bishop stood beside me, quiet since we'd deplaned. Everything had come out in that long flight back.

How Vincent had been responsible for giving the orders to kill Bishop's uncle, and had put the word out that Bishop would be hunted until he paid back double what he'd won counting cards. Dom hadn't had a clue.

Bishop had wanted my father dead for ten years, for a reason that was no longer valid. I felt the anger drain out of Bishop as my father explained the inner workings of his organization and that he wouldn't have been bothered with the details of something like that.

Ignorance was no excuse, but Bishop had a choice— continue to hold the grudge, or let it go.

He'd made his choice, and that choice was me.

"You two ready?" This came from Con, who held open the back door of Lord's Hemi 'Cuda.

Was I ready? Ready to start over with this new life and not worry about it being snatched away from me at any second?

Yes.

Ready to be with Bishop and not keep any more secrets?

Yes.

But was he?

He'd shown up in New York, walking into the belly of the beast to face what he'd run from for ten years—all because he loved me. And then he'd sat in front of my father and told him that he wouldn't be content in this life until he made me as happy as I'd made him. That the only thing he wanted was to watch me fly, so long as he could soar beside me. His words had given me hope like nothing else possibly could.

I thought it was safe to say he was ready.

We slid into the backseat of Lord's awesomely cool car, and Con took the front.

"We're going to pretend none of this ever happened, right? You're not going to make me tell Vanessa? She'll be pissed she didn't get to go."

I wondered if he was crazy. "What did you tell her you were doing?" I asked.

"Helping a friend."

"Then I guess it depends on how many questions she's going to ask when you get home carrying a duffel bag of guns."

Con shrugged. "I'll leave those in the trunk. Lord can

explain them to Elle."

Lord looked at him sideways. "Which means Vanessa will know by morning."

"Good point. I guess I'm gonna play up this hero angle pretty hard-core."

I pressed tighter to Bishop's side. "I don't mean to be rude, but this guy is the hero in my book."

Bishop looked down at me. "You don't need a hero, Eden. You've got that covered." He pressed a kiss to my hair. "But I'll be there by your side all the same."

"So, where am I dropping you off this fine evening?" Lord asked.

"My place," I said. "If you don't mind."

Bishop nodded. "The boss lady says her place, so that's where we'll be."

Boss lady. I liked it.

I didn't break down until I stepped into the shower and everything that had happened today came crashing down on me. I dropped my forehead against the wall, and my chest heaved when I thought about how close I'd come to losing everything.

Bishop. My father. My friends.

I cried for Angelo—the version I'd known before.

The door creaked, and a breeze told me Bishop was inside. The curtain slid open a foot and I turned my head sideways.

"Breaks my heart to see you cry, cupcake."

"I'm sorry."

He shook his head. "Don't ever apologize for how

you're feeling. You own that. It's yours." He stripped his shirt over his head and shoved his jeans past his hips before stepping into the shower. "But if you're gonna cry, at least do it where I can hold you."

The water beat over us both as I clung to Bishop's shoulders. He pressed his lips to my forehead and held on but said nothing. Nothing needed to be said. I just needed to let it all flow out and down the drain.

When the water started to run cold, he moved us out of the stream and turned it off.

"You need to go to my place where we have more hot water?"

I shook my head, a smile tugging at my lips. "No, I think I'm good."

"You're sure?"

"I'm positive."

"Then let's get you dried off and dressed."

We stepped out of the shower, and Bishop wrapped me with a towel before grabbing one for himself.

"We're going to have to do something about the fact that you have no clothes here," I said when he pulled his jeans and T-shirt back on.

He gave me a look. "I was thinking more along the lines of how we need to do something about the fact that we don't sleep in the same place every night."

Bishop had a point.

"We haven't really talked about what's next for us. Except, you know, the fact that you told my father you love me and basically dared him to stand in our way." I was still smiling inside over how adamant Bishop had been on the plane. "So, what do you want to do?"

"I'm not going to rush you. You've wanted your

freedom for a long time, and I'm not going to take that from you. You decide when and how we handle this. I'm on your timetable. I'm sure as shit not going anywhere."

The fact that he wasn't trying to push me made it all the better. "Do you kill spiders?"

Bishop looked at me like I might be crazy. "Say what now?"

"Do you kill spiders? Because honestly, I'm all for being independent . . . until spiders are involved. Then I want a big man in my house to kill them for me and carry me away and give me a dozen orgasms so I can forget about the horror of spiders."

Bishop's booming laugh filled the small space of my apartment. "Is that right?"

I nodded.

"So are you telling me you want me around?"

"Yeah. I do. But it'd be even cooler if we could both keep our places and just go back and forth for now. Maybe see which one suits us better?"

Bishop studied me, and I realized he got what I was saying without me actually saying it. I wasn't ready to give up my place just yet. It was tiny, but cute and awesome, and I loved it.

"I think that works just fine for me, cupcake. I'll bring over a bag, and you can take a bag to my place."

"I'm going to have to go shopping." I thought about all the stuff in my apartment in New York. Designer clothes perfect for the life I no longer wanted. "Yeah, I'm definitely going to have to go shopping."

He pulled me into him and squeezed me tight. "I think your girls would be more than happy to help you with that."

My girls.

My man.
My life.
My everything.

67

Eden

THEY AMBUSHED ME JUST BEFORE THE END OF MY shift. In all honesty, I wasn't surprised. Charlie, Vanessa, Elle, Valentina, Yve, and Delilah strode into Your Favorite Hole like they were on a mission. The window had been replaced, and the events of three days ago seemed like just a bad memory now.

"It's time for details, sugar." Delilah stopped in front of the register and pressed both palms to the counter. "Bishop isn't telling me a damn thing."

I was actually surprised they'd held off this long, but then again, I'd been *busy* in the best way possible with Bishop at my place. Complain about my man-bunned giant keeping me trapped in bed for hours and hours? *Not likely.*

Fabienne wiped down the counter around the espresso machine and nodded at me. "You might as well knock off now and tell them everything. Make sure to do it loud enough so I don't have to work too hard at eavesdropping."

My boss had been incredibly patient, taking the incomplete explanation I'd offered her and my apologies about bringing the crazy into Your Favorite Hole in stride. I'd offered to pay for the window damage, but she'd just huffed.

"That's what insurance is for. You might've attracted the nutjobs like a magnet, but that doesn't mean you're responsible."

I lifted my apron over my head and slipped out from behind the counter.

They picked the cozy seating area, and Charlie, Yve, and Valentina crammed in on the loveseat. Vanessa took a chair and Delilah settled on the footstool, leaving the last chair for me.

"So, what the hell happened? And why the hell didn't you tell us you were some badass mobster's daughter?"

Delilah went straight for the jugular with her questions. Given that it was her brother who I'd dragged into it, I wasn't all that surprised. Before I could gather some kind of answer together, Charlie responded.

"Because some people don't like to talk about their fathers. Especially when they're infamous or notorious." She looked at me with understanding clear on her face. "I've been there. I get it."

I nodded. Charlie understood better than anyone what I'd been grappling with, except on a much crazier scale. Dom had kept me in the shadows, but she'd been thrust into the limelight during her father's trial. I supposed, in a strange way, I owed Dom for that. But now I was ready to live in the light.

"Dom was never a true father. I'm the youngest of his illegitimate kids, and I was never allowed to meet my half siblings. I wasn't really allowed to meet anyone. I think it was his way of keeping me safe, but . . . well, we all know how that worked out."

"We will when you tell us . . ." Delilah prompted.

So I told them as much as I could, and by the end, jaws were nearing floor level.

"We're thankful as hell you're okay, and that you didn't bring our guys back with any bullet holes," Yve said. "Although Titan would probably claim to be bulletproof."

I laughed, thankful she broke the shocked silence.

"Are you sure he's not? Because he did stare down some mobsters like he had no fear."

Yve's tawny eyes widened a fraction before rolling. "Of course he did."

"So, what's next?" Valentina asked.

I smiled, but Delilah answered for me.

"Bishop is going to lock her down and never let her out of his sight again."

I wasn't going to argue with that.

With perfect timing, the front door chimed, and the man in question walked in. Bishop stopped behind my chair, lowered his hands to my shoulders, and squeezed.

"Have you finished your interrogation?"

Delilah made a noise that I was pretty sure qualified as a harrumph. "We can keep going for hours."

Bishop's grip tightened. "Not gonna happen. I got a date with my girl."

His sister sent him a look that promised she wasn't letting this go entirely. "I suppose we can let you have her. For now."

Bishop released one of my shoulders and his hand slid around to my collarbone. "For now?" He laughed. "Fuck that. With Eden, it's all about forever."

A collective *aww* released on a sigh from the girls as my heart sped up.

Vanessa rose. "On that note, I think it's time for us to go." She met my gaze. "I would invite you to join us for girls' night, but you've clearly got other plans. Know that you're welcome anytime. We take turns hosting."

Bishop released his hold as I stood.

"Thank you." I shot a look at the man behind me and said to Vanessa, "You better believe I'll take you up on it sometime."

"We'll hold you to it," Charlie said. She stepped forward and wrapped her arms around me. "If you ever need to talk, I'm here."

I squeezed her and then stepped back into the circle of Bishop's arms, and my heart was near to bursting. I'd never had this. The overwhelming support. Friendship. *Love.*

It truly was everything.

We climbed off the back of Bishop's bike, and I unlocked the gate to the courtyard at my place. Harriet was coming out her back door as Bishop pushed his bike inside.

She clapped her hands. "I'm so glad I caught you! I wanted to take one last look at the place before I jet off."

"Jet off?" I asked.

"In the flurry of all your excitement, I must have forgotten to tell you. I'm headed to Machu Picchu to expand my landscape watercolor skills. After that, I'm going to hug a few tortoises in the Galapagos and then see those crazy heads at Easter Island. I've got a lot to check off my list before I kick the bucket." She came forward and wrapped me in a hug. "Now, keep yourself from getting kidnapped again while I'm gone. I don't want to miss it."

From inside, her front buzzer sounded.

"That's my car to the airport. I'll see you kids soon."

"Safe trip, ma'am."

"Not too safe, I hope. Life is all about taking chances." Harriet winked, whirled around, and disappeared inside.

Bishop looked down at me. "She's a nut, but she's a cool old lady."

I was thinking the exact same thing. Her comment about checking things off her list made me think of all the ones I had pinned to my bulletin board in my New York apartment.

"And here you probably thought I was crazy with my list of things to check off."

He shook his head. "Not at all. Why not experience everything you can?"

It was the opening I needed. "I have at least dozen more lists. Cities all over the world. By the time I'm Harriet's age, I want to check everything off."

Bishop studied me. "Is that right?"

I nodded.

"Then I guess we're going to have to get our hands on those lists so we can start planning."

A smile stretched the corners of my lips. "Really?"

Bishop slid a hand under my hair and curled it around the back of my neck. "A lifetime of adventures with the most amazing woman I've ever met? Sign me up. I'm ready."

I threw my arms around his neck and pressed my lips to his. When I pulled back, I met his green gaze. "So, about this date . . . what are we doing?"

"You'll find out when we get there."

By the end of the night, Bishop had inked us both with new tattoos—his was a cupcake, worked into the sleeve on his left arm, closer to his heart, he said. Mine was a beautiful bird on my shoulder blade, flying free. No more gilded cages or clipped wings for me.

I also finally checked off the last thing on my New Orleans *Must Do* list. I learned how to say *I love you* in Cajun.

68 Bishop

Six months later

"**A** FEDERAL COURT HAS FOUND DOMINIC CASSO not guilty of all pending charges. Should we start calling him Teflon Dom?" a news anchor asked his co-host.

"I don't know how he did it. I really, truly don't," Eden whispered from beside me on the couch with her gaze glued to the TV.

"He successfully pinned everything on Vin and Angelo, who didn't exactly have a chance to refute it."

"I'm not sad about it. I don't know what that says about me as a person, but I'm not sad at all."

I pressed a kiss to her forehead. "You don't need to be sad. Angelo was a creepy fuck."

We'd found more and more evidence of that once we'd gone back to New York and cleaned out Eden's apartment. That was, after the Feds had let us in. Thankfully, we knew people who knew people.

Cameras had been installed in every room, including the bathroom, as well as in her office at the spa.

The head of one of the crime families who was supposedly engaged in the so-called "power struggle" that had been happening to take control of the Casso empire had come forward. He confessed to Dom that it had all been orchestrated by Vincent with Angelo's help. Dom had cleaned house, identifying more associates and soldiers on Vincent's separate payroll.

I hadn't pushed too hard for more answers because, quite frankly, I wanted Eden as far away from the entire thing as possible.

Her father agreed, and had given his blessing.

Not only did he not want me dead, he wanted me very much alive for Eden. I didn't want him dead either. Enough blood had been shed.

"Did you check the mail I left on the counter? There was a big envelope for you."

She shook her head and pushed off the couch. When she made it to the counter, she lifted it. "This one?"

"Yeah."

Eden tore it open. "What the hell?"

I stood and strode toward her. "What is it?"

She handed me a piece of paper. "A deed."

"What?"

I grabbed the envelope, which didn't appear to have a return address, and dumped out the rest of the contents on the counter. A picture, a brochure, and a set of keys fell out.

It was a house in the French Quarter. The picture didn't look like much, but the brochure was a whole different story. From the outside, it looked like a simple brick building, but the pictures of the inside showed a completely renovated townhouse. The *ten thousand dollar a square foot* kind.

The deed was in both our names.

Eden flipped the picture over, and a note was stuck to the back.

An early wedding present. Don't keep my girl living in sin for too long, Bishop.
—DC

Eden's eyes practically bulged out of her head. "Holy shit. My dad just gave us a townhouse. In the Quarter. You've got to be kidding me."

I thought about the ring I'd bought last week at an antique store on Conti Street and had been carrying everywhere with me since. I shook my head. *How did the old man do it?*

"Oh my God, we have a house!" Eden yelled and jumped into my arms. "Not yours, not mine. Ours."

"We sure do." I stared down at her. "Did you see the note?"

She nodded. "You don't have to. I mean . . . if you don't want to. I know that's not really your thing."

"What the hell are you talking about?"

"Getting married. We don't have to if that's not what you want."

"Why the hell would you say that?"

Eden shrugged. "I don't know. I just . . . Delilah told me you said you never wanted to settle down."

I set her on her feet. "*Before you.* Every fucking thing changed when I met you, Eden. Stay here. Hold on."

I headed for the door.

"Where are you going?"

Eden came outside as I ran down the stairs to where my bike was parked in the courtyard.

I unlocked the hidden compartment and pulled out the tiny silk bag. It hadn't cost a fortune, but it was too perfect for her.

I came back up the stairs as she was coming back out the door with her flip-flops on. "I told you I'd be right back."

"But—"

She stepped inside the apartment and I dropped to one knee. "This isn't how I planned to do this. Actually, I hadn't yet figured out how I was going to do it. But I don't ever want you to think that this wasn't what I wanted. You've always been what I wanted, Eden."

I pulled the ring from the bag and held it up. A pink morganite stone set in an antique platinum band of vines.

"You . . . you bought that?"

"Yeah. I did."

"You want to marry me?"

"When you're ready and not a day before." Her eyes shimmered with tears as I slid the ring on her finger. "If you'll have me."

She nodded. "Always."

I looked up at the ceiling, wondering if somehow Casso had known. Didn't fucking matter. He'd given his blessing, and Eden was mine.

The End

Go to http://www.meghanmarch.com/#!newsletter/c1uhp to sign up for my newsletter, and never miss another announcement about upcoming projects, new releases, sales, exclusive excerpts, and giveaways.

I'd love to hear what you thought about Eden and Bishop's story. If you have a few moments to leave a review on the retailer's site where you purchased the book, I'd be incredibly grateful. Send me a link at meghanmarchbooks@gmail.com, and I'll thank you with a personal note.

Also by Meghan March

BENEATH Series:
Beneath This Mask
Beneath This Ink
Beneath These Chains
Beneath These Scars
Beneath These Lies

FLASH BANG Series:
Flash Bang
Hard Charger

DIRTY BILLIONAIRE Trilogy:
Dirty Billionaire
Dirty Pleasures
Dirty Together

DIRTY GIRL Duet:
Dirty Girl
Dirty Love

STANDALONES:
Bad Judgment

Acknowledgments

Every time I go back to New Orleans with a Beneath book, it feels like I'm going home. Not because New Orleans has ever been my home, but because this Beneath world is one I love so dearly. Without the most amazing readers on the planet, I wouldn't have the opportunity to keep revisiting that world. Thank you so much for taking a chance on me and picking up this book. You allow me to have the best job imaginable, and I'll endeavor never to take it for granted.

And like with every book I write, *Beneath These Shadows* would not be what it is today without the help of a fabulous team of people.

Special thanks go out to:

Pam Berehulke and Angela Marshall Smith, for once again being everything I needed at all stages of the editing process.

Angela Smith, Jamie Lynn, and Natasha Gentile, for your enthusiasm and insight.

Danielle Sanchez, for being straight-up awesome. I love having the privilege to work with you and the Inkslinger team.

Golden Czermak, FuriousFotog, for a kick-ass cover image.

Sarah Hansen, Okay Creations, for another fabulous cover.

Stacey Blake, Champagne Formats, for going above and beyond in your work every time.

My Runaway Readers Facebook Group, for being my home on the interwebz. You're not only my cheerleaders, but a huge part of the reason I keep writing. With your enthusiasm behind me, I feel like there's nothing I can't accomplish.

My crew of fabulous bloggers, for tirelessly spreading the word about books simply for the love of books. You deserve all the thanks in the world.

My family, for supporting even my biggest dreams.

And last, but certainly not least, JDW, for being my rock and an amazing inspiration for the sexy-as-hell alpha heroes I write. I'm the luckiest freaking girl there is. I love you.

Author's Note

UNAPOLOGETICALLY SEXY ROMANCE

I'd love to hear from you. Connect with me at:

Website: www.meghanmarch.com
Facebook: www.facebook.com/MeghanMarchAuthor
Twitter: www.twitter.com/meghan_march
Instagram: www.instagram.com/meghanmarch

About the Author

Meghan March has been known to wear camo face paint and tromp around in the woods wearing mud-covered boots, all while sporting a perfect manicure. She's also impulsive, easily entertained, and absolutely unapologetic about the fact that she loves to read and write smut.

Her past lives include slinging auto parts, selling lingerie, making custom jewelry, and practicing corporate law. Writing books about dirty-talking alpha males and the strong, sassy women who bring them to their knees is by far the most fabulous job she's ever had.

She loves hearing from her readers at meghanmarchbooks@ gmail.com.